William—
Congratulations
on winning—Hope
you enjoy the book!

Happy Reading!

Ann
Jenna

The Siege of Kwennjurat

A M Jenner

Thanks and Dedication

A very big thank-you is in order to our readers who waited, mostly with patience, for four years for the sequel. Special thanks to those who recognized the necessity of a certain death in Tanella's Flight, and forgave us for it.

This book is dedicated to our friend Dallyn, who at fourteen, looked exactly like Crispin.

Books by A M Jenner

Tanella's Flight
Fabric of the World
Clues to Food
Deadly Gamble
Reading Sampler
A Heart Full of Diamonds
Assignment to Earth
Inherit My Heart
The Moms Place
The Siege of Kwennjurat

Author's Note

This is the second book of The Kwennjurat Chronicles. I strongly suggest you read the first book in the series, *Tanella's Flight*, before commencing this book. It will make more sense to you that way.

If you really can't wait, I advise you go first to the end of this volume and read the section titled "catching up to the story".

Calendar of the Ten Kingdoms

The year is a twelve moonatt cycle; each moonatt has thirty days. The moon has a 28-day cycle. The moonatts are listed below in chronological order throughout the year.

Daatha, Golorinn, Arysa, Pleig, Corith, Beltaine, Monleth, Aidorth, Trymmyl, Peschnorr, Garnneth, Samhain.

The Ten

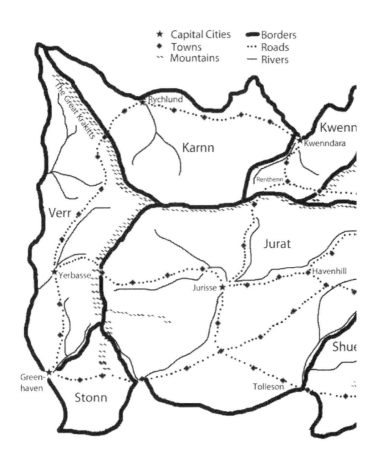

Kingdoms

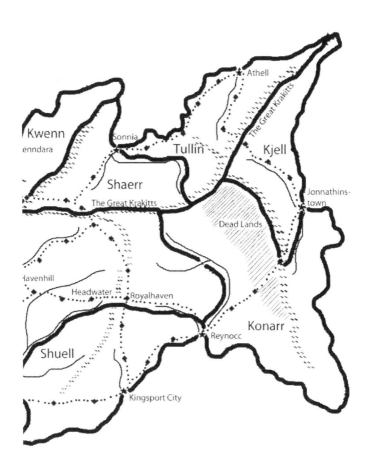

The Siege of Kwennjurat

A M Jenner

Chapter One

First Flight
24th Day of Pleig, 2448

The coach rocked from side to side as Rocnar whipped up the horses, pushing them as hard as he dared. Hitting a deep pothole, it lurched violently, nearly overbalancing. A loud snarl came from the prince within; reminding him he needed to be more careful or he'd suffer stiff consequences. As the fear of being tortured later that evening was more immediate than the fear of their pursuit and arrest, he finally slowed a bit, gaining greater control over the horses as they raced on through the bright, cloudless day.

If they'd gotten away early enough, no one would yet suspect them for the murder of an innocent courier or their part in the kidnapping of the Princess of Kwenn, or that they had left the kingdom for a destination Rocnar prayed the prince had in mind.

Chapter Two

Search and Seizure
19th Day of Corith, 2448

Torresson pulled on the final bit of his blue and gold livery, smoothing the last of the wrinkles of travel from the seat of his breeches. The ride from Renthenn to Jurisse had been a pleasant one and he looked forward to the day with delight.

He opened his soft leather courier's pouch and verified that his letter of credit was still nestled against the royal decree King Fergasse had provided, giving him full authority to carry out the detailed instructions the king had imparted to him. This assignment was very different from anything he had done before.

He settled the pouch in place against one hip, the long leather strap across the opposite shoulder. Quickly dragging a comb through his hair, Torresson grinned at his reflection in the small mirror the innkeeper had hung on the wall. Today was going to be fun!

Today, Torresson had instructions which would greatly overstep the usual boundaries behind which couriers abide. His current commission on loan to King Fergasse of Jurat would put him in a position to make certain demands on the upper servants who usually looked down upon couriers. Yes, today was certainly going to be fun!

Torresson ate a hurried breakfast and then located the innkeeper.

"I'll need the use of a small carriage for the next two weeks or so; also a team to pull it, and one of your sons to care for the horses. Additionally, I'll need my own horse to remain here while I'm gone."

The innkeeper's eyes had grown wider with each request Torresson made.

"What business does one of Kwenn's couriers have making this sort of demand? Your own horse will be much faster for you to be getting on with your king's business."

Torresson smiled. The fun was beginning already. He pulled the letter of credit King Fergasse had given him from his pouch, and showed it to the innkeeper.

"I have been loaned to King Fergasse, and it's his errand I'm on. The service you give me is given to your king, and the bill will be taken care of by his Majesty."

The innkeeper inspected the document and seal carefully, then handed the paper back to Torresson.

"In that case, sir, I'll be most happy to provide you with all you've requested." The innkeeper quickly gave directions to his ostlers, and within a dozen minutes, a still smiling Torresson was being introduced to Jornn.

The innkeeper's son was a likely lad of 18 with curly blonde locks. Of medium height, the boy's wrist bones protruding from his too-short sleeves showed he'd not yet attained his full growth. Introductions complete, Torresson climbed onto the box next to the boy and told him their first stop would be King Fergasse's palace.

Jornn proved to be an excellent driver. Before any great space of time had passed he was pulling up in front of the palace. Torresson told him to wait nearby then moved confidently toward the doors. He was well known to the door stewards and they admitted him without question. The footman stepped toward him, smiling a greeting as he teased, "What brings you here when all the Ambassadors have joined the nobility in Renthenn for the royal wedding? Are you lost?"

"No, Kendonn, not lost at all. I'm just here on a little business for the king. Could you fetch Michaals for me?" Torresson grinned wider, knowing the butler he'd just asked for usually avoided what he termed 'the common rabble of couriers'. "It's all right, man! King's business." He gestured and the footman left with haste to summon the butler.

As usual, Michaals treated Torresson as though he were lower than the lowest scullery boy, even though technically all couriers worked directly for the king and were not part of the household staff. Ordinarily Torresson simply avoided Michaals, but this assignment was his one opportunity to put Michaals in his place, and Torresson wasn't going to miss it.

Michaals peered down his long nose at Torresson and his blue and gold uniform. "His Majesty is not in residence," he informed the courier in lofty tones which left no doubt about his opinion of Torresson's intelligence. "He is in Renthenn, attending Prince Fergan's wedding."

"Yes I know, Michaals; he borrowed me from King Jameisaan and sent me on a special commission. I have most explicit instructions to be admitted to Prince Liammial's rooms."

The butler sneered. "Prince Liammial is also not in residence at this time. I'm rather afraid you'll have to wait until his return to be admitted to his chambers." He made as if to turn away.

Torresson reached into his pouch and withdrew the royal decree King Fergasse had provided him. "Wrong again, my good man," he said cheerfully, clapping the startled butler on the shoulder. "This missive from your Liege gives me authority to enter Prince Liammial's holdings and remove from them anything I see fit." He presented the document to the man with a flourish.

The butler eyed the parchment with a suspicious look. He gingerly accepted the document, unfolding it carefully in order to read it.

The further down the parchment the butler's eyes traveled, the further out of his face they bulged. Soon his face was very nearly the same color as the parchment he held, and his mouth parted slightly in his astonishment. Known as 'Iron Face' by underlings in the staff for the rigid control he held over his features, any emotion registering on the austere face was a testament to the degree of his distress.

"I see," the butler nodded to Torresson as he reached the bottom of the parchment, "Kendonn will direct you to his Highness' rooms at once, and see to all your needs."

Torresson's grin nearly split his face in with delight. He followed Kendonn to the prince's personal chambers where he didn't really expect to find much of value. He gathered up a few unopened notes, most of them perfumed, which had been collecting since Prince Liammial's departure.

When they reached the prince's ambassadorial offices, Torresson looked around with satisfaction. He dropped the perfumed letters on top of the desk where their scent added to the office's stale air.

Folded and rolled parchments bearing a number of different-colored dispatch ribbons covered most of the flat surfaces of the room. "I'll need a small trunk," Torresson said. Kendonn nodded and disappeared.

Torresson located a dispatch pouch and put the perfumed missives within, along with a hastily penned note stating where he'd found them.

By the time Kendonn returned with the trunk, the widely scattered documents had been neatly stacked on the desk. A note stating the origin of the contents went on top of the papers, and the dispatch case lay on top of everything else.

Torresson securely latched the lid, then hefted the container and personally carried it out to his waiting carriage.

Only after they'd left the palace grounds did he give directions to the boy Jornn as to their next destination.

Chapter Three

His Majesty's Townhouse
19th Day of Corith, 2448

King Fergasse's descriptions and directions were so accurate that Torresson was able to visualize the entire city laid out in his mind, a large red "X" marking his goal.

As they drove, Torresson issued instructions to his young helper.

"The safety of the trunk in the carriage is the most important thing," he said.

Jornn nodded, most of his attention on his driving.

"If anything goes wrong here, leave me. Take the box back to your father's inn and then send help for me."

Jornn nodded again. "I'll do it," he answered, "but I don't like leaving you."

"The box is more important even than my life," Torresson replied. "Should I die, or become incapacitated, Jornn, the trunk must go to the king."

"I'll not fail you, or his Majesty," Jornn vowed, his freckled face serious. When the boy stopped the horses a scant thirty minutes later, Torresson wondered if he'd misheard or misunderstood King Fergasse. Perhaps he'd merely taken a wrong turn.

This part of town was shabby. The narrow houses all nestled against each other as though each depended on its neighbor to remain upright. Most of the buildings had a narrow gap between them too small for even a young child to squeeze through, but many shared a common wall. There were no yards of any sort; the door of each dwelling opened directly onto the street. There was nowhere to leave a carriage save on the street itself. Though he could not see them, Torresson could feel watchful eyes on him, and knew this was a neighborhood where you had to be very careful of both person and possessions.

Torresson was glad Jornn was with him. He didn't dare leave the carriage, or its precious contents, unattended in this street even for the length of time it would take to knock on the door. This was surely not the private home of a prince of any realm!

Torresson clambered down and knocked sharply at the door. For a long while there was no response.

Torresson hesitated to break into the home in broad daylight. Even if the watch were called, they would be slow to respond in this area; he was more afraid of the neighbors' rough justice. Although he had royal permission to enter, he didn't want to attract attention to himself. It would only cause delay to his mission.

He rapped again on the door, as loudly as he could manage with his fist. Torresson could hear the empty sound echoing through the room beyond. Still there was no response.

Torresson retrieved the whip from the carriage. Reversing his grip, he raised the leather-bound wooden handle in preparation to beat upon the door panel with it.

At that precise moment, the door swung silently open. The look of shock on the wizened little butler's face was priceless as he observed the courier on the doorstep, whip raised above his head.

Torresson laughed at the awkwardness of the situation, lowering his weapon at once. "Good day, sir."

The tiny, ancient man cupped his hand behind an ear and peered at Torresson through rheumy eyes. "Eh?" he inquired at what was undoubtedly the loudest volume he could manage.

Torresson answered in kind, his voice echoing through the corridor.

"Is Prince Liammial at home?"

"Nay, Sorr," the butler yelled back, "His Majesty be not at home."

"May I come in?" Torresson hollered.

"Nay, Sorr," the butler reiterated, "His Majesty be not at home." His volume had not diminished in the slightest.

Not wishing to announce his business to the entire street, Torresson tossed the whip to Jornn, then agilely pushed past the squat servant and stepped inside. The servant yelped and quickly moved into the house after Torreson, who closed the door behind them. Looking around, Torresson's mouth fell open in surprise. Everywhere he looked were paintings, furniture and other accessories as luxurious as those found in any palace he'd ever been in; richer than some by far.

It was made more impressive by the squalor outside its doors. Fleetingly, he wondered who

Prince Liammial entertained within these walls, but had the feeling they were people he didn't want anyone at the palace to see him with.

"Wot's this?" the servant bellowed at the top volume his wheezy lungs could manage, recalling Torresson to the moment and bringing his eyes back to the servant before him.

The man continued, his raised voice echoing back from the far end of the entry hall. "I telled ye, Sorr, his majesty be not here. Now be orf wit' ye afore I calls th' watch."

Torresson smiled grimly. His commission for King Fergasse was at odds with this aged retainer's loyalty to his master. "Is there anyone here, apart from yourself?" he inquired, still yelling loudly enough to be heard by the old servant. Why anyone would keep a butler employed after age had rendered him deaf was beyond him.

"Nay," he said, shaking his untidy grey head, "jess' me an' ma wife, Liza, be here, an' her gone ta th' market th' lass' two hours." The butler's volume rose, as though he feared Torresson was also deaf.

"Does she hear better than you do?" Torresson felt scratchiness at the back of his throat and knew this one conversation might render him hoarse for the rest of the day.

"Aye. Ye'll be wantin' ter wait an' tell 'er yer bidness wit' his majesty then? I'll tell yer boy ta tyke yer carriage roun' ta th' mews. He kin put it by th' back door fer ye."

"Thank you!" Torresson bellowed, then made his own way into the parlor and seated himself to await the absent Liza.

Some considerable time later, during which he had neither seen nor heard the butler, the parlor door opened and a woman entered. She was of an age with the butler, but that was the end of any similarities. While the man was gaunt and stooped, with large hairy ears that made him rather resemble a large bat, his wife was very nearly as wide as she was tall. Her kindly face was creased from many smiles, where his was dour and disapproving.

Her voice was mellow and pleasant to hear, especially as she moderated her volume. "'Tis my understanding you're here to speak with His Majesty, Sorr."

Torresson was curious about the servant's error in protocol. Princes were properly addressed as *Highness*, while *Majesty* was customarily only applied to kings.

"Nay, good lady, I did not come to speak to Prince Liammial. I am here by special commission of King Fergasse, to collect Prince Liammial's personal papers."

The woman looked puzzled, and then gave him a sad smile. "From King Fergasse? Ah, Sorr, tis a pity ye be touched in the head, with our good king dead these many months."

It was Torresson's turn to be puzzled. "Dead? Not hardly. I was in his presence not three days ago."

Hope dawned in her face. "Yer certain it was King Fergasse an' none other? Ye wudden be foolin' an ol' lydy now, wud ye, boy?"

"No, ma'am, I would never try to fool a woman of your wise years. When I left Renthenn three days ago, I had just come from an audience with King Fergasse. He is alive and well and was in Renthenn for Prince Fergan's wedding to the Princess Tanella of Kwenn."

Liza clasped her hands together in joy and then a small frown creased her brow.

"That rascal Liammial! He was ever telling tales in th' nurs'ry; doan' know why I shoulda believed that one. Well!" her happy demeanor returned. "Ye said ye was on th' good king's errand, young man, so you just be telling me what yer about, an' we'll be seein' to it."

The door of the study opened and the gnomish butler appeared. "Wot's he want?" he hol-

16

lered at his wife, ignoring Torresson's presence entirely.

"Haint sed yet," Liza yelled back at him. "He were jist about ter tell me." She looked at Torresson and shook her ancient head.

Torresson opened his mouth to speak, but his words were drowned out by the old man's screaming as he pointed a finger at Torresson's face and waved it around.

"Well! Speak yer bidness, young fella!"

"Shut up, Henry, cain't ye see he's a-tryin' ter talk at ye?" the housekeeper screeched at her husband.

Torresson gave up and began laughing. Never in a thousand lifetimes could he have imagined a pair like this!

Immediately two sets of accusatory eyes pinned him to the chair in which he sat, their facial expressions matching their indignation. Torresson's laughter died off, and he was finally able to speak his business.

"His Majesty, King Fergasse, has charged me to collect all of Prince Liammial's papers and bring them to him. If you'll kindly direct me to his chambers and his study and anywhere in the house he might have left any documents, I'd appreciate it."

Neither the lean man nor his fat wife moved. Torresson reached for his courier's pouch. "I have a decree from King Fergasse, instructing me to take possession of the documents, if you'd like to see it," he said, beginning to draw out the rolled parchment.

"Nay, that be not needful; I trust yer from his Majesty," the woman said quickly.

"What ye be a-givin' her writin' for," Henry yelled, "when she's never bin able ter read a word in all her life?"

"Shut up, Henry!" Liza yelled at her spouse. "It be this way, Sorr," she said to Torresson, switching volume automatically with the familiarity of long practice.

Liza turned and shambled from the room, Torresson following in her wake. Three doors down the hall, she ushered him into a parchment-strewn office.

"I'll need a small trunk to take this away in," Torresson said to Liza. She departed at once in search of the container.

As he began collecting and stacking the documents, Torresson briefly wondered what had prompted Fergasse to give this strange order and what information he hoped to find among the prince's papers.

Torresson shrugged off his curiosity as he always did. It was really none of his business why or what; his only task was to complete his assignment in a professional manner. He turned his thoughts to the journey on which he would embark on the morrow; a week-long trek to Prince Liammial's estate at the eastern end of Jurat and back again with yet more parchments. At least on this trip he would have the comfort of the carriage seat and the company of young Jornn, instead of the vagaries of changeable spring weather and only a horse for company; conditions which usually plagued couriers at this time of year.

Chapter Four

Shadowy Listener
21st Day of Corith, 2448

The night was coming on chill and stormy, a good match for both the day's weather and his present mood.

Rocnar the Incompetent had hit every rut in the soggy road, and each muddy bog in between, and Liammial's royal backside had been battered to a very painful pulp.

In the month since Rocnar had killed the Kwenn courier, Liammial hadn't dared to stay in any one place for very long. He was sure his brother was searching for him, and he knew in his bones if Fergasse found him while he remained in power, Liammial's life would be forfeit.

He'd stayed for a short time with two of the many who'd sworn their loyalty to him in return for greater tracts of land and higher titles once he'd ascended the throne.

There was an entire kingdom which his brother and the other reigning monarchs knew nothing about: men from many kingdoms who'd sworn their fealty to him, and addressed him royally as *Majesty* when alone.

Liammial desired that all the wealth and worship of the Ten Kingdoms be his, and no one would have a greater reign than he.

In the last day or so he'd been formulating plans to take control at Jurisse; an exercise now imperative, considering his first plans had gone so badly awry.

The army in Shuell would be a great advantage, but it wasn't the only resource at his disposal.

Because he still held the delicious princess of Kwenn captive, he expected there to be trouble between Jurat and their northern neighbor very soon. The wedding had been scheduled to happen five days ago, and with the Princess stuck in that little run-down cottage, Kwenn and Jurat should be declaring war on each other for the broken treaty at any moment. He smiled at the thought. What he needed most now was news.

Liammial's musings were interrupted as the carriage slowed and pulled into an inn yard.

There was a loud squelch as Rocnar hopped down from the box, and Liammial realized the mud must be deep, and probably, he sniffed fastidiously, infiltrated with all manner of dung as well. His lips tightened with disgust at the mud, his sore backside, and the entire situation.

The carriage door swung open and Liammial pulled up the hood of his cloak before exiting. Making sure the hood was well forward, more to guard against recognition than the rain, he slopped through the mud and into the inn. Seeing no private parlor, he walked to a table in the corner furthest from the fire where the shadows would be the hardest to penetrate.

Rocnar entered shortly, having made arrangements for rooms and dinner, and depositing the small trunk he'd carried from the coach in their chamber. He brought drinks to their table, setting them carefully on the table's surface before helping his master to be seated. A serving maid appeared with two trenchers of a thick, hearty stew, still steaming as she set it on the table before them.

A small commotion at the doorway caused most of the room's occupants to focus their attention on the new arrivals.

Liammial, his side to the room in general, watched from the depths of his hooded cape as a man, his wife and two nearly-grown daughters entered, laughing and brushing the rain from their brightly colored clothing. The women waited at the entrance of the common room while room arrangements were made, looking for a good table near the warm fire. As her parent joined the group, the younger of the daughters discreetly pointed to an empty table and all nodded in full agreement with her choice.

Removing their cloaks at the doorway and hanging them on the pegs to drip onto the straw-covered floor, the family made for the table, chattering gaily to each other as they walked. The husband gallantly seated his wife, then each daughter in turn before taking the head of the table for himself. Liammial turned away and barely noticed their actions, now intent on his food.

The serving maid attended the family and left for the kitchen. As they settled themselves into the chairs about the scrubbed table, it appeared they were continuing an earlier conversation.

"But it does make sense, calling the new country both names. Don't you think so, Papa?" one girl asked.

"Quite, my dear, quite!" he boomed down the table. "I must say, the name *Kwennjurat* is much easier to say than the other way about, is it not? No, *Juratkwenn* just doesn't have the same feel to it all. It will take a bit of getting used to, though, and saying the *Nine Kingdoms* instead of the *Ten Kingdoms* after all, yes, quite a lot to swallow in one go, I'm afraid. I do wonder deep down what it is all about, though."

Liammial, still shrouded in his cape and hood, froze in place with his wooden spoonful of stew half-way to his mouth as he listened intently to the family's discussion, his eyes locked onto their table. Rocnar had paused with a chunk of biscuit mid-way to his mouth.

"It does make sense when you think of the fact that both kingdoms each had just one child to inherit the titles, don't you agree, Arthur?" their mother said practically, addressing her husband.

"Well, that's sort of interesting, too," said Arthur. "King Fergasse had a brother who could easily have taken over Jurat, but it seems he's up and gone somewhere. He certainly wasn't at the wedding. That young Ambassador Sommersby had been at court in Jurat right before the wedding and told me Prince Liammial suddenly just vanished a month ago. No one seems to know where he's gone but I'll tell you what I've heard, though. Lady Autr…, I mean, there are some who were very upset when the prince left in such a havey-cavy manner."

"Arthur!" his wife said sharply. "Enough of court gossip! You're posted in Kwenn and you can't be sure exactly what happened in Jurat, after all!" She jerked her head toward the girls, apparently reminding him their innocent ears shouldn't be listening to court gossip regarding the prince's love life.

"Ahem," he said, looking at his family guiltily, "did you girls, ah, notice what an attractive couple the Prince and Princess made?"

As the girls went into raptures about the princess's dress and veil, the sounds of a throat being cleared reached Liammial's ears, and he observed the man looking at his wife. Her back was to Liammial, but Arthur's heavy sigh of relief let Liammial know the dolt was grateful he'd averted a storm of recrimination from his spouse. The clod now beamed at his table companions.

The girls continued to rhapsodize about the wedding.

Liammial began shaking with his rage. How had the princess escaped? When had it happened? More importantly, who was responsible for her escape? His spoon handle snapped, some of the splinters entering his palm. He showed no signs of pain, but threw his mangled spoon upon the table, the stew slopping onto the boards. He set his tankard down with enough force that some of its fluid slopped over the rim and onto the boards of the once-clean table planks, joining the stew.

Rocnar simply gulped a lungful of air and seemed unaware of the bread still suspended between table and face.

Long moments passed before either man moved again. Liammial now stared deeply into Rocnar's eyes, measuring for himself the strength of his courage and the depth of his loyalty, and found both sorely lacking. Rocnar's face showed only fear.

Neither man consumed any further food, but left their utensils on the table and raised their goblets. After draining three tankards in rapid succession, Liammial spoke, pleased to see Rocnar shudder from the anger in his voice.

"Hear me now." He dropped his voice low so the family at the fireplace couldn't hear him, and Rocnar, even as close as he was, had to lean forward to hear him.

"They. Will. Pay! Every. Last. One of them. Will. Pay. They are sitting on *my* throne, and I *will* have it. Twenty-five years of stealth have failed, but force shall triumph! Mark these words and mark them well, Rocnar. *I will get them. I will be king! On my oath I swear it!*"

Liammial stood abruptly.

"Find out all they know about the wedding and," he paused, barely able to form his lips around the word, "Kwennjurat!" He spat the word from his mouth as though it had a putrid taste, then swept from the room in disgust, his long, black cloak causing eddies of dust and dried straw to swirl in his wake.

Late in the evening, Rocnar pulled his weary bones up the inn's stairs. His skillful questioning of the Ambassador and his foolish family had yielded much information, and none of it would be to his highness's liking. He only hoped Liammial would be content with raging at his enemies, and decide a beating wasn't necessary for the bearer of the bad news.

A forlorn sigh escaped his lips as he neared the door of their rooms, his mind forming the wording of his news with care. He knew the way it was delivered was almost more important than what he had to say, if he wanted to keep all his body parts intact and out of pain. He paused a moment, then squared his shoulders and entered the room.

Chapter Five

A Royal Conference
24th Day of Corith, 2448

The rays of the midmorning sun peeped over Fergan's shoulder and crept between the lids of Tanella's eyes. She squeezed them shut tighter and buried her face against her husband's chest, unwilling to arise and begin a day which would no doubt be full of meetings and plans of war, so unlike the past week, which had held only love.

Fergan's arms tightened around her and his mouth swooped down to capture hers, and for a few more shining moments, Tanella's world was perfect. She watched the appreciation in Fergan's eyes before he smiled down at her, then saw his smile turn to regret as he turned away to leave their warm and comfortable bed.

The royal couple made their way to the small dining room where Fergan shocked the servants by serving Tanella with his own hands as they ate breakfast.

Finished, they stood and moved toward the door.

"Where is your father likely to be at this hour?" Fergan asked.

"Either in his office or the throne room." Fergan offered his arm and Tanella tucked hers through it, snuggling close to her husband's side, before leading him off through the passages.

The corridor outside Jameisaan's office held the regular door sentinels, and Tanella nodded to them as she stepped past to the closed door. Long used to Tanella's comings and goings in her father's office, they knew she preferred to announce herself. She rapped lightly on the door, and then opened it slightly, poking her head through the doorway.

"Papa?" she quietly queried.

"Come in, Tanella, and Fergan, too, if he's with you. We have need to speak with you both." Her father's voice pleasantly welcomed the young people within the room.

Tanella listened as the two kings outlined their plan. When they finished, silence drew thick blankets around the four as they sat, each with their own thoughts for long moments. Tanella felt Fergan's fingers squeeze her hand gently, and she turned to look into his beloved face. Something passed between them which was felt, but she couldn't put a name to it. She knew, as he had known, they would be serving their country together. They had discussed many different aspects of it during the past week while they were alone together, but neither saw the possibility they would be in separate places. The plan was a sound one, even though she disliked being away from both her new husband, and the center of action. Her hand tightened on his for a moment longer and then she turned to her father-in-law.

"How soon do I need to leave?" she asked, a little apprehensively.

"First thing tomorrow morning, I'm afraid," Fergasse said. "If you'd like, the reports are all there on the desk, and the two of you can spend some time right now reviewing them, then spend the early part of the afternoon together making your individual diagrams for what lies ahead. Jameisaan and I would like to meet with you both following dinner for a review of plans before we separate for our different areas. Is that acceptable?"

Tanella and Fergan looked at each other for confirmation. Tanella nodded, and Fergan answered for them both.

"We'll be ready, Father."

"Thank you, Son. I'd rather not have to separate you this soon after the wedding, but I have no choice in the matter. I thank you both for your willingness to help us save the country!" Bitterness filled his voice, his face a stern mask.

"Come, Fergasse," Jameisaan said, rising. "We have our own preparations to make before we leave for Jurisse in the morning."

Fergasse looked at his hands, and Tanella watched him slowly unclench his fists. "Coming, Jameisaan," he said, and rose from his chair.

He looked at the pair before him, his eyes lingering momentarily on their fingers still entwined. A heavy sigh left his parted lips, and he raised his gaze to theirs and smiled a bit sadly, Tanella noticed. "There are times it isn't much fun being the king!" he sighed. He nodded his head to the two of them and followed Jameisaan out of the room.

Chapter Six

Arrival at Royalhaven
25th Day of Corith, 2448

The sun was balanced on the edge of the land, painting the sky pink and orange in its last fiery protest before sinking out of sight and plunging the world into darkness at day's end. Torresson welcomed the warm caress of the last rays on his back as the boy Jornn skillfully guided their small carriage along the road.

Jornn's voice broke into his musings. "There's a village up ahead."

"That will be Royalhaven. We'll stop there for the night."

"I thought you said Royalhaven was the prince's estate?"

"It is. Many times the village takes its name from the estate it's located on. We're likely on the prince's land already."

"Then why not go on to the manor house? Or are we still too far?"

Torresson chuckled. "No, we're not too far, but I'm sure the prince's people here won't give up his documents easily, and that's a battle I'd rather fight on a good dinner and a night's sleep."

Chapter Seven

Preparations and Promises
25th Day of Corith, 2448

Princess Tanella sat on the carriage seat with her eyes closed. A person who looked closely at her might suggest the color of her pale face was tinged a delicate shade of green . Those who knew her best, who were around her on a daily basis, did not look closely at her. They eyed her gowns to be sure all was presentable, saw to the dressing of her hair in the current mode, even made sure her jewelry was the appropriate cut and color of stone for the occasion; but they did not search her face closely each morning.

The wheel of the coach hit a particularly deep rut, causing the carriage to sway to a precarious angle before righting itself. Janna grabbed the strap hanging just inside the doorway to keep from slipping onto the floor of the coach in a shameful heap.

Tanella pressed a handkerchief-covered hand to her lips and prayed she wouldn't disgrace herself by being sick before they could stop for a rest. She couldn't understand why a journey in a comfortable carriage along a mostly smooth road was making her feel so ill when she'd never before been susceptible to illness while travelling. Perhaps it was simply the sheer amount of time she'd spent travelling in the last moonatt, but a feeling in the pit of her stomach told her that was not the answer. Something else was wrong with her.

As soon as they got to Kwenndara and she'd rested a bit, she would seek out the healer.

Chapter Eight

The Pig In Poke Inn
26th Day of Corith, 2448

Torresson lay still on his bed and checked the window again, looking for any hint of dawn lightening the sky.

A good meal and a restful night's sleep came nowhere near describing their stay at the Pig in Poke Inn of Royalhaven.

The meal had been exactly that, meal. To be more precise, it was a thick, lumpy, mealy gruel which very nearly glued his mouth shut. When he'd enquired whether there was meat or fresh bread, the innkeeper had whined an excuse that his Highness's taxes were such there had been neither meat nor leavening for bread in the inn for a thrice of moonatts. Torresson looked at the girth of the man and doubted the truth of the statement, but remained silent. He didn't want to start a fuss while on the prince's estate.

Upon being conducted to their room, Torresson had shuddered in revulsion and asked to be taken to the Inn's best room. The innkeeper had hastily and most profusely insisted that this *was* the best room and Torresson would receive no better and no worse than the innkeeper himself had, the better furnishings having been sold for food. The servile manner was so overdone, Torresson doubted his word on any matter. He noticed the innkeeper was verbose when it came to settling the bill, which included their breakfast, he was assured, before the unkempt man quit their room to leave them in peace.

The thin straw-tick mattresses were threadbare, the straw poking through in places. They looked none too clean, and Torresson wondered what sort of insects might abide within. The ticks lay on rope-spring beds which hung slack. He was not at all sure the bed would hold his weight. He considered tightening the ropes, but the wood looked rotted and the ropes were frayed. The rags pretending to be blankets lay any which way across the beds as though the last human occupant had left hurriedly.

Rodent droppings were piled high in the corners of the room and lay scattered across the center of the floor as well. Lack of funds from high taxes didn't excuse pure laziness.

Jornn had silently set one of the trunks in the center of the floor and returned to the carriage for the other, his dismay written plainly upon his face.

Torresson considered once again trying to find a comfortable part of the bed, or at least a bearable spot. He declined to move, recalling when they had first lain down in the hope of rest the air had filled with straw dust which had risen from the ticks with each tormented movement of their bodies.

The broken window let in the chill night air. Wrapped in his own warm cloak only his face was exposed. Hopefully the thick wool would also help protect him from the creatures he was undoubtedly sharing the bed with.

Torresson kept his eyes firmly on the window as it slowly lightened toward dawn. Soon there would be sufficient light to quit this poor excuse for an inn. If they left at first light and drove slowly, it would be an early but decent hour when they arrived at Prince Liammial's manor.

The sky in the window brightened slowly but steadily, and he found his eagerness to be gone strengthening apace with the dawn's illumination.

Just as he judged it was time enough to be on their way, Jornn's voice came from the other bed in the cramped room, sounding somewhat groggy from lack of sleep.

"Do you think it's late enough in the day to be gone from this place, sir?"

Torresson grinned. Apparently the lad shared his distaste for this establishment. The pair arose and did their best to smooth the wrinkles from their clothing. Each hefted one of the small trunks and Torresson followed Jornn down the stairs of the silent inn and across a rock-strewn yard to the stables.

Together they secured the trunks in the coach and removed each horse from its stall. Carefully checking each horse for signs of rodent bites and inspecting their hooves for soundness, they soon had the team hitched to the carriage and were in readiness to depart.

As yet, they had seen none of the regular inhabitants of the inn. Not being in a mood for more of the lumpy gruel for breakfast, they declined to wake anyone before leaving.

After climbing up to the box Jornn started the horses moving on their way out of the village; neither looked back for a last glimpse of the Pig in Poke Inn. As they moved slowly down the road, Torresson gave Jornn explicit instructions.

"This is a letter of credit from King Fergasse." He handed the document to Jornn. "I want you to hold it for us."

Jornn, a surprised look on his face, gave the parchment one more fold and tucked it into the purse at his belt.

"I don't know what we'll encounter at Royalhaven, but I've a feeling it won't go easy. If there's trouble of any sort, I want you to leave. Go back to the inn at Headwater where we stayed the night before last. I'll join you there if I can. If I haven't come in three days, take the two trunks back to Jurisse.

"Give the trunks only to King Fergasse or King Jameisaan of Kwenn and tell them all that has happened. It's imperative they learn of it immediately."

"I understand, sir, but what of you?" Concern marked Jornn's voice.

Torresson grimaced. "I'll make my own way to Jurisse, if I still live. These are dangerous times, but great events are happening, and it makes for a good life to be involved in great things."

Jornn split his face with a grin, no doubt brought on by the strong emotion engendered by loyalty and the passion of one in service to the king.

"It's magnificent to be even a small part of great things," he agreed.

They traveled a ways in silence. Torresson could feel the boy was bursting to ask something, but Torresson was content to wait for the question. Finally Jornn gathered his courage and broke the silence.

"Sir?" His voice seemed unusually tentative, as though he thought the question might be met with derision or laughter.

"Yes, Jornn?" he said encouragingly.

"Do you think, well, that is to say, there's not much future for me at the inn in Jurisse. Horses and I get on well enough, but I find more joy in riding than caring for them." his voice trailed off in apprehension, as if he felt he was being too forward.

"And?" Torresson felt he knew what might be coming, but was determined the young man should actually ask for what he wanted.

"Well, sir," Jornn gulped down his fear and continued. "I was wondering if you would take me on as an apprentice. I think a courier's life might suit me. Not just this trip, sir, but how you've told me it usually is," he ended breathlessly.

Torresson grinned. "I have found you to be a pleasant companion on the road and think you'd make a good courier. I'd be glad to take you as an apprentice, providing your father has no objections."

"He has naught to say on it as I'm of age," Jornn protested.

"Perhaps," Torresson replied, "however, if he can't give you a good recommendation, I won't take you on."

Jornn nodded his understanding.

Chapter Nine

The Battle of Royalhaven
26th Day of Corith, 2448

Torresson pointed off to the left at the large, two-storied manor house which featured a wide, straight, tree-lined drive. "That'll be Royalhaven."

Jornn slowed the horses to make the turn. Within a very few minutes they had pulled to a stop in front of the massive, intricately carved front portal.

Torresson slid from the box, adjusted his tunic and courier bag, and walked confidently to the front entrance, rapping smartly on the door.

There was a short pause, then a butler dressed in pure black livery opened the intricately carved door and sneered down his long nose at Torresson.

"The servant's entrance is in the rear." He started to close the door again, but Torresson stepped quickly forward and blocked it with his body.

"I am here on His Majesty's business," he exclaimed "and I will not be treated as a common tradesman!" He pushed into the house as he continued. "Now; you may show me to the parlor, and send for the steward of the estate."

The butler didn't show him anywhere, but summoned a footman and whispered something into his ear. The footman bowed reverentially and withdrew.

Within a trice of minutes, three large, well-armed men entered the rear of the hall. Recognizing the trap, Torresson leaped for the front doors, getting one partially opened before the massive butler was there to fight him for possession of it.

Realizing his own escape was, for the moment, doomed, he screamed out the closing portal for Jornn to go. Torresson was rewarded with the immediate sound of hooves retreating down the drive at full speed before the thrown knife nicked his arm and stuck, quivering in the doorframe.

Torresson froze, understanding his life depended on making the right choices and saying the right things in the next few minutes.

The butler was no longer sneering, his face now the cold mask of a man-at-arms.

"Just exactly which 'His Majesty' are you here on business for?" the butler demanded. "And what exactly is that business? Couriers wearing colors from Kwenn have no call to be in this place."

Torresson swallowed and assumed his most humble voice and demeanor. What was going on here? He must play for time to discover it. They must think him harmless.

"Tis most true I wear Kwenn colors, and wear them proudly. My master, King Jameisaan the Good of Kwenn, very kindly lent me to the service of His Majesty, King Fergasse of Jurat, your own Monarch. King Fergasse was visiting in Renthenn and had need of a courier; I was fetched."

The butler thought that over for a minute or two before replying. A few droplets of blood flowing down his arm had made their way as far as Torresson's fingers; he flicked them so they fell to the floor with a splat. By now, his sleeve must look terrible, though he could feel the flow had nearly stopped. He hoped it would work in his favor.

"Well, then," the butler finally began, "state your business. His...Highness Prince Liammial isn't in residence, so I cannot fathom why you'd be sent here."

The slight pause as he considered what title to apply to Liammial was scarcely noticeable, but it put Torresson in mind of the retainers in Jurisse who had been told Liammial was King. He could hear feet scuffling nearby and knew in addition to the butler and the three armed men who lurked in the shadowy recesses of the hall, others listened, waiting for the butler to decree his fate.

"What I cannot fathom," Torresson replied infusing his voice with as much innocence as he could, "is why royal servants such as yourselves should attack and injure a king's courier before you even ask what his commission is? As it happens, I was sent to retrieve some of Prince Liammial's papers and bring them to his Majesty in Jurisse."

A pregnant pause burdened the air in the hallway for the space of several breaths before the butler spoke again. "You'll be taking none of Prince Liammial's papers with you. In fact, you'll not be leaving here yourself until I get instructions from his Highness on what to do with you." His voice was strong, implacable.

Torresson allowed himself to sway as another few droplets of his life's blood spattered on the marble floor, hopefully giving the impression the loss of blood had left him weaker than he truly was.

"Ranjit!" the butler barked, looking at the bloody mess that was Torresson's arm and the flecks of red now staining the floor. One of the hulking men at the rear of the hall moved smoothly forward at the sound of his name.

"Sir," Ranjit replied, his voice full of obeisance.

"Take our royal courier," the butler's sneering voice commanded, "to a guest room and confine him there. See that he has what's necessary to bind his wound. We wouldn't want to be accused of being uncivilized hosts."

"Yes, M'lord," Ranjit murmured, taking hold of Torresson's uninjured arm and pulling him roughly across the entrance hall.

Torresson stumbled twice while ascending the stairs, mostly from the haste his escort demanded. He hoped he appeared weak from loss of blood. Torresson tried to appear feeble and ungainly as he was hustled down the wide hallway.

Ranjit proceeded quickly to a door and shoved Torresson into what was obviously a sumptuously appointed guest room for a lady.

"Y'should find sumtin' in ta dressin' room ta use fer a bandige," Ranjit muttered in a surly tone, then stepped back, slammed the door behind Torresson and twisted the key in the lock.

Torresson straightened, gave the room a hasty glance, but found no obvious means of escape. He quickly explored the dressing room and the small maid's quarters beyond, and then settled down in the dressing room.

Removing his jacket and shirt with some difficulty, he stepped to a small cabinet against the outer wall of the room and poured water from a pitcher into the basin beside it, hoping the water was at least mildly fresh.

He rummaged in the cabinet and found cleanly folded linen cloths probably used in the bathing of the lady who would most likely use this room. He tore one into strips and laid them aside momentarily. He picked up another of the linen cloths and wet it in the water now in the basin. Bathing the slight cut on his upper arm, he also rinsed the blood from his lower arm and hand, then bandaged the wound the best he could one-handed.

Torresson grimly smiled as he completed the task. He'd always bled copiously from even the smallest scrape. Many times it had worked to his advantage; he prayed this would be one of those times. He knew those below stairs who had witnessed this wounding would have no idea how little actual damage the cut had done. Struggling a bit, he put shirt and jacket back on, wanting to be ready to flee if the chance appeared.

He took time now, moving as quietly as possible to avoid the sounds being detected by anyone posted outside his door, and looked through the suite in more detail. He noted the distance to the ground and the lack of trees convenient to his windows. His view from those windows told him the room he occupied was at the rear of the house, and he could see no guards posted at the stable doors. He filed the information away in his mind.

Torresson looked at all the clothing available; various sizes of women's garb, and took note the maid's door to the servant's back hallways was not locked. That could be either an oversight or a trap.

He also discovered an easily moved panel in the dressing room, with a narrow passage behind it. He'd wait a bit before investigating that possibility. Considering the accuracy of thrown knives in this household, he'd be better off waiting until all were sleeping before making his bid for freedom.

Chapter Ten

Flight!
26th Day of Corith, 2448

Jornn sat tensely on the box of the small carriage and watched as Torresson knocked on the ornately carved door.

Torresson hadn't told him much about this commission from the king, but Jornn was neither deaf nor stupid. Even in the stables of his father's inn they had heard about the army in Shuell, and a few made speculations on whether this had anything to do with Prince Liammial's sudden disappearance from the capital during High Court, an unheard of occurrence in anyone's recent or past memory.

He knew the trunks in the carriage were filled with parchments taken from Liammial's other holdings; now they were at his principle estate, obviously to collect more of the same. The massive front door swung open, then nearly closed again as Torresson skillfully talked his way into the manor.

Torresson had seemed less open this morning as they dressed; a touch more snappish. Of course, that could have been caused from the lack of sleep last night, but Jornn rather thought Torresson had a lot on his mind and was anxious about this day's work going well.

The directions he'd been given to safeguard the documents, even at the cost of Torresson's life, seemed to stem from over-anxiety, but he would follow them to the letter, as a good apprentice should.

Without warning, the door was snatched open. A blue and gold clad arm and leg emerged briefly, and then disappeared back into the house. Just as the door slammed shut, he heard Torresson's voice yelling at him to go.

With a heavy heart and complete obedience to the man he considered his master, Jornn snapped his whip above the horses' heads and set them to their quickest pace in the direction they'd come from.

There were no signs of immediate pursuit, but Jornn did not ease the pace until he was well beyond the village of Royalhaven and the unfortunate Pig in Poke Inn. It would be evening before he arrived in Headwater. He worried about Torresson as he traveled, praying his mentor would be safe, hoping they'd be able to join up in three days' time. Jornn had no wish to go to the king alone to give him the trunks he carried and tell him Torresson was missing and perhaps even dead. Jornn shivered in the morning air at the thought.

Chapter Eleven

Escape Attempt
27th Day of Corith, 2448

It was well past midnight and the sounds of people settling in for the night had long since ceased. From the sounds he'd heard, there were about ten times as many people here as there needed to be for a country estate whose Lord was not in residence.

There had been an argument in the next room amongst five male voices over which of them would get the bed tonight. The victor had won by claiming his rank entitled him to the bed every night, and if they didn't like sleeping on the floor, they could be put on patrol duty instead. The arguments had ceased abruptly at that point.

Torresson recalled the description of the black uniforms of Milord's Army the couriers had been given when Princess Tanella had been kidnapped last month. Every courier had given special attention to watching for such men and listening to all they could learn.

The clothing the so-called servants wore here had the same look to it. Their attitude was definitely wrong for members of the serving class, though it fit what he'd seen of professional men-at-arms. He'd bet most anything he owned the men on this estate were an advance party from the army. The only question in his mind was whether Prince Liammial was their victim or their willing host.

Once the men had all settled in for the night, the house had adjusted, too, squeaking and groaning as it breathed out the heat of the day from its tired frame and contracted in the cool night air.

Torresson had watched the patterns of movement in the garden throughout the day. Although men had come and gone from the stable, there didn't seem to be anyone guarding the horses within.

There were regular patrols through the grounds and gardens, the men moving in groups of three. The timing was such he felt he could avoid them, especially as they'd all been carrying lanterns since the sun had set, and would be easy to see.

An honest man, it had disturbed his heart to contemplate the thefts he would need to accomplish in order to effect his escape tonight. He had finally quieted his conscience by reminding himself that technically, everything within the borders of the kingdom belonged to King Fergasse, and furthermore, Torresson carried a royal decree allowing him entry to Prince Liammial's estate, and permission to remove anything from the premises which he felt was necessary to remove.

Of course, the king had been thinking of documents and containers to transport them in, while Torresson was currently thinking about a change of clothing and a horse; both were now necessary for him to take in order to complete his royal commission.

Torresson took a pillow from the bed and pulled the embroidered linen pillowcase off, tossing the exposed pillow back on the bed. He did the same with the other two pillows, leaving him with three handy bags.

Two of these he folded and placed in the courier bag which still hung from his shoulder. It seemed that even though the men in the house were willing to lock him up, they were not willing to risk the penalties attached to disturbing the contents of a courier's pouch. Torresson removed his boots and tucked them into the third pillowcase. He looped the top of the boot-filled pillowcase through his belt so his hands remained free. He spent a long moment considering the light blue color of his cloak, and then silently removed a black cloak hanging in the dressing room. It was light-weight, definitely feminine and wouldn't afford much in warmth, but the color was perfect for his needs.

Stepping softly in his stocking-clad feet, he entered the dressing room and pushed aside the hidden panel he had discovered earlier in the day. He lit a candle he'd found in a desk drawer during his earlier search of his prison quarters, re-secured the bundle of boots at his belt, and slipped into the secret passage.

Torresson carefully crept through the narrow corridor, placing his stockinged feet as near the wall as possible to prevent the floor from squeaking, if he could. It wasn't long before he'd reached the other end of the passage.

He puffed out the flame of his candle before easing the door open. The full moon streamed through the windows of the bedchamber into which he now peered. The dark velvet bed-curtains, heavy furniture, and sumptuous fur throw on the bed told him without doubt these chambers belonged to the master of the house. Prince Liammial certainly had a taste for luxury.

There were no soldiers sleeping here other than one body sprawled across the bed. In the fitful light of the fire Torresson could identify the butler who quite obviously commanded this bit of Milord's Army; Torresson suddenly recalled that one of the soldiers had called him "Milord" while they were capturing him this morning. Could he have stumbled across the army's headquarters, right here in Jurat?

He toyed with the idea of killing this "Milord". It would certainly cause a lot of problems for the army, if this were their commander-in-chief, but the odds that he could accomplish the deed in total silence were small, and Torresson decided the information he carried was worth more to the kings than one dead man. Torn between regret and relief, he decided to let the man live, hoping he'd made the right decision.

Torresson eased himself back into the secret passage. He'd likely have more success using the servant's back halls and stairs to reach his freedom. With no way to relight his candle, he was armed only with the knowledge there'd been nothing in the passage to trip over and no side openings.

He grasped the dark candle in his left hand, trailing a couple of fingers along the wall as he walked with his right hand outstretched before him, feeling for the door he'd entered by.

He was shortly back where he'd begun, in the sumptuous and feminine guest room. Relighting his candle from the embers in the fireplace, Torresson slid it into a candlestick and placed a glass chimney over it to protect the candle from stray drafts.

Chapter Twelve

Second Attempt
27th Day of Corith, 2448

Making sure the black cloak with its frilly feather trim completely covered his own more practical garment, he pulled the hood up and was immediately rewarded by a face full of feathers. He nearly sneezed from their tickle as he blew at the offending trim and after some effort got the pair of cloaks arranged to his satisfaction.

Checking to see his boots were still secure, Torresson picked up his candlestick and slipped through the maid's door. He crept out into the servant's back hallway, moving towards the rear of the house.

The bare floor was chilly through his stockings and Torresson moved as quickly as he could along the dim passage, locating stairs and moving down them to the main floor of the house. The stairs ended at a single door which he opened cautiously.

He found himself at the end of a corridor with a long blank wall facing four arched doors spaced on the left side of the hall. Red eyes gleamed in the candlelight from a crack low in the wall, but the span was devoid of human inhabitants. He heard muffled scurrying sounds from behind the panel and shuddered to think how many rodents were living in the space.

He swallowed, then crept along the hall to the first archway. Listening, the air carried no human sounds to his ears. He peered around the corner and saw the shelves of the small room piled with crockery and dishes of all sorts neatly stacked and awaiting use. Stemmed crystal goblets glistened from the rack where they hung upside down and drawers which would contain the cutlery lined the stone walls of the butler's pantry.

The next arch opened into the scullery with its large cauldrons for heating water and all sorts of pots, pans, knives, and other implements of food preparation.

A quick glance through the third arch showed the food pantry with shelves piled high with dry goods and foodstuffs of all sorts, including smoked meats hanging from the overhead beams. Closer inspection of those showed none had been cut into, and he resisted the urge to cut a large chunk from one to take with him. Torresson moved further into the room and appropriated other food for his journey, cutting a large slice from a partly used wax-covered cheese, then wrapping it in a bit of linen and tucking it into his courier's pouch alongside a small round loaf of bread. A basket of carrots sat on the counter, and he took two of them. One of the carrots went into his courier's pouch, while the other was snapped in half and tucked into his purse before he slipped silently back into the hall.

The fourth and final arch opened onto the kitchen as he suspected it would. Although there was bread rising on the hearth, there was no other evidence of human occupation. Torresson padded across the room wondering how much dirt his stockings had collected in his stealthy travels through the house with his boots at his side instead of on his feet. He carefully tried the latch on the outside door to test if it had been secured. The lever moved, and thankfully was well-oiled; no creaking, raspy noise split the kitchen's dark stillness.

Leaving the door closed for the moment, and still cautious of making sounds, Torresson set his candle down on a sideboard near the door where others were kept for easy access for the servants entering and leaving the house. He stepped back a few paces. He removed his boots from the frilly pillowcase and donned them, folding the case neatly and adding it to his courier's pouch. Turning, he blew out the candle's flame, leaving the smoking wax stick in place and still moving carefully to avoid noise, he strode the final steps to the door. Easing it open just far enough to admit his body's passage through the portal, he felt the cool night air caress his face as he closed the door quietly behind him. He stood still, listening to be sure he heard the latch snick back into place. If the door were found hanging open, his escape would be discovered that much quicker.

He moved onto the grassy verge alongside the path and slid into the concealing shadows surrounding a large bush, then settled himself to wait on the patrol. He'd been watching their movements as they patrolled the grounds in duos and trios all day long. It would be easier to get to the stable if he knew exactly where they were and which direction they were moving.

He must have just missed the previous patrol because it was very nearly half an hour by his best reckoning before he heard careless footsteps approaching his position, crunching on the gravel of the path.

"Jeeze," one man's voice grumbled, "there ain't nobody here. There ain't bin nobody here for the two moonatts we bin here. An' there ain't gonna be nobody here. So tell me why we gotta keep lookin' alla time!"

The trio paused in the path near Torresson. He dared not move even deeper into the shadows for fear the movement itself would attract their gaze. He breathed as shallowly and slowly as possible and prayed the guards would resume their patrol soon.

"Acuz his lor'ship sez so!" Jeeze replied. "An ah dunno 'bout yer, but ah lahk to stay healt'ee, so ah does whut his lor'ship sez ta do. Now hesh, Pesker. Iffen any o' th' reg'lars heer ya, then healt'ee iddn't whutcha gonna be. Ye wuz there. Ye seed yer own self whut they dunn ta Kingsport Ciddy. Me, ah lahk breathin' so's ah does whut ah'se told to do an ah keeps ma mout' shet. Now move on. We gots ta finnish th' patrollen afore we're found a-loiterin'." His voice held more than a tinge of fear.

"Yea, Pesker," the third man added. "Me an' Jeeze want ta keep livin', so shet yer trap!"

Jeeze set off down the path, gravel crunching beneath his feet, his two companions scurrying in his wake to catch up with him and the light he carried.

Torresson remained motionless in the shadows until the men were well out of both sight and hearing. At last, he cautiously withdrew from the shadows of the bush and began moving in the general direction of the stables.

He crept slowly down the pathways from one patch of deeper shadows to the next. He knew there were several hours yet of darkness and he wasn't about to sacrifice his freedom, or his life, for the few minutes he may gain by moving too quickly across the garden.

Twice more he paused to allow patrols to pass him by, and counted himself fortunate none had noticed him in the shadows with his ridiculous feather-trimmed cloak fluttering gently in the slight pre-dawn breeze.

When finally he entered the stables, he was delighted to see no guards had been posted over the horses. He'd worried over it all day since he hadn't been able to see the men's faces clearly enough to know whether they were relieving guards inside, or just checking on the horses.

Torresson paced silently down the row of stalls, seeing a goodly number of strong black horses filling the stalls. The sight strengthened his feeling that this was, indeed, a nest of soldiers from Milord's Army. He dared not steal one of them, knowing it would be harder to blend in with the general horses in this region, and easier to find were he pursued.

Continuing to pace silently down the row, he looked for a horse more likely to belong to Royalhaven and Liammial than the current army in residence. He would prefer one which looked to be swift, strong, and amenable to a midnight gallop with a stranger on its back. He reached into his purse and took out one of the pieces of carrot from the kitchen.

Nearing the end of the stables, a horse stood with his great head over the stall's door, and as Torresson cautiously approached him, he whickered softly, quietly pawing the ground with a front hoof.

Torresson whispered, "There big fella, easy, easy." He reached a hand out to the horse to touch his nose, bringing the other hand with the carrot piece up to the horse's head, his palm flat and the carrot resting on it. The horse nodded his head as if to thank him for the treat, and then with gentle lips slurped the carrot into his mouth. Torresson patted him on the neck, whispering softly to him, praying the crunching of the carrot would not alert others to his presence. The sound filled the stall, nearly echoing off the walls in the dark silence of the building. To his great relief, it didn't seem to bother any of the horses, including those in the next stalls.

Breathing a nearly silent mutter of thanksgiving, he made a cursory search of the immediate vicinity but found no readily accessible saddles or harnesses. He returned to the stall and with a sigh, pulled the soft rope halter and rein from its hook on the wall. It had been many years since Torresson had ridden bareback, and he had no doubt his nether regions would soon be reminding him.

The horse wolfed down the second piece of carrot, then seemed eager to don the harness; and with very little urging, followed Torresson from the stall and into the stable yard. The horse was tall, and lacking a stirrup to aid in mounting, Torresson led the horse to a wood fence, scrambled atop it and from there slid onto the back of his borrowed mount.

The horse remained docilely in place, accepting Torresson and the lack of a saddle with equal aplomb, surprising his rider and generating another prayer sent heavenward from the rider bent low on the horse's back.

Hiding against the line of trees as much as possible, Torresson walked the horse around to the front of the manor, listening for any sounds of discovery from the patrols. Keeping to the grassy side of the drive, he maneuvered the horse to the edge of the front gates. Slipping through them, he set his steed to a faster pace, staying on the softer ground at the edge of the road. After he'd made the first turn he lowered the hood of the frilly black cloak and raised the pace as he fled Royalhaven, heading for the open road.

Once on the main road, Torresson settled into a mile-eating but easy pace for the horse. In the dim light of the waning moon, he hoped the horse wouldn't stumble. Jornn would have reached the Headwater Inn early in the evening, and Torresson wanted to make the best time possible in order to catch up with him and their precious cargo.

He would certainly have a great deal to tell the king. Too bad he couldn't retrieve the papers from Royalhaven. With the army in residence, undoubtedly the documents there would have yielded much. Ah well, he'd done the best he could, and had at least escaped with his life and limbs fully intact. Another prayer of deep gratitude wafted heavenward on the early morning breeze.

Chapter Thirteen

The Mayor's Council
27th Day of Corith, 2448

Princess Tanella waited patiently while Janna fixed her hair. Her father had given her no guidance for this assignment; for the first time, she had been left totally on her own to carry out a royal directive.

She straightened her spine and took a deep breath. She must not fail; she had much to do, and very little time in which to do it.

Janna patted a last curl into place, and stepped back.

"You're finished, Milady," she said, offering a quick curtsy.

"Thank you, Janna," Tanella said, rising and giving Janna a hug. "I'm so glad you're here with me."

Janna giggled. "Now that you're ready to go, what do I do with the rest of my day?" Her face took on a little crease of a frown between her eyes.

"I honestly have no idea," Tanella answered. "What did Shayla tell you?"

"I really need to press the clothing we brought with us, both yours and mine as well."

"That sounds good," Tanella said. "I'd much rather be here pressing clothing than meeting with the mayor and his council. I've no idea what I'm going to say to them."

"Just tell them how things are and what they need to be doing," Janna suggested. "Don't let them argue with you; just be the imperial princess they're expecting to meet. Don't worry; I'm sure you'll do fine."

"I certainly hope so. I'd hate for Father or Fergan to be disappointed in me if this job isn't done properly."

"I've known your father all of my life," Janna said, "and I know that if you do your very best then he won't be disappointed, no matter what the outcome is. Mother always told us there was no single right way to accomplish a task, that the results were the important thing."

Tanella took a deep breath. Janna was right, she would simply do her best, and everything would turn out right. She hoped; and prayed fervently.

Within half of an hour, she was walking into the meeting hall in the heart of Kwenndara.

There was a goodly group of people seated around a long table, and with much scraping of wooden chair legs against the slate floor; they all leapt to their feet to bow and curtsy before her.

"Please be seated," she called out, and the room was again full of screeching chairs and then an expectant silence fell. All faces turned themselves toward their princess.

Tanella took another deep breath, settled her thoughts in her brain, and began.

"First of all," she said, "you should know that just above a week ago I was married to Prince Fergan of Jurat."

There were murmurs of surprise throughout the hall, the sounds echoing from the stone walls.

"Our kingdoms have become one, ruled now by my father, King Jameisaan, and my husband's father, King Fergasse. The name of our land is now called Kwennjurat."

The mayor raised an almost timid hand to catch her attention, and she nodded at him to grant him leave to speak.

"What will become of Kwenndara, your Highness? Where will the new capital of this Kwennjurat be located?"

Tanella smiled. He was probably worried about the possibility of lost revenue.

"That has not yet been decided," she explained, "because there are matters more dire facing our new, young kingdom. For the moment, the royal families are dispersed with our separate duties to prepare for the coming war."

"War!" one man gasped. By his clothing, Tanella guessed he might be head of the Smith's guild.

"War," Tanella confirmed. "Our Kingdom of Kwennjurat is at war with Milord's Divine Army." She looked at each of them seriously for a long moment to give weight to her words.

"This army has already consumed the entire kingdom of Shuell, and now stands poised on our southern border."

There were murmurs among the assembled group, but they were more expressions of astonishment than chatter between neighbors.

"My father, King Jameisaan, has gone to Jurisse to oversee the army along with King Fergasse. Prince Fergan is in Renthenn overseeing the formation of the new courier service for a more efficient way of communication between us all. Our job here is to gather fighting men to send to the army in Jurisse, and to succor the refugees which will soon be coming our way."

"Refugees?" one woman asked.

"From Jurisse," Tanella explained. "Both kings will be evacuating everyone not in the army from Jurisse, and they'll be coming here to stay until our kingdom is safe once again. We'll need help from everyone in Kwenndara, but I know we can accomplish the task my father has set us," Tanella said quietly. "I'll need each of you to send word to the palace by tomorrow morning as to what space and supplies the members of your guilds have to offer for the care and keeping of the refugees."

A more comforting murmur echoed around the room now, as people accepted what she had to say, and prepared themselves emotionally for the onslaught to come.

Tanella was relieved the meeting had gone so well. Perhaps her father had been right after all and she was really needed here. She breathed out a quiet sigh as she looked at the people before her. She let them have a moment more to talk softly between themselves before she garnered their attention once again.

"As I've spent most of my life in Renthenn, I don't know you as well as I should. I want to learn who each of you are as we will be working closely with each other in the next few weeks. Please do me the great favor;" she asked of them, "as you leave today, tell me your names and what guilds you represent. That way, I'll know which person to ask for when I'm confronted with a particular challenge. By the time the refugees arrive we need to be a smoothly-working team and be able to handle any and all situations which must be faced. I ask this favor of you because I can't possibly do this by myself.

"Kwenn has always had the reputation for courtesy and adaptability. Together, let us step forward and show the Nine Kingdoms we are still dependable, courteous, and compassionate with one another. It's up to us to set the tone for the consolidation of our countries. Please help me show my father that his trust in us is well-placed." She paused, looking at each one in turn before she closed her address. "Thank you. I shall await word from each of you by tomorrow morning."

She smiled at them, hoping they couldn't tell she was shaking in her boots and her stomach was rebelling against the food she'd eaten for breakfast. She only hoped she wouldn't disgrace herself before she got back home and in her private quarters.

Chapter Fourteen

Reunion
27th Day of Corith, 2448

He rounded the corner and the westering sun caught Torresson full in the eyes. Momentarily blinded in the ruby light, he closed his eyes as he slowed the pace but pressed on, trusting his steed to avoid obstacles in the road. The feel of the horse beneath him and the clipped sound of the hooves told him he was still progressing along the hard-packed earthen roadway.

The horse was a well-behaved mount, responding to his every command, verbal as well as with prompting from knees, thighs and the soft rope halter he'd managed to steal with the horse. With his eyes closed against the sun's brightness, the exhaustion he'd been fighting momentarily overtook his tired frame and he dozed, leaning heavily to one side as the horse plodded along. Head sagging onto his chest, Torresson swayed on the horse's back and the movement jerked him into wakefulness. Trying to right himself before he slipped from the horse, he reached frantically for the horse's straggly mane and dragged himself vertical, eyes squinting into the still-bright sun.

Surrounded as he'd been by his enemies last night, he'd dared not sleep. The scant minutes he'd been able to snatch the prior night at the Pig in Poke Inn had been neither restful nor abundant. Torresson raised his hand against the glare of the sun and peered down the road. He was rewarded with the distant view of a small village. Bone weary with fatigue, he cared not where he was, he would stop here for a night's rest. If he had not yet caught up with Jornn, he could do so on the morrow. Torresson pulled himself straighter on the horse and urged him to a greater speed.

Shortly, he drew near and entered the village. The shade of the double-floored buildings where shopkeepers had comfortable apartments above their business establishments was a blessed relief to his dry, irritated eyes.

He quickly located the inn and gratefully slid his aching body from the back of the horse, too tired in mind and body to make explanations to the ostler for the lack of saddle and proper leather bridle. Silently handing the horse over to the stableman who came to fetch it, Torresson turned and plodded into the inn's common room.

The slight figure which was instantly beside him belonged not to the innkeeper, who was assisting another patron at the moment, but to the boy, Jornn.

"Master Torresson! Are ye all right, sir?" Concern marked the young man's voice and appeared in his eyes as he stepped to Torresson's side.

As the youth looked full into his tired face, Torresson was aware that Jornn realized he mustn't say too much here, although he looked to be bursting with questions. Torresson was grateful Jornn was using such admirable self-restraint. He was too tired to talk or answer any query put to him. He hoped he'd remember to compliment the boy on the morrow.

"Fine; just dead tired, Jornn. Where's our room?" His vision, blurred from tired eyes, caused Torresson to squint, but he was just able to focus on the young face before him.

"I've food on the table, sir," he said, pointing to one of the nearby tables.

"Need sleep more'n food, Lad." His tired body swayed as he spoke.

"This way, Master Torresson," Jornn said as he quickly led the way down the hall and to the stairs leading to the rooms above. "We're on the next floor at the back so's it's a bit more private-like and quieter; but only one flight of steps."

Torresson mumbled a sound and then followed mutely up the stairs and along the hallway to a room at the back of the building. Opening their door, Jornn quickly moved out of the way and Torresson entered, sat on the edge of the bed and dropped his hat onto the floor in front of him.

Jornn, apparently sensing the complete fatigue of his employer, hurried forward and grasped a booted foot to help his master. Grateful, Torresson mumbled a weary thanks and fell back onto the bed, asleep even before the second boot left his foot.

Chapter Fifteen

For Lack of a Saddle
27th Day of Corith, 2448

Jornn gently lifted his Master Torresson's leaden legs onto the bed, covered the slumbering body with a quilt, and tiptoed from the room, softly closing the door behind him. As he walked down the hall, his intent to return to his interrupted meal, he met the innkeeper coming toward him.

"Hold, young Jornn," he said gravely. Jornn halted, a questioning look on his face. The innkeeper continued, his voice commanding.

"I mus' speak wit' yer Master Torresson 'twonce." His face was stern, almost angry.

"Hold, Innkeeper; Master Torresson is asleep and too tired even to eat. What may I help you with, sir?" Instinctively, Jornn stepped a pace more into the middle of the hallway to protect his sleeping master. He drew himself up to his full height.

"Yer master jist rode in on one of Prince Liammial's mounts wit' no saddle ner bridle. It looks ter me 'at th' horse be stole, an' we here 'bouts perteck our royal fambly. I mean ter find out how he gots hold o' th' horse." He stood, glaring at the lad.

Jornn, not being privy to that information himself, dared not answer in exactness, but felt he could probably give enough of an answer without disclosing their mission, to satisfy the innkeeper.

He smiled to charm the man. "If you'll recall, we're here on king's business and have a letter of credit signed by his majesty. Therefore, I'm certain it's not unusual to use resources of the royal family to carry out the monarch's commission." He widened his smile as he put both hands out, palms up, to give the impression of complete innocence, yet watching carefully to see how his words were accepted.

The innkeeper stood silent, appearing to mull the information over. Jornn knew he'd seen the letter of credit, not only when he'd returned alone, but prior to that, when they'd stopped here several nights ago and from the hand of Torresson himself.

Making up his mind, he gruffly said, 'At's so, but I still be a-wantin' a word wit' 'im meself, come th' mornin'. Jist ter hear it from 'is own lips, yer unnerstan'."

"I'll make sure to tell him as soon as he awakens, my good man, I assure you." Jornn's grin widened, but in secret relief. The innkeeper stood irresolute for a moment longer, and then with a muttered grunt he turned and walked back down the hallway and descended the stairs.

Jornn's eyes watched until the beefy man was out of sight before dragging much needed air into his lungs. He let it out slowly, muttering a near silent but thankful prayer to his Maker that his head was still attached to his neck, before heading down the hall himself to finish his now cold meal. He prayed he had done the right thing, hoping Torresson would be pleased Jornn had kept him from being awakened by a surly innkeeper.

Chapter Sixteen

Grace and Truth
28th Day of Corith, 2448

His Grace Anconn Kovach, The Lord Mayor of the great city of Jurisse, Crossroads of the Ten Kingdoms, sat uneasily in his chair at the head of the long table and watched the members of the council arrive.

Portly Ernnest, head of the Bakers Guild was chatting away merrily with diminutive Widow Hanna, who ruled the city's Washer-Women with an iron will. The mayor shuddered at the memory of the tongue-lashing he'd received on the only occasion he'd ever crossed the widow.

Quickly he turned from the recollection and surveyed others. Jonn Cooper was here, representing the barrel makers of Jurisse as he stood in a corner earnestly talking shop with Wayland Smith, descendant of the first blacksmith to set up shop in Jurisse. He liked Jonn and Wayland. They were diligent men, willing to listen and think about things before expressing their opinions. Hard workers they were, too.

His eyes continued around the room, noting who was in attendance, and saw all had arrived save for Sally Taylor, the seamstress, when her cheery face arrived at the door, slightly out of breath. She glanced around the room and quickly headed for the empty chair next to the Widow Hanna and demurely slid into it. Anconn nearly snorted. Sally might appear timid, but appearance was all it was; she was nearly as headstrong as the Widow Hanna, though somewhat easier to reason with. Once she'd made up her mind, however, it was nigh impossible to get her to even consider changing it. He left the thought and watched the assemblage a few moments longer as he pondered the implications of the unusual summons which had arrived at his door by special courier before sun-up this morning. He took in a long breath and expelled it silently. Best begin.

He cleared his throat and silence fell in the room; each of the members of the council was a professional in their field, and acted the part.

Each also took quite seriously their duties to their guilds and to their city. Good people, all. In view of the unusual summons he'd received this morning, he was certain their mettle was about to be tested.

The council members still standing in little groups around the room took their assigned seats at the long table, faces turned toward the mayor as they awaited his pleasure.

"Welcome, all," he began with a smile. "I appreciate your coming on short notice."

"Stow th' flowery speakin' an' git t' th' meat o' it. What's th' fire about? I gots ter git back t' me shop. Yer costin' me coins, ye are!" Tomm Cutter, the butcher, growled in his gravelly voice with heavy jowls wobbling slightly.

"In point of fact," the mayor said, "I don't know where the fire is myself. I was awakened before dawn by a messenger from the palace; the note he bore said only that the king wished to address the council at mid-morning, and so I called you to assemble."

"Whatever for in the middle of the work-day?" Widow Hanna called shrilly down the table, her black eyes snapping.

"You know as much as I do, Widow, for I've told all I know. Being a loyal subject of his Majesty, I've done as he commanded and I'll be content to wait upon His pleasure."

A wave of muttering swept up and down the table as people turned to their neighbor, but the assemblage remained in place in anticipation of the king's arrival.

They didn't have long to wait. Just as the mid-morn bells rang out through Jurisse, the door of the council chamber opened to the king and two of his men.

Lord Mayor and the council alike jumped to their feet and bowed before their king.

Fergasse moved to the head of the table, instructing them all to be seated, his personal men stationing themselves behind but on either side of the chair he'd taken.

As he'd never anticipated the need to be seated before the king, the Mayor had neglected to provide an extra chair for the meeting, and, so as not to hold things up by having one fetched, promptly seated himself on the floor at the king's side.

The king, however, noticed the action and called for a chair. One quickly was brought and added to the table. The king turned then, and looked down the table at each of them before he began.

"Ladies," he nodded to them, "and gentlemen, also, it is with a heavy heart I bring you ill tidings. For the first time in our history, we find ourselves at war."

He paused a few moments until the shocked gasps had quieted and he regained the attention of the assemblage.

"Some of you may have heard rumors of it already. I am confirming to you there is a large and vicious army which, having conquered and swallowed Shuell in a matter of weeks with much bloodshed, is now poised and preparing to fall upon Jurat."

Once again he waited a moment or three for the people to master their astonishment and fears before he continued.

"As I have no desire to see my people killed or enslaved, I've been working closely with King Jameisaan of Kwenn to find a way to save both our peoples from this army."

A collective sigh of relief rippled around the table, and offers of assistance followed from each of the gathered community leaders.

"You have no idea," Fergasse said, his voice close to breaking with the depths of his emotion, "how it warms my heart to see your willingness to work together in this time of trouble." He cleared his throat before continuing.

"You should be aware that my son Fergan has just been wed to Princess Tanella, and we have combined Kewnn and Jurat into a new kingdom named Kwennjurat. King Jamiesaan and I will be ruling jointly for the present.

"For our defense, all males above sixteen years and who are sturdy enough to wield a weapon are requested to join our army. We will be adding the men from Kwenndara and the rest of the country to the north, as well as all throughout our own kingdom who desire to fight and can be spared from the farms."

He shifted in his chair and leaned forward earnestly before continuing. "Everyone in Jurisse and not in the army will be evacuated to Kwenndara. We will be moving through the city quarter by quarter. We'll need every available horse, carriage, coach, and wagon, and we'll need to transport supplies as well as people.

"Many will have to walk, but we need the city cleared by sundown on the Second of Beltaine, which gives us four days, not including today. I'm sorry, but many of your possessions will have to be left behind. We're hopeful we can keep the bulk of the city intact, so that when this is over and the army vanquished, we can bring you home and you'll have homes and belongings waiting." The audible gasp was immediate.

One of the king's men stepped forward, handing a bundle of parchment to the king before stepping back into his place. King Fergasse handed the stack of documents to Jonn Cooper, on his right, who took the top paper and passed the rest along.

"Now, these are lists of what must be done, and by when. Anyone among you who cannot read should send word to the palace, and I will assign you an assistant who can. The north quarter goes first. We'll need some of your tradesmen to spread the word. We need every person in Jurisse to do their part and help, or there will be delay, and delay means innocent people will die. We can't allow it. There's plenty here for everyone to accomplish, so let's begin! Mayor Kovach, see to it without delay."

With these last words, King Fergasse rose from his chair and swept from the room. Immediately a babble of voices broke out, only to be silenced by the Lord Mayor's overriding tones.

"As his Majesty said, we all have work to accomplish, so let's get moving! Have your guilds get the word out to the people. I'll go to the orphanage. If we need to have a quarter of this city ready to leave by tomorrow, there's not a spare moment. Report back to me this evening at mid-evening bell. We must be in readiness for the king."

The council cleared the chamber at once, members scurrying in every direction, their papers grasped tightly. The Lord Mayor folded his parchment and slid it into a pocket as he all but ran toward the orphanage, organizing in his mind the steps required to get these children to the safety of Kwenndara.

Chapter Seventeen

An Unsuspecting Spy
28th Day of Corith, 2448

Torresson woke late in the morning, much improved for the sleep he'd had. His leather courier pouch was digging into the small of his back, and his full bladder was no doubt what had wakened him.

The inn room was small but neat, the other bed was empty and neatly made. He rose and made use of the chamber pot, then turned to a small table under a mirror. He poured water from the pitcher into its matching basin and then used it to wash his face and hands. He drew his comb from his pouch and, moistening it in the basin, tamed his unruly hair. Torresson grimaced at the wrinkles in his tunic; he oughtn't to have slept in it. His breeches were similarly creased. He flicked water on his clothes and pulled them as straight as possible. His growling stomach reminded him he needed breakfast.

Turning away from the mirror, he saw at the foot of his bed the small trunk containing Prince Liammial's papers they'd collected in Jurisse. Sitting on top of the trunk were the two battered leather cases containing his and Jornn's spare clothing. Sitting on the floor next to the trunks were Torresson's boots, newly cleaned and polished.

Gleefully digging into his bag, he discovered Jornn had seen his clothing cleaned and pressed. Taking on an apprentice suddenly had some advantages! Torresson gratefully doffed his wrinkled and dirty raiment and then made liberal use of the water in cleaning himself more completely before pulling on his crisp, clean clothing. Never before had he realized how heavenly a fresh change of fabric could feel against his skin!

His dirty clothing, folded as neatly as possible, he crammed it into his small bag, then sat on the edge of the bed while he pulled on his boots. Now he was ready for breakfast.

Proceeding down the hall and stairs Torresson made for the common room. As he entered the nearly deserted room, Jornn waved him over to a table near the fireplace and then hurried off toward the kitchen to bespeak breakfast.

The meal arrived shortly, crisp bacon with fried eggs and potatoes, and a small basket of soft rolls. A large flagon of sweet water was also set before him. Torresson reached for the basket of rolls with one hand, and the dish of butter with the other, but as he broke the first roll in two, the innkeeper himself arrived at his side.

"I be needin' ter speak wit' ye," he said in a low voice, "'bout th' horse ye brought in lass night. I be a-thinkin' 'tisn't yer horse." His look said much more than his tongue had.

Torresson nodded and immediately stood. "I'll speak with you in the private parlor. Jornn, watch my meal, if you would."

Jornn acknowledged the direction with a nod, and Torresson followed the innkeeper to the private parlor.

As soon as the door was closed, the innkeeper set in. "I wanted ter talk ter ye privily, Sor, acuz I know yer a king's courier, an' I never did hear of a courier goin' bad, but the fack is thet ye come in lass night on one-a Prince Liammial's horses, an wit' no saddle ner tack, an thass trouble like I doant need. So afore I accuse ye of horse thieving, I wanna know yer story an' how ye come by th' prince's horse, wittout no

94

acouterments, like." His eyes were serious, never leaving Torresson's face.

Torresson smiled disarmingly. "I can certainly understand your concerns; it's never good to be involved in a theft, particularly when the owner is as powerful a man as the prince. It happened this way: the trunk the boy and I are carrying on a private commission for the king contains items which he values highly. I can say no more of the contents than that. I was afraid that if highwaymen learned of my passage, they might try to steal what we carry for King Fergasse. I had instructed the boy Jornn that if we were stopped, I would climb down from the carriage, and appear to be opening the coach for the men, at which point he should leave quickly and wait for me at an inn of my choosing. As we set out yesterday, no, 'twas the day before, we were set upon in the road."

The innkeeper listened, his eyes bulging from his head in his excitement at being told such a thrilling tale.

"The boy carried out our plan," Torresson continued, "and left me in the road with the brigands so as to safeguard the king's trunk, alongside which my own life is of no moment in its importance.

95

"Their dismay at losing the carriage, and a valuable prize, quickly turned to anger against myself. They set about to beat me, and from their words I feared they meant to kill me. I managed to break free of them and ran for my life. I spent much of the day hiding in ditches and under bushes, and, late in the night I was able to make my way into the prince's stable.

"There were no lights on, neither in the stables nor in the house, so late was the hour. I was afraid to call out, for fear the highwaymen were still nearby. I couldn't see any tack at hand, except the rope bridle, so I took it along with the horse I needed in order to make my escape a certainty."

"Then ye did steal 'at horse from hiz highness!" the innkeeper started with incredulity.

"Well, yes, and then again, no," Torresson continued swiftly, holding up a hand to stay the innkeeper's protests. "You see, I have in my possession a royal decree, signed by the king himself, which authorizes me to borrow what I need from the prince in order to complete my commission. So in truth, I did not steal the horse, although the prince is not aware I have borrowed it."

He placed a hand on the innkeeper's shoulder to engender the man's confidence in the facts being presented, and continued.

"In fact, I didn't see the prince's banner flying at Royalhaven, and so believe he isn't in residence. What I require from you, good sir, is to care properly for this horse; it's been ridden hard the last day as I was making my escape. The poor thing needs rest and proper food.

"The king's letter of credit I carry should see to the horse's good care here at your stables while you await the prince's arrival. We wouldn't, after all, want to send the prince's mount back into an area infested with highwaymen who know good horseflesh. Prince Liammial will probably appreciate your hospitality for his horse and thank you in his own way with some reward. When Prince Liammial passes here on his way home, send the horse home with his entourage and send the bill to the palace in Jurisse. King Fergasse will pay you promptly."

The innkeeper puzzled out in his own mind the statements Torresson had made, thinking deeply and at length before he answered. "'Tis a good account ye gives of yerself, master courier, and I be doing as ye say. I'll keep a good account o' th' feed an' boardin' an' I be sending word to the palace then, as soon as I've delivered the horse to his highness."

Torresson sketched a shallow bow to the innkeeper. "Thank you for your aid in this matter; and now, if you'll make our carriage ready, the boy and I'll be leaving as soon as I've finished my breakfast."

The innkeeper bowed deeply and bustled off, and Torresson returned to his long-anticipated meal. If the innkeeper did as he promised, Torresson anticipated King Fergasse would be pleased to learn not only when the prince was back in Jurat but his exact whereabouts.

Chapter Eighteen

The Evacuation Commences
29th Day of Corith, 2448

Chaos reigned supreme in the North quarter of the city of Jurisse. People ran in every direction completing last-minute chores. Those with carts provided space for the belongings of the many who were walking. Even the smallest children carried small bags of food or skins of water. Every animal native to the quarter was loaded with as much as they could carry, or hitched to hastily improvised conveyances.

Carts were piled as high as possible, with extra boards added to extend their sides. The atmosphere was at once tense and jovial. Although some of the cheerfulness was forced, most people were grateful their king cared enough for their safety to evacuate the city, and the friends, family, and neighbors all did their best to finish preparations and leave according to their schedule.

With mutual assistance, the entire north quarter of the city had been emptied by mid-afternoon, and those who were staying behind as newly commissioned members of the Kwennjurat army were set along the boundaries of the emptied quarter to guard against looting by any of the less scrupulous among the remaining populace.

King Fergasse looked on the guards with satisfaction, and hoped they realized their work in guarding their homes would also guard their king and country. He surveyed the work done this day and hoped the next three days would go as smoothly, then turned wearily toward the palace; his day was not yet finished.

Chapter Nineteen

The Thayne of Liammial
29th Day of Corith, 2448

The small, nondescript carriage trundled
down the road in Verr. The occupant had no liking for this part of the world. The land was low
and flat, and it flooded regularly. A profusion of
plants grew in every crevice that held the least
amount of dirt or water. Many grew, bare-rooted,
clinging to the rocks themselves. One couldn't
move without brushing up against something that
would instantly release its particular odor to add
to the already ill perfumed air unless you had a
vigilant gardener who cleared living space for
humanity on a daily basis. In Liammial's opinion, none of the gardeners were vigilant enough;
the entire country was one giant, stinking swamp.

Nevertheless, it offered something of value to him. One of the many noblemen in his secret kingdom lived here, and would offer him not only a place to shelter, but a base of operations where he could get information and direct the last stages of his work, setting the timing for the final act. The coach slowed and turned into the estate, and Liammial relaxed fractionally. Here among his loyal vassals, he should be safe from the persecution of his brother. Very shortly, Rocnar brought the carriage to a halt in front of the stone steps of the manor house. The vehicle swayed as Rocnar scrambled down, and Liammial waited, listening.

There was the pounding of the knock at the door, and the sweeping sound of wood against stone as it was opened. Two indistinct voices lightly punctuated the air with sound as Rocnar conversed with the doorman, extracting information as well as announcing their presence. A pause of peaceful stillness followed the low voices. Hurried steps approached the coach, effectively stomping on the quietude surrounding Liammial and then the door was flung open by the Baronet himself, his non-stop blathering not slowing as he offered aid to Liammial in exiting the coach and blessing his lucky stars that his

Majesty had come to stay, gracing his humble dwelling with his august presence.

Liammial dug out his court manners and smiled at the man, and was offered the best bedchamber and his choice of any of the ladies on the estate for his own personal amusements. He accepted both, and wearily made his way to his bedchamber, announcing that he wished to rest after his journey, and would not be down for dinner this evening but would take a tray in his room.

Chapter Twenty

A Rude Awakening
1st day of Beltaine, 2448

His Royal Highness, Prince Liammial of Jurat and recently resigned Ambassador to Kwenn opened his eyes. The bed was sumptuously soft, the velvet coverlet warm and for one brief moment he imagined he was awakening in the palace in Jurisse.

A scowl darkened his pale features as his eyes contemptuously picked out threadbare spots in the hangings and the slightly scuffed finish on the dresser. His hope came crashing down around his ears as he recalled his recent reversal of fortune.

It was no secret to his particularly close associates that, above all else, he desired possession of the throne of Jurat, along with all of the privileges which accompanied that golden seat.

There were, however, a few minor obstacles between himself and his legitimate inheritance of crown and kingdom. Of prime consideration, of course, was the fact the throne was currently occupied by his elder brother. What did it matter that Fergasse was a scant few hours older? It should have been obvious to all Liammial was far more fit to rule.

The path to the throne had also been blocked by Fergasse's two children. Years ago Liammial had arranged an accident for his niece, Diantha, just before her marriage, insuring she produced no heirs. It was a great comfort to him that his interfering sister-in-law had perished in the same accident when the highwaymen had become a little rambunctious and overstepped their instructions.

His nephew, Prince Fergan, had proved to be a more elusive prey. Liammial had learned early on it was impossible for anyone to arrive unremarked at the young prince's country estate, Havenhill. King Fergasse had set additional watchers over his only remaining child since the time of Diantha's death. Undoubtedly Fergan was unaware of how closely he was guarded, but much to his chagrin, Liammial had discovered no way to remove the young prince, either at court, or at Havenhill without the finger of blame pointing directly at himself.

Until now, Liammial had not been willing to come out in open opposition to his brother, but his attempts to stop the marriage of Fergan to the brainless bit of fluff in the next kingdom over had been discovered, and Liammial had been forced to flee. Time had run out, and the children were wed. They must be dealt with before they produced yet another presumptuous claimant to *his* throne.

Prince Liammial rose from his bed and donned a deep blue velvet dressing gown. He padded across the room to a chair by the fireplace and sat before the ashes within the grate. The couriers he'd borrowed and sent to those who had sworn fealty to him in return for the promise of titles, land, and power upon his ascension to the throne had not yet had time to deliver their messages; he expected none of them to return for at least a week. Therefore, today he would concentrate his not insubstantial attentions on the twin challenges of aiding Milord with his upcoming invasion and dealing once and for all with the newly wedded pair, Fergan and Tanella.

What he really needed most for either venture was information, and he had various ways to gather that. He rang for Rocnar.

The cringing, mousy man hobbled into the room, bowing and fawning. For some reason Liammial found the servile behavior irritating. He frowned, and the servant flinched as if expecting a blow. The man was impossible! After all, it wasn't as if Liammial had given him undeserved beatings. Good help was hard to find, and though Rocnar was only an indifferent valet, he was an absolute genius at extracting information and remaining discreet when about his master's bidding.

"You'll need to pack for several days." Liammial began, "I have a little errand I need you to accomplish; a matter of some essential information."

Rocnar bowed again. "Yes, Your Highness. Where will I be going?"

"Jurisse. You are to return to the palace. I have a note for you to deliver to Lady Autrancia. There will be a reply. Also see if any dispatches have arrived for me from Shuell. They will have the black and flame-red ribbons on them. Find out for me when my dear brother will be returning from the wedding in Kwenn. Most importantly, I need to know where Fergan and Tanella will be making their home, where they are now, when they're likely to be travelling, and by what route."

Rocnar had nodded his head as Liammial had stated each one of his points, but he looked up sharply at the last demand, his eyes widening in fright and understanding.

"Do you mean to kill them, Milord?"

"Of course I mean to kill them," Liammial stated casually, in the same manner he would discuss whether or not to attend a dinner party. "How can I inherit the throne while Fergan lives? And we can't discount the possibility that they've been wed two weeks and the frivolous little slip of a princess may already be carrying the next heir; an heir which I will not allow to be born. So be off with you to Jurisse, and bring me what I need to ensure that I am the only living heir to the throne of Jurat."

Chapter Twenty-one

Arrival in Jurisse
1st Day of Beltaine, 2448

Torresson stretched contentedly in the late afternoon sun. It was Jornn's turn to drive, and Torresson had nothing to do other than watch the passing scenery and keep a lookout for trouble. With luck they should reach Jurisse tonight and get a bath and have a long night's sleep before meeting with King Fergasse at the palace tomorrow. He'd be able to deliver the precious papers he'd gathered, along with the more urgent information that there appeared to be a contingent of Milord's Army staying at Prince Liammial's royal estate, possibly led by Milord himself.

He gazed for a while at the backs of the horses. They'd traded teams each night at the different inns and were using the pair they'd begun with two weeks ago on their out-bound journey. He really was looking forward to a long soak in a hot tub.

His practiced eye noted the harness straps on the right side horse were somewhat looser than they should be. He instructed Jornn to stop and as soon as the carriage had been pulled to the side of the road, he jumped down while Jornn remained on the box.

Torresson inspected the harness. Now that the carriage was stationary, the straps were properly tight. The horse, therefore, hadn't been pulling its full share of the carriage's weight. He bent down to inspect the animal's hooves and found a fairly large stone lodged in one shoe. It was no wonder the horse hadn't been pulling correctly; he knew *he* wouldn't be putting his full weight on a shoe with a rock in it!

Torresson drew his dagger and carefully pried the stone from the hoof. There wasn't any blood, but when he released the hoof, he could see that damage had been done. The horse had developed a bruise and wouldn't put its full weight on the hoof. There was nothing more to be done here on the roadside; the horse needed hot compresses and rest. The next inn would be the closest place to receive aid for the animal which, if Torresson was not mistaken, was in Jurisse.

Swinging himself back onto the carriage box, Torresson briefly explained the situation to Jornn, and they set off again, moving now at a walk. He drew in a deep breath and sighed. It looked as though his bath would be much delayed.

The sun was long gone by the time they reached the outskirts of Jurisse. Torresson couldn't see a single light at any window and judged the time to be nearing the midnight hour. As they approached the gates, lit with a pair of torches, he was unsurprised to find the heavy planks closed. He climbed down from the box as Jornn pulled to a halt, and then walked to the side of the gate, intending to rouse the keeper.

He rapped firmly on the gate-keeper's door. To his surprise, instead of the single man who usually tended the city's gates, a small knot of armed men stepped around the corner of the gatehouse, several of whom carried torches.

One of the men holding a torch approached the gate, accompanied by three of his silent fellows.

"Who goes there?" the man with the torch demanded.

"Torresson, king's courier of Kwenn, on a commission for King Fergasse." Torresson replied, "and Jornn, my aide." He eyed the arms a bit nervously, not knowing who held them.

The man signaled to the others still stationed at the corner of the gatehouse and the gate slowly opened, but only barely wide enough to admit Torresson's equipage. As the gate swung shut behind them, Torresson noted it must have been recently oiled because the usual squeak was missing. He climbed back up on the box with Jornn and they continued on their way.

Jornn drove through the silent, dark streets to his father's inn. In view of the lateness of the hour, they didn't have concerns when no one emerged to take the horses. Together they unhitched the beasts and led them into the stable. Jornn stopped by the doorway long enough to light a lamp.

He turned and held it up, then gasped, his mouth hanging open. Torresson could see why. In all the length of the stable, there wasn't a single horse in any stall. They quickly stabled their animals and then hurried to the inn to raise the alarm for the missing horses.

Entering through the kitchen door, their befuddlement was compounded. There were no lights within. The fireplace contained no glowing coals, but was dark and cold. Jornn pulled a small tin from his pocket and working by touch, struck a light. He soon had a lamp lit, and was gazing around the empty kitchen. Concern for his family filled his face.

It was obvious the inn was unoccupied. The fireplace had been completely cleaned of ashes. The dishes were neatly set in their places. Jornn called out for his mother and father as he dashed into the pantry, then returned, fear evident on his face.

"No one's here! The food's all gone! What's happened, Torresson?" his voice wavered on the edge of tears. "My family!"

Torresson shrugged and reached out to lay a hand on the boy's shoulder.

"No idea, Jornn. There's a lot that can have happened in two weeks, and not necessarily bad things," he said. His voice was measured and he strove to keep it level to give the boy a reassurance he couldn't find within his own heart. "Because everything seems put away and the food taken in an orderly way, it looks like they left of their own will and not because they were forced to get out in a hurry. I suspect we'll get our answers at the palace."

Jornn headed for the door. "Let's go then."

"Hold, Jornn. We can't show up at the castle at this time of night," Torresson argued. "They'll hardly open the gates for anyone less than the king. Your lame horse needs to rest, as do we. Best we sleep here and go on in the morning."

Jornn nodded, unshed tears bright in his eyes. "You're right, Torresson. I'll get some wood then, for a fire. At least we can be warm and comfortable tonight, if not well fed. Sorry about that."

"Not to worry, Jornn. We'll do for the night. Come, let's get our gear."

Together they brought their bags of clothing and the small trunk in from their carriage and built a fire in one of the better rooms. Jornn fetched blankets and made up their beds. Wrapped securely in a blanket he said his grandmother had made, he cried silent tears of worry for his family until he fell into a light and restless slumber.

Torresson watched the firelight catch the tear-streaks on Jornn's face. Though he'd tried to make light of the situation, he knew there were precious few reasons the inn would be empty like this. If the army had come and Jornn's family had all died fighting in the streets; no, then he wouldn't have known the gate men. They wouldn't turn against the king and serve the army, and they wouldn't have just let him in without giving him a warning of some sort.

They'd find out more at the palace tomorrow, but until he knew what the true situation was, he would be ready to bolt at a moment's notice.

Chapter Twenty-two

Inn Trouble
1st Day of Beltaine, 2448

Torresson awoke abruptly. Someone was moving quietly nearby. A few feet to the left of him, Jornn's sleeping lump, curled in his grandmother's quilt, was outlined by the light from the dying embers in the hearth. He couldn't have made the sound which had penetrated Torresson's sleep, nor were Jornn's quiet, snuffling snores enough to have brought him to this stage of vigilance.

A soft creaking sound penetrated the otherwise silent inn. Torresson slipped from the blanket he'd thrown over his own tired body an hour earlier and silently stepped towards the room's entrance. He'd covered more than half of the distance when the door was thrown open and men were rushing in, one knocking him aside as he passed by. Torresson banged into a chair which threw him more off-balance as he crashed to the floor, rolling away from his attackers.

The room was filled with loud yelling and the splintering sounds of furniture crashing asunder. His own yell to alert Jornn was unheard in the din, and as he scrambled to his knees he saw two men grab the quilt and dump Jornn onto the floor.

Jornn's arms flailed out, trying to ward off continued attack by the two who'd upended him. A blow to the side of Torresson's head brought his attention to the solid shadows attacking him. As he tried to roll away, he used his feet to kick the legs from beneath one of his assailants. He got at least one good punch to the innards of the other, judging by the whuffing sound just above his own head as the man toppled to the left. He scooted out of the way as the fallen attacker regained his footing and came back toward him.

Torresson jumped to his feet, his knee meeting with the oncoming man's upper leg, twisting the man away from him. The yelling sounds had ceased as the fight increased, and Torresson yelled for all to hear;

"Couriers! We're couriers!"

Abruptly the aggressive action halted, and only the sound of heavy breathing was heard in the sudden stillness.

"What's that?" one of the marauding men asked, wheezing slightly.

"We're couriers of the king." Torresson repeated, less loudly but just as firmly.

"Can they prove it, Dromminilva?" a different man asked.

"Do you have the proper letters to show it?" First Man asked, still rather breathlessly.

Torresson realized this Dromminilva must have been the one he'd hit in the guts and who must be the man in charge.

"Yes, we can. My tunic with Kwenn's colors is, or was, on the chair at the foot of the cot near the window. The pouch on the seat holds letters proving it. Let me get them for you." He didn't move yet, but awaited office to do so.

Dromminilva considered but a moment. "Get the papers," he said, still more aggressively than Torresson liked to hear, but he moved towards his belongings as Dromminilva continued, "Pittarrs, stoke up the fire so's we can see."

As Torresson moved toward the chair which had been shoved away from the bed and into a nearby corner, he saw another man head for the hearth.

He opened the pouch he'd retrieved from the floor as the sound of wood being tossed onto the coals met his ears. Grasping the parchment with the king's seal on it, he turned to the men in the room. The stance of each told him they were still ready to fight.

He lost no time in holding the papers up. One stepped forward; a slight hunching told Torresson the man's innards were still hurting. Mentally he shrugged. He should have simply knocked on the door and asked what they were doing instead of rousting them in such an aggressive manner.

Dromminilva plucked the parchment from Torresson's outstretched hand, stepped closer to the now brightening fire and opened them.

From the length of time he had the pages tilted towards the fire, Torresson figured he was either a slow reader or he'd read them through thrice.

Sighing, Dromminilva re-rolled the parchment and handed the roll back to Torresson.

"They seem to be in order and not forgeries. We're sorry about jumping you, but this whole section has been evacuated, and we're to make sure no looting goes on. The odor of burning wood brought us to this block and smoke from the chimney pointed to your being here. Why didn't you just go on to the palace?"

Torresson noticed the men relaxed marginally, but were still alert. "We didn't get here until after the gates were closed, and we wanted to present clean bodies at the palace in the morning. They don't need to smell the week's hard travel on us."

"Why did you choose this particular inn, instead of one in an area still populated?"

"No one told us about the evacuation, and this is Jornn's home. It seemed a logical choice at the time. It now makes sense there was no food here. If his family was evacuated, they would have taken everything with them."

"Sorry about the intrusion," Dromminilva repeated, "but with the evacuation, there are strict curfew rules. While you're in the city, don't be out after dark, and don't go into the evacuated sections."

"Thanks for the warning," Torresson answered.

The men turned to leave, the one closest to Jornn helping him to stand and untangle the quilt still twisted around his legs.

A sharply indrawn breath made Torresson aware Jornn was injured, but as he'd not made a sound or a word of complaint, Torresson said nothing. The men left the bedroom, clunking down the stairs in their heavy boots, their muttering voices becoming more indistinct with distance.

They heard the firm thud of the front door closing, and both men let out the air they'd trapped in their lungs.

"How badly are you hurt, Jornn?" Torresson asked.

"I don't know. My ankle feels mangled."

Torresson stepped to his side, supporting his young friend as he limped once and then hopped over to the bed. Jornn sat on the edge and pulled his foot up to place it on his knee. Torresson could see the swelling already well advanced, and glanced around to find something to prop the injured foot on.

Two of the four chairs had been reduced to splinters, but the chair his clothing had been resting upon was still whole. He dragged it over and gently stretched out Jornn's leg, placing the foot itself on a portion of folded quilt to pad it for maximum comfort while he assessed the damage.

Jornn made very little sound as Torresson prodded the lower leg, ankle and foot. His face was ashen in the firelight, and beads of sweat dappled Jornn's forehead. Torresson guessed the pain must be severe. Finished with the prodding, he swung both of Jornn's legs over onto the bed, being as careful as he could be and instructed Jornn to lie back on the bed. Although there was heavy swelling and some discoloring already in evidence, it did not appear to be broken.

"Is that the only place you hurt?"

"Yes."

"Well, as far as I can tell, your ankle will need a healer, but we can get that done at the castle tomorrow. For now, about the best we can do is try to get as much sleep as possible in the hours of this night we have left to us."

He picked up the quilt and laid it over Jornn, gently tucking the edges in, trying to give comfort without treating him as less than a man. He'd comported himself well in the skirmish, and hadn't cried or complained even though Torresson knew damage like that to an ankle would hurt like the devil himself had stomped on it.

Returning to his own bed, he straightened the covers and slid down, finding the best position he could, but knowing he'd not get much sleep himself. His stomach growled with his hunger, and he hoped they hadn't sent the castle's best cooks with the evacuation party. A good wash and a tasty breakfast would go a long way to make life cheerier.

What a hectic and dangerous excursion this had turned out to be, but interesting. Yes, highly interesting, Torresson thought as he lay quietly, listening for sounds of the night, but finding few. He wondered what the morrow would bring, and if the kings would find much of interest in the papers they'd brought with them.

He heard one small sound from the other bed, and Torresson contemplated the time he'd have to be without his young friend as Jornn's ankle healed at least enough to walk on. He hoped the boy would be able to garner at least a little sleep before the sun split the sky.

Chapter Twenty-three

At the Palace
2nd Day of Beltaine, 2448

"Will we have access to a healer once we get to the palace?" Jornn's voice held doubt considering he was just an innkeeper's son who hoped to become a courier.

"It shouldn't be a problem, lad," Torresson said as he guided the horses through the silent streets of Jurisse. Are you all right with us going this slowly?" he asked, glancing at the young lad next to him on the box of their small carriage.

"Yes, I'm fine. It only hurts when we find an especially large bounce," he said, "and with the injured horse setting the pace, we shouldn't have too many to contend with. Actually," he grinned impishly up at Torresson, "going this slow makes me feel a bit like I'm supposed to wave at the peasantry, except there doesn't seem to be anyone to wave at!" He raised an arm and waved at the empty air beside their coach while Torresson laughed.

"Well," Torresson snorted in his amusement, "we definitely are moving with a slow and stately grace, which is, indeed, how the royalty travels about the city!" His laughter rang out across the quiet street. "Don't get too used to waving, Jornn, we'll be at the castle's entrance in a few minutes."

The palace guard recognized Torresson and at once opened the gates for him, the horses maintaining their snail's pace as Torresson directed them toward the stables.

There seemed to be a fair amount of activity at the stables, and Torresson was encouraged. A stableman appeared as he drew the carriage to a halt. Tying off the lines, Torresson vaulted lightly from the box.

"Torresson, how've ye bin?" the older man asked as he shoved a hand forward, grasping Torresson's hand. "What kin ah do fer ye?"

"I need you to look after this horse, Geoffrey," he said gravely. "He picked up a rock yestereve, but we still had a ways to pass before we could get him seen to. I know you'll know exactly what to do."

The man grinned to hear Torresson's praise. "Go 'long wid ye," he said. "I'll look attar th' harse wivout all da palaver!" He looked pleased just the same. He barked orders to several of the stable lads standing nearby, and they began to ready the horses for unhitching.

"One other thing; may I borrow a couple of your lads to help? I've a pair of small trunks besides our clothing to get into yon castle, but more important is young Jornn here. He's badly injured his ankle and can't take a step on it. The bones may be broken. We won't know until a healer attends him, but in the meantime, I'll need to have him taken up and settled on whatever bed Michaals assigns him. He'll probably send for the healer then."

The man nodded his understanding, and pointed to several others within his sight to help Jornn and Torresson. A litter was fetched and Jornn was carried, over his protests, to a bedchamber in the palace Michaals assigned for their use.

With Jornn settled onto one of the two small beds, his face white with the pain of getting him there, Torresson quietly spoke with the butler regarding the healer. Michaals had given Torresson no argument this time, remembering their last encounter. Torresson appreciated the consideration, and showed deference to him in return.

"I'll send for him immediately, Torresson," he said. "Is there something more you need than this room and the healer?"

Torresson smiled gratefully. "Since the city is completely deserted, we were unable to have supper last night, nor food to break our fast this morn. If a plate of something warm could be foraged and brought to us here, it would be fully appreciated!"

Michaals nodded and added, "Would some cool lemonade be welcomed as well? I think there was some freshly brewed this morn, and mayhaps there's a bit left."

Torresson's smile stretched into a full grin. "It would be most welcomed, Michaals! You have the best lemonade in the Kingdoms, I'll swear it! My mouth is already wet with the anticipation of the beverage!"

Not a short while later, Torresson and Jornn had received an excellent meal. The dishes of bread and cheese were tasty and the juicy meat which, though it had cooled since the last meal was served, was still delicious. They topped the whole with cups of the fresh lemonade.

The healer arrived shortly, and after careful examination of Jornn's painful ankle, put their minds at ease.

"In my opinion," he announced, "nothing has actually broken. You need to keep the limb propped upon pillows until the swelling subsides and do not place weight upon it until the pain is gone. I've some liniment here to rub onto the ankle soundly," he said, matching action to word, "and then bind it tightly. Repeat this every third hour," he said as he finished the binding. "I'll be back tomorrow morn to see how he goes on." He busied himself packing up his medicaments, not paying heed to those around him, as Jornn proclaimed his ankle was on fire.

Jornn was in such obvious pain from the examination, that Torresson ignored his inclination to laugh at the boy's discomfort. Jornn's antics as he tried at once to yell like a scalded dog and grit his teeth and bear it like an adult were entertaining.

The healer finished gathering his equipment and elixirs and then hurried off to present his bill to the steward.

As the healer left the room, Jornn, threatened Torresson with bodily harm if he came anywhere near his ankle with the smelly devil's brew.

"Rest easy, Jornn," Torresson said calmly. "I'll only put some on you if the swelling hasn't gone completely by the time you're supposed to have your next treatment."

"Do you promise me, Torresson?" Jornn said, wiping the tears from the corners of his eyes with a shirt sleeve.

"I promise, Jornn. In the meantime, I want us both to rest until supper. Michaals said the kings will be busy until at least that time. Then we can give our report and turn over the documents."

He yawned widely, doffed his outer wear and dropped his weary frame into the small bed opposite Jornn's, falling at once into a deep and untroubled sleep.

Chapter Twenty-four

Torresson's Report
3rd Day of Beltaine, 2448

A gentle hand touched Torresson's shoulder and he came awake at once. A manservant in the black and red livery of the King of Jurat stood before him, leaning slightly toward Torresson's recumbent form, his hand outstretched still from the considerate awakening shake. The man straightened and took a step back from the bed. He gestured to his right, where a covered tray sat upon the night stand, delicious breakfast smells wafting from beneath the cloth.

Jornn was already awake and sitting up in the bed across from Torresson, the habitual smile upon his optimistic face, but the pallor of his skin bespoke his pain.

"The healer will be returning momentarily to see to the young man's injury," the servant was saying, "and King Fergasse bids you attend him as soon as you have washed and broken your fast. He is in his study. Would you have need of a guide?" The servant raised an eyebrow in question, his clear gaze upon the courier's face.

Torresson shook his head. "I need no guide to the study; however, I will need assistance carrying these two small trunks to the king," he said seriously, indicating the pair of containers in the corner. "I'll ring when I'm ready. The breakfast smells wonderful; thank you for bringing it here, and please inform the king I will be there directly."

The servant bowed slightly and withdrew.

Torresson rose from the bed and moved toward Jornn's side, and then the healer bustled through the door and peremptorily jostled Torresson to the side.

Muttering under his breath, the curative man removed the wrappings, applied more of the salve and bound the ankle tightly again. "The swelling is disappearing nicely despite the colored marks now blooming on the boy's foot and ankle," he said to the room at large, as though Jornn's hearing was the injured item and not to be trusted with the direct knowledge.

Jornn's wrist received like attention from the healer and Torresson saw the perfect hand-print shape of the bruising there. He clamped his teeth tightly together in frustration and anger to keep his tongue under control; it wouldn't do to speak of their man-handling here, he'd wait until his audience with the king.

Having been shunted to the side, however, Torresson busied himself washing the dust of the road from his body. To his surprise and delight, the clothing he'd shed the day before had been brushed free of the dust of the road and pressed, and his boots cleaned and polished also during the night. He pulled them on with pleasure, checking his appearance in the mirror between the beds.

Once the healer had gone, Torresson uncovered the breakfast tray and split the contents with Jornn, the two talking quietly as they ate.

Torresson rang for the footman who would help him heft the trunks, then took his leave of Jornn. Together the footman and Torresson, laden with the trunks full of Liammial's papers, made their way through the castle, seeking the king's study.

As they approached the correct door, Torresson was surprised to see Tinne, King Jameisaan's secretary, and a good friend of his, sitting just outside the closed portal.

Tinne looked up at their approach, and his face broke into a wide grin.

"Torresson, my friend! The kings said they were expecting you, and if you'll wait, they'll be out in a moment or twelve!" His audacious grin indicated a wealth of shared knowledge of those who'd served the vagaries of royalty together.

Torresson laughed. "'A moment or twelve!' I like that, and it's definitely the way things are when one waits upon kings! As a matter of fact, I had expected to see them at supper time last night, but they put me off until this morning."

Torresson indicated to the footman where to set the small trunk, and the fellow deposited his burden then left the pair to await their meeting. Torresson set his trunk beside the other.

Tinne and Torresson fell to quietly catching up on each other's adventures since their last separation, as much as could circumspectly be shared without breaching confidences.

Few minutes passed before the door opened and a page in Jurat's livery beckoned Torresson in.

Torresson directed the page to take one of the trunks while he hefted the other, for what he hoped was the last time. With a deep breath to organize his thoughts, he entered the presence of the kings.

Torresson bowed low before the monarchs, his body slightly more angled toward his own liege.

Jameisaan spoke first. "Be at your ease, Torresson. Sit here, near us and tell us of your journeying." His voice was kind, but Torresson could hear the tension in the tones.

"Sires," he said, straightening, "let me open the trunks and then I'll sit, by your leave." He looked at each in turn. They nodded their assent.

He walked to the side table and retrieved one trunk and set it on one end of the table then fetched the second and placed it beside the first. He opened them both, extracting the pouch from one, setting it beside its trunk. He turned back to the men and walked to the chair they'd indicated, perched on the edge of it, mildly uncomfortable sitting in the presence of the monarchs.

"Here is some cool lemonade for when you need it," King Fergasse said, indicating a tray with several crystal goblets residing beside a pitcher of clear water. At Torresson's negative head shake, he settled back into his chair, and then continued.

"Now, my good man, please begin and leave nothing out. Not only do I want you to tell us exactly what happened at each residence, I would like to know your feelings; how things struck you or your impression at each place." He became silent, his dark eyes intently probing the courier's.

Torresson began speaking, commencing with the day of the wedding when he'd left Renthenn. He detailed the important points; the old couple who had been told Liammial was already king; the men from Milord's Army at Liammial's estate; the arrangements he'd made with the innkeeper to track Liammial's movements. He indicated which documents came from which place as he reached it in his narrative.

He spoke, too, of the arrogant, unprofessional way the guard Dromminilva had treated Jornn and the injuries Jornn had suffered needlessly because of it. He informed the rulers he'd taken on Jornn as apprentice, pending his father's recommendation. At the end of the report, he took a drink from the crystal goblet, pouring each sovereign one of the same, at their request.

Each king asked several questions, clarifying this point or that, and then Jameisaan spoke.

"Torresson, we've set up a relay system of couriers and way-points. You've been assigned to Renthenn. You'll need to leave on the morrow, which is going to be hard on young Jornn's ankle, I know, but I want him with you as he's your apprentice. Once in Renthenn, he can rest until it's completely healed then he can join you on the road."

"As far as his father's recommendation," Fergasse chimed in, "you may need to wait a considerable time to obtain it. I'm not positive just where everyone's been relocated. However, I can give you *my* endorsement. I have had dealings with Jornn's family for years, and found the entire lot of them to be honest and hard-working. I can well imagine Jornn would prefer the life of a courier to that of working in his family's inn; he's always had a curiosity about the world outside Jurisse." He looked steadily at the courier before him. "As for his father's permission, though, I cannot give it."

Torresson's grin split his face. "Jornn is of age, Sire, and needs no permission. I did tell him I wouldn't take him on permanently without a good recommendation from his father. I was thinking more as to his work ethics, integrity and temperament than parental consent. Your words are sufficient for me, and I thank you for the both of us. Jornn will be pleased, as well."

He rose, bowed, and left the chamber, his mind turning at once to the preparations required for them to leave the city in the morning.

Chapter Twenty-five

A Horse! A Horse!
4th Day of Beltaine, 2448

Torresson awoke and lay unmoving, listening carefully to his surroundings. The morning was still, and unnaturally quiet for a city of this size.

There were no carriages clattering, no vendors in the street crying their wares. Even the morning light in the window seemed subdued. Pulling on his shirt and tunic, he stepped quietly to the window.

The sky was covered by a thick layer of heavily laden clouds, their dark bottoms threatening to rip open and dump cold water upon all who were foolish enough to be outside. He wrinkled his nose at the heavens. It looked like it was going to be one of the less-pleasant days to travel.

He finished dressing in his usual economical manner, pulled a dampened comb through his tangled hair, and moved away from the cabinet housing the pitcher and basin.

Moving to Jornn's bedside, he examined the injuries. Though still swollen, the foot was definitely decreasing in size. It was plain to see, however, that the ankle would not be going into Jornn's boot.

Torresson gently unwrapped the bandages and applied some of the salve the healer had left. Jornn made no noise, but bit his bottom lip as he allowed his mentor and friend to complete the ministrations.

Torresson re-wrapped the ankle as tightly as possible and washed the salve from his hands. Whatever was in it had made his fingers first burn, then go numb. He hoped it was bringing the same numbness to Jornn's ankle and relieving some of the pain.

Torresson helped Jornn rise and assisted him in his necessary morning ablutions. With Jornn leaning heavily on his master's shoulder, the couriers made their way to the kitchen, seeking breakfast.

Their meal finished, Torresson left Jornn in the kitchen while he returned and retrieved their belongings from their chambers. Jornn was to spend his time profitably begging travel rations from the kindly cook.

Torresson returned to the kitchen, collected the packet of food on his way through, and proceeded to the stables. There were no stablemen in evidence.

"Hello?" Torresson called. His voice didn't carry far, the sound almost completely absorbed by the piles of soft hay set out for the horses' nourishment.

A shuffling noise to one side caught Torresson's attention and he turned. He watched as an incredibly ancient man, wrinkled and worn by the years, scuffed across the hay-strewn floor, raising a small cloud of dust with each step. One of the nearer horses sneezed.

"Whotcher be a-needin'?" the wizened old man asked, his cheek bulging with something he was chewing on.

"Pair of horses," Torresson replied pleasantly.

"Ain't got none," the antiquated stableman stated. He turned his head slightly and spat on the stable floor, just missing Torresson's boot before turning back in the direction he'd come.

"Hey!" Torresson said, sharply, moving his foot out of the way quickly.

The old man turned back toward him, a closed look on his craggy face. He eyed Torresson for a long moment, and then said once more, "Whotcher be a-needin'?"

"I need a pair of horses. The king has commanded me to leave this morning for Kwenn."

"Then you kin walk, same's ever body elset. Ain't got no harses." He stared straight at him, almost daring him to make something of it.

"What's your name, my good man?" Torresson asked, pasting what he hoped was a tolerant smile on his face.

"They calls me 'Old Josh'," the man said after a considerable pause. "I be th' head o' th' stables fer th' king," he added, as though making sure Torresson knew he had the authority to grant or deny permission regarding the horseflesh under his care.

"Well, then, Old Josh, I need a pair of horses this morning. Please set about filling my request without delay." Torresson congratulated himself that his voice was still on an even tone; respectful, but firm.

"Cain't."

"And why can't you?" He lightly gnawed the softness of his inner cheek, striving to show no irritation, although it was increasingly more difficult with the ancient's stubborn demeanor.

"Ain't got no harses." Old Josh continued to stare at Torresson as though he were indistinguishable from the stable walls surrounding them, all the while never missing a beat in chewing the wad within his cheek.

Without moving his head, Torresson pointed at the row of animals contentedly munching their morning hay. "What do you call those?" His voice, although still level, now showed a ragged thread of frustration.

Old Josh snorted, sounding much like one of the steeds he'd probably tended all his life, a lopsided grin splitting his face, some of the substance within his cheek nearly dripping down his weathered chin. He waggled his greyed head at the apparent stupidity of the man standing before him.

"Dem be harses, be ye blind?" He spat once again onto the straw-strewn floor, wiping the drizzle on his chin with the back of one gnarled hand.

"Then you do have horses, and I'll have two of them." Torresson spit out the words in his exasperation.

"Nay, yer will not!" the stableman shot back. "Dem harses be spoked for an' ye can walk, same's all th' rest! Dat's whot th' king said 'bout dem harses. Ye'll not git these ter ride, no sir, nary a one!" His stance was aggressive; his eyes blazed with his determination, once again daring Torresson to differ with him.

Torresson looked at him for a long moment, then turned away from the old man and walked down the row of animals. He paused before the pair he and Jornn had brought with them. This pair belonged to Jornn, not the king, and could not be commandeered without Jornn's consent. He felt confident of his ground.

He opened the stall of the horse which had been lamed by the stone and examined its foot. The horse shied a little when Torresson pressed on the center of the hoof. He released the hoof and left the stall, knowing the horse wouldn't be leaving with them today.

Jornn's other mount was well-rested and in good condition. Torresson led the horse from the stall and began saddling the beast, a calmness restored to his innards by the mere action of preparing to carry out the kings' request.

"Hey now, young feller!" Old Josh roared. "Whotcher be a-doin'? Oi'll call the watch, Oi will! Thet thar harse hain't be yer'n, an' ye ha' no bidnez a-sattlin' it!" Spittle sprayed the floor as he tried to stop Torresson from saddling the mount.

"No, it isn't my horse," agreed Torresson pleasantly. "It belongs to my young friend who is sitting in the kitchen waiting for me to bring his horse to him."

"Ye cain't tyke th' harses!" Josh wailed. "Ye has ta walk like th' rest of 'em. Ye was 'spozed ter be gone already! Ye cain't take 'em, Oi tells ye!" He made a grab for the reins.

Torresson turned to face the ancient retainer, leaning close, his eyes never leaving the man's face. He spoke quietly but with determination, danger adding to his tone as he enunciated each word clearly, the threat behind the words nearly a tangible thing between them.

"Listen to me, old man. I'm leaving this morning on the king's business. I am a king's courier. Do not get in my way." He leaned a little closer still, letting his body language add additional weight to his words.

His eyes now bulging in fright, Old Josh scrambled smartly out of Torresson's path. Torresson watched him scuttle before making his own move. He walked to a stall on the end of the last row and led out his own beautiful bay mare, grateful that Jornn's father had sent the horse here rather than sending it with his family to

Kwenndara. He saddled her and strapped his and Jornn's bags behind the saddles.

Old Josh watched, looking totally confused about how he should proceed. Finally, he fell back on one of the threats he'd used on Torresson earlier. "Oi'll call th' watch!" he shrilled, pointing in the general direction of the castle's guard house.

"Fine!" Torresson snapped, his irritation back in full force. "You call the watch, and I'll call the king, and we'll see who ends up with the horses." He continued to saddle his horse.

"Ye cain't be a-botherin' his majesty over a pair of harses, not inna middle o' a war. There'll be a-fightin' here soon an' he's busy plannin' how ta save th' kingdom," Old Josh whined now, looking frightened.

"I shouldn't have to bother his majesty in order to take my own horse from the stable," Torresson agreed, "but trust me, Old Josh, I'll do anything I have to do in order to leave this morning, on horse, for Kwenn, as his majesty commanded me."

The old stableman looked up into Torresson's eyes; Torresson hoped the man could see his implacable resolve. Apparently he could.

"Tyke 'em, then," the ancient retainer spluttered, hanging his head in defeat, "but Oi'll not be hung fer yer thievin' o' th' harses; ye'll get yer jist dezzerts! Ye'll see!" He turned then, and shuffled back to his corner of the stable, muttering imprecations and invoking curses to rain steadily upon Torresson's poor head.

Torresson finished preparing the mounts and led them to the kitchen door, where he helped Jornn to mount before swinging himself into his own saddle.

Their cloaks tight around them, they rode from the palace together, into a mist which was almost, but not quite yet a drizzle.

Chapter Twenty-six

Refuge for the Weary
5th Day of Beltaine, 2448

Tanella sat in solitary splendor at the breakfast table, dubiously eyeing the poached fish. Lately she'd had a difficult time eating anything without feeling ill afterward. Perhaps she was simply overly anxious for the safety of her father as he labored in the midst of what would soon be a battlefield.

She decided against the fish, and pointed at the mound of fluffy yellow eggs that lay in the bowl. The footman standing behind her chair quickly transferred eggs to her plate until she gave him a sign signifying there was enough. She stabbed one of the puffy nodules of scrambled egg with the small fork she held in her left hand,

and transferred it to her mouth. As she chewed, she wondered how the chef managed to balance the flavors of butter and egg so perfectly every morning.

A servant tapped at the door, then entered followed by one of the young ragamuffins who had been pressed into service as messengers. The scruffy boy made his best approximation of a bow, and Tanella gestured to him to speak as she hurriedly swallowed her eggs and washed them down with a sip of water.

The boy stood, apparently awestruck, his excited eyes fastened on the princess. Tanella smiled. "Did you come to bring me a message?"

The boy nodded.

"Is it written down?"

He shook his head.

"Well, then I'm afraid you'll have to just tell me who sent you, and what the message is."

The boy gulped and took a deep breath.

"Beggin' yer pardon, Princess, I guess you wuz just so beautiful I plum forgot how ter talk fer a minute. My da, Jummpion, the Smith, sent me ta tell ya there be a buncha smoke an' dust on the road, an' he thinks them from Jurisse be comin' at last."

"Thank you. You can run along now, and tell your father I'll be in the central square shortly to welcome our guests and help get them settled, according to the plans we've made."

The boy nodded, made another try at a courtly bow, turned, and all but fled from the room. The servant followed the boy, closing the door carefully behind them.

Tanella quickly finished the remaining eggs and then motioned to the footman she wanted some fish after all. She didn't really want to eat any, but if the refugees were finally arriving, her morning might go on long past the nooning hour. She might well need the nourishment of the fish to tide her over until supper.

Breakfast complete, she rose. "Please have Janna meet me in the library, dressed to go out," she instructed the footman as he hastened to open the door for her. The man nodded, and Tanella made her way to the library to wait.

She was so tired of the formality the servants here treated her with. It was as though they were impressed by their own importance because they served in the king's official residence. What she really needed was a friend, and she knew just where to find one.

It wasn't very long before Janna entered the library.

"Where am I going?"

"Nowhere until we've had a talk."

Janna's face screwed up with apprehension.

"Have I done something wrong?"

Tanella chuckled.

"No, not at all, but I've decided I don't want you to be my maid any longer." The look on Janna's face made her laugh again.

"Close your mouth, I'm not firing you. I'm promoting you."

"Promoting me?"

"Yes. You're not my maid any longer. You're my lady-in-waiting."

"I can't be a lady-in-waiting, I'm not a Lady!"

Tanella laughed again.

"I was under the impression that the Right Honorable Darrynn, the Duke of Shields is your uncle?"

"Well, yes, but..."

"And I believe that another uncle is a king?"

"Only by marriage."

"So you really do qualify to be a lady-in-waiting. Janna, if you'll let me do this, you can come with me and help me as we settle all these people. I won't be quite so alone here. All my friends, except for you, are in Renthenn."

Janna bit her lip, indecision written all over her face.

"Please?"

Janna nodded at last. Tanella rushed forward and embraced her cousin.

"So what does a lady-in-waiting do, anyway?"

"I don't know; I've never had one, so we'll make it up as we go along. Mostly, I'll want you to be a companion, and help me out with all the hordes I've just been told are descending on us this morning. With your training from the inn, you're good at organizing things, and you already speak with authority. Most will do your bidding as a matter of course, in addition to that you'll be by my side and reflect my authority as well. You'll get on just fine. I have full confidence in you; I know just how bossy you can be when you were in charge of one of our projects!"

Janna nodded, her face creased with a sassy grin. "I can do that. All the underlings at the inn knew better than to cross me if I gave them an order. I guess the difference here is in title only, and who gave me leave to give the order initially."

"Besides, *Lady Janna*," Tanella said with emphasis on the new title, "you'll get a bunch of pretty clothes to wear as your official uniform. I know how much you like beautiful things. In fact, growing up, it was your only complaint about being the daughter of an innkeeper; you wanted clothes that matched mine! Remember?"

"Vividly," Janna said. "I also remember every single word of reproof my mother gently laid on my ears where my father could not hear her words. 'Fine dresses do not bring the happiness of true love.' She was always right, too."

"Yes, she was. Once you passed the age of twelve, though, Janna, you stopped worrying about clothes because you were having so much fun bossing everyone around; and before you try to talk your way out of that, know that we need to be gone from here right now to meet with the lord mayor before the refugees knock on the castle door!"

"You know me too well, Tanney! Do you really think I can do this?" Green eyes met green eyes, both searching each other's face.

Tanella smiled. Janna had called her by her childhood nickname, and she found the feelings attached to it brought her strength and courage. "I have no doubt you can do this, Janna; and I really need it to happen. The only way I can have your help, strength and good advice is to have you with me as my lady-in-waiting. Will you do it?" Tanella held her breath until Janna nodded.

"Good, let's go." The cousins left the library, and the butler opened the front door as they approached it. Tanella motioned Janna out the door and then turned to the butler.

"Goodsill, I've just promoted Lady Janna from my maid to my lady-in-waiting. As one of her uncles is Darrynn, the Duke of Shields, and another is my father the king, she is to be known as Lady Janna from now going forward. Please inform Mrs. Howsse of the changes. Lady Janna will need proper quarters, adjoining mine, if possible. Also, we'll both be in need of ladies maids, and Lady Janna will need to be supplied with appropriate clothing for her new station."

"Yes, Your Highness."

"I trust it will be seen to by the time we return?"

"Yes, Your Highness. May I suggest?" he stood silent and respectful, awaiting her leave to speak further.

Tanella blinked. This was the first time she was aware the butler knew words other than "yes" and "Your Highness".

"Please; what do you suggest?"

"If Your Highness is willing, we could move the pair of you into her late majesty's suite, which has an adjoining room for a lady-in-waiting. We've kept the room in complete readiness, Your Highness, so it won't take long to make the changes you desire. I think you'll be pleased with everything."

"Perfect! See to it then, Goodsill."

The butler bowed. "Yes, Your Highness."

Tanella turned and went out the door to where Janna waited. A footman followed not far behind them. They walked the short distance to the central square in happy companionship. Jummpion hailed them as they arrived, and broke off his conversation with the mayor as the two dignitaries hastened to Tanella's side and bowed before her, stopping her party in a bit of shade in the square.

"Do please rise."

The mayor consulted several lists of parchment in his hand.

"Highness, we sent some runners out to see the cause of the dust, although we're fairly certain it's the refugees. They should be entering Kwenndara at any moment now."

"Are we ready, Lord Mayor?"

"I believe we are as ready as we can be, Your Highness, given the short notice."

Tanella nodded. "Are those your lists of hosting families?"

"They are."

He held the lists out, and she took them from him, glancing down the slim sheets of parchment.

"We'll need all our young urchins to guide our guests to their new homes."

"The call has gone out, Your Highness; the children should be on their way here."

Tanella nodded, and then handed the lists to Janna.

"These are the names of our host families, Lady Janna," she said by way of allowing the Lord Mayor and the others surrounding them to know of Janna's standing. "You'll note each name and how many people they can take in. Please keep track of how many we send, and where, and cross the hosts off your lists as their homes become full. We'll settle the first arrivals in homes, then others in the spaces we've cleared out as dormitories, and the last-comers will have to be tucked into the inns and palace outbuildings."

Janna nodded, and quickly gave orders to several of the nearby men. In short order she had a small barrel to sit on and a plank across two others to use as a makeshift desk. A child was sent to a nearby shop to procure ink and pen. She spread the slips of parchment out on her desk, and sat studying them intently.

The first of the wagons and carriages pulled into the square, and Tanella greeted the refugees warmly, inquiring how many were in each party, then discovering where they should go, and sending them off with one of the small local children to guide them to their final destination. The time they'd spent in preparation was well worth it, as their methods proved successful. The long train of people was settled by the evening meal.

Tanella was tired but pleased as they trudged back to the palace. According to the information brought by the group's assigned leader, the next group should be only a day's travel behind the first, and the refugees from each quarter of the city should arrive in a steady stream for the next three days. There might then be a respite from housing people until those who had to travel slower were able to complete the long trek up and over the Great Krakitts.

Chapter Twenty-seven

Royal Arrival
7th Day of Beltaine, 2448

The sound of his horse browsing on the bushes woke him. He rose unsteadily to his feet, and checked the surrounding area for any plants that looked edible. There were a few handful of berries left on the bush he'd slept under, and he quickly stripped and ate them, licking the juices of the over-ripened berries from his fingers and hoping they hadn't gone bad on the vine.

A small streamlet trickled nearby, and he smiled. He would be able to slake his thirst, and begin the morning with a full belly, even if it was only water that filled it.

Having drunk his fill, a little more of the water served to clean himself up a little. The small pool wasn't deep enough to bathe in, but he removed his tunic and splashed enough of the icy water on his face and arms to wash a goodly bit of the dusty road from his person. He sat carefully next to the pool and bathed his legs and feet also, where they hung naked from beneath the faded and worn breeches.

The young man doused his hair, combing it with his fingers and trying to tame the wild brown waves. When the water stilled, he stared into the pool for a long moment at his reflection. He didn't recognize himself. He looked more like a wild creature than a human being. His face was thin, and his shoulder bones protruded sharply from his skin. He was accustomed to being well muscled. His face was darker brown than usual, and he cursed the loss of the broad-brimmed hat that he'd customarily worn any time he left home. He doubted anyone who knew him would recognize him, if any of them still lived.

He pulled on the dirty and torn velvet doublet which had once been a deep emerald green. It hung loosely from his thin shoulders. He checked the makeshift rope belt that secured the matching, now ill-fitting breeches to his hips.

Finally, as prepared for the day as he could be, he mounted his horse and rode warily through the bright morning. The horse he sat upon was a fair beast; tall, well colored, yet also showing signs of recent privation in his dull coat and dispirited walk. Having the ability to graze on roadside vegetation had been an advantage the horse had over his rider, for he looked the better-fed of the pair.

They topped a slight rise in the road, and the walls of Jurisse came into view. The young man reined in, halting their progress momentarily and sighed in relief, then patted his mount's neck.

"Only a little further, Trueheart, and we'll be able to rest," he promised the horse. The pair set off again much lighter of heart at the nearness of their destination.

As he entered the gates of Jurisse, the young man looked about him in consternation. The street was choked with carriages standing in line. Horses with riders and carts of all descriptions filled every available space.

A young boy of perhaps eight years chased a piglet through the confusion, seemingly unaware of the danger of being trampled by an animal or flattened by a vehicle. He disappeared into the sea of legs and wheels, calling out to his pig.

Other children and not a few adults ran this way or that, clutching bundles and seeking one another.

An argument broke out in front of a chandlery. The merchant was busy loading household furniture into a cart, and several of his neighbors were loudly protesting they'd been told to take only food and supplies and clothing with them.

The chandler retorted the furniture had been a dower gift in his family for five generations and he'd die before abandoning it to be burned by the army. It was his cart and he'd carry what he pleased to in it.

His neighbors said they'd be willing to help him die if that's what he wanted, but he'd best not waste valuable cart space which should hold provisions with a load of wood. One went so far as to suggest the chandler bring the furniture, as it would make a wonderful cooking fire along the way.

Fists were flying before the thin stranger and his horse had picked their way through the crowd and turned the corner.

Slowly but steadily he made his way toward the palace. He shook his head dismally as he passed through the palace gates unchallenged.

He slid from his mount at the front portal. A stableman appeared and took the horse away among much clucking over its condition.

The lean man straightened his tunic and brushed off as much of the dust as possible before presenting himself to the door steward, who stood imposingly in front of the castle doors.

"Is King Fergasse in residence?" he asked, then winced. His voice sounded almost rusty from disuse and dusty roads.

"Yes, sir," the door steward responded, "but he is not in at present. Would you care to wait?" His voice came to within a whisper of a sneer.

"It looks as though I'll have to wait," he said, a wry smile twisting his lips. "If you would be so kind as to have me conducted to a place I can rest comfortably while waiting, and send to inform your liege that Prince Kezele of Shuell seeks audience at his earliest convenience, I'd appreciate it. Also," he said, looking down at his dusty attire and indicating the state of it with a wave of his begrimed hand, "if I could at least have some water to wash off the worst of the dust, it would be well received."

The expression on the steward's face never wavered, though Kezele could see the consternation in his eyes. Well did he know that he didn't look like anything resembling a prince. The steward turned away, then opened the door and summoned a footman.

"Kendonn, His Highness, Prince Kezele of Shuell," he indicated the waiting young man, "needs water to wash with, a room to rest in, and a message to His Majesty informing him of his highness' arrival." His voice was even closer to a sneer than it had been a moment ago.

The footman bowed and waved the self-named prince into the hall. He led the visitor up several staircases before opening a door for him.

"Could you please send for some refreshment, also water for a bath would be well as I have been traveling for some time and I'm sure I reek." His voice was low, but firm.

The footman nodded.

"Also," the prince continued, "I'll need my clothing cleaned, if possible, and would there be anything I could borrow to wear in the interval?"

The footman nodded once more, and then withdrew from the chamber.

Some considerable hours later, Prince Kezele checked his appearance. Scrubbed clean, well fed for the first time in recent memory, and attired in plain and ill-fitting though clean clothing, he began to feel more like a human being again.

Ready for an audience, he rang for a servant. The footman he'd seen before reappeared.

"Yes, Highness?" he said politely, his eyes taking in the changed appearance.

"Kendonn, isn't it?" At the footman's nod, the prince continued. "Has his majesty, King

Fergasse returned yet? When will it be possible to see him?"

"King Fergasse sends his regrets that he is too deeply involved in the evacuation efforts to see anyone today, but sent word that King Jameisaan will see you as soon as you were refreshed." His quick bow of the head and palmed gesture to follow him were respectful.

Confusion clouded the prince's brow. "King Jameisaan? Does he not rule Kwenn, to the North? Or is my reckoning of how far I have traveled incorrect? This *is* Jurisse?"

The footman straightened and faced the prince. "Nay, ye are not mistaken. Ye are in Jurisse, but perhaps news has not reached ye that a pair of weeks ago our Prince Fergan married Princess Tanella of Kwenn, and our two lands are now one. I bid ye welcome to Kwennjurat, where Kings Fergasse and Jameisaan rule jointly."

"I see." Prince Kezele absorbed the new information. "Then I would be delighted to see King Jameisaan, Kendonn. Lead away." Prince Kezele smiled.

The startled look on the footman's face was expressive; his smile must have made a difference. From the slightly deeper bow he was given, Kezele could only suppose so, at any rate, and followed as the footman turned with another gesture of his gloved hand.

"This way, Highness," Kendonn said, a tone of deeper respect coloring the footman's voice as he bowed once more then left the room, Prince Kezele trailing in his wake.

Chapter Twenty-eight

Prince Kezele's Tale
7th Day of Beltaine, 2448

Several flights of stairs and corridors later, the footman bowed him into a chamber which was comfortably appointed, but not extravagant. A large table occupied the center of the room, and seated behind it was a man who, though dressed simply, was obviously a king; his majesty and power radiated from his very presence.

Prince Kezele bowed to him as the footman announced his presence.

"Come in, my boy, and have a seat." King Jameisaan gestured at a comfortable chair placed across the table from him. His bright blue eyes beneath the craggy brows surveyed him as he spoke. "Prince Kezele, now, you'd be, hmmmm," his voice trailed off as if in thought of trying to place the prince, but the watchful eyes never wavered. Prince Kezele stepped forward, but continued to stand.

"I am the youngest son of King Anthonny of Shuell, Sire, as well you know, doubtless having looked up my pedigree before consenting to send for me." The prince had a twinkle in his eye and a lightness to his voice to remove the sting of rebuke from his words, knowing as he did that he must provide positive identification of himself, especially considering his appearance when he'd arrived. "Shall I recite the names of all my siblings in order, or will it be sufficient that I show to you my ring, which bears our family crest?"

He dug into the purse at his belt and removed a ring and proffered it to the king, and his smile increased in size as Jameisaan accepted the ring and he continued speaking.

"Of course, the crest is small, my being a younger son." He sketched another bow to the king before seating himself in the chair Jameisaan had indicated, his easy manner showing a long familiarity with being in the presence of royalty.

Jameisaan examined the ring closely before returning it.

"What can you tell me of conditions and happenings in Shuell?" His vigilant eyes were back on the prince's face.

Prince Kezele frowned, the pain of his memories sliding across the surface of his mind. He wondered if his pain showed in his eyes. He took a deep breath and looked straight into King Jameisaan's face. "Some three moonatts ago, I had dressed simply, in hopes of a good day spent hunting. As I left the city, I saw a fleet of merchant ships approaching, but thought nothing of it save it was a large fleet.

"Around noon, I began to smell smoke drifting on the wind, and thought perhaps a fire had broken out among the forest trees. When I investigated, I found it was coming from Kingsport City. It looked as though the entire city was ablaze, and I knew not what I should do. I rode toward the city with all the speed I could get from my horse, but while still a distance away, I saw many who were trying to run from the city but were being turned back by an army at the gates, or slaughtered by their swords. Some managed to escape the melee on the roadway."

His voice cracked with emotion, and he paused to swallow. The torture of self-recrimination was thick in his voice as he continued.

"I could not reach the castle nor my family. Guards at every gate were butchering any and all they could reach. There was nothing I could do to help my people by being dead, but I thought if I reached Jurat, perhaps I could get help to come back and fight the army who had taken over our city.

"I spoke with several who escaped, and from what I learned of each, have put together a tale of what happened, but as to how accurate it is, I'm not completely certain, having seen as little of it as I did." He stopped to wipe the moisture from his eyes and gather his composure.

"The army came from the ships I'd seen that morning. Numerous men simply got off the boats, and then walked through the town. All the men wore black.

"The men walked peaceably through the market, and then went into the inn closest to the castle. All this, of course, was as unremarkable as the ships' arrival.

"Suddenly there was much shouting, and they left the inn, running. They carried burning torches, and the inn was aflame. Everywhere they went in the city, fire followed. They burned homes, shops, everything they could reach with their torches.

"Their swords were busy also, hacking the life from our people, not only those who bravely tried to fight back, but innocent children and old people. One man told me the streets near the palace flowed with the blood of our people as they assembled quickly to try to protect the royal family. I was told the palace burned, but as to who of my family might have escaped, as I did, I know not. I have tried to find word of them, but none I've spoken to have any knowledge of what has befallen the rest of my family."

The young man stopped once more, choking on his words, the pain and grief of those words a torment to him. Even as moisture seeped out of distress-laden eyes, the young prince gathered his composure about him and continued.

"In the last three moonatts, I've been traveling to Jurisse by a round-about route to avoid capture, not knowing for certain how far inland the army may have come. I've had to stay in hiding much of the time. When I became too hungry, I would stop and work a day or two here and there for farmers in return for food. I have heard how this so-called 'Divine Army' has swept across Shuell, pilfering supplies for their men. They've stolen away most of our young men, telling them they must join their army or die. I don't know how many innocent people have been killed simply to frighten the young men into joining the army.

"They have also," his voice became ragged and he wiped moisture from his eye with a trembling hand, "taken many of our fair young maidens; I'm sure for no wholesome reason. None of the maidens have been seen again by their families.

"Their leader is seldom seen. He resides in a white tent in the center of his force. His lieutenants often go in and out of his tent, bearing fresh orders from him for deployment or whatever else he has in mind. There are often couriers seen going hither and yon to the white tent. They all wear black, and no one knows from whom they come. It's clear to me some other agency is at least giving the army information, if not steering their movements while sending instructions and information to the white tent. The Divine Army lines much of the border between Jurat and Shuell, especially near the roads. They have swept most of Shuell clean of food and young men.

"King Jameisaan, there is no war-treaty between our people. There never has been need of one before, as the people of the Ten Kingdoms have lived peaceably one with another from the time of the Great Krakitts. Being the youngest son and having no direction from my father, I do not have authority to make a war-treaty with you. But I would beg you, from the bottom of my heart, and in light of the centuries of friendship between our people, I beg you for any aid you can give to remove this army from our shores. I also bring you a warning that your people may be next to fall to these atrocities."

Determination and purpose now filled Kezele as he made his plea to the king seated across from him. He continued to look into the king's face as earnestly as he could while he waited for the king to speak; so much hung in the balance.

The king searched his face carefully for a long moment, his brow furled in concentration. He finally spoke.

"Do you know what they seek?"

Prince Kezele shook his head. "They've destroyed to instill fear. They've taken our men to make their army greater; they've taken our food to feed themselves. They've taken our women for their pleasure, but I have heard of nothing they seek, nor any goal they wish to achieve."

Kezele rubbed a shaking hand over his tired face, letting the gesture tell of his concern. He shook his head once again, and then drew in a deep breath, expelling it quietly.

Slowly, he turned his eyes back up and looked deep within the steady blue eyes of King Jameisaan, suddenly missing his own father more than he could have predicted.

"It struck me as very odd that the bulk of the army seems to have stopped at our border. From time to time, however, I've seen a few men who looked to be from their group deep within your borders, which kept me in hiding, and prolonged my journey to you. Why would they suddenly stop like that, especially given the speed of the unprovoked attack on my country? One would think they'd simply continue, rather than give anyone a chance to prepare for them. I can think of no reason for them to have gone as far as the perimeter of Shuell and then stop." He shook his head dropped his eyes to his ring, realizing he was twisting it around and around his finger and stopped the action. He sighed dejectedly before looking back up at Jameisaan.

"I didn't know what else to do, Sire, other than come here for help. I just don't have the training for this; as the youngest son, I was never expected to be in a situation of ruling, especially in the midst of a war."

Jameisaan looked at the young man a long moment, and seemed to make up his mind. "First of all, Prince Kezele, I thank you for your perseverance in making your way here. In the hour of your great distress you came, bearing grave tidings, but though you sought help for your own people, you have also thought to bring a warning to your neighbors of what awaits to befall them. This is a noble and kingly action." The brief smile only lifted one mouth-corner of the otherwise solemn face.

Prince Kezele felt his face warm and knew he'd flushed.

Jameisaan continued. "We're already taking measures to protect our people, as much as we can, and we're laying plans to deal with this army. I will make sure King Fergasse is aware of the contents of your report. I'm fairly certain he'll wish to speak with you at some length. After you've rested a little, if you could show us on a map your approximate course of travel and any further details you may remember, that will serve to help us all even more." His smile was kind, and Kezele was relieved.

"For now, I can see that even this short interview has wearied you. Your journey has been long and full of hardships. I'll have you conducted to a place you may rest and recover."

"Thank you. I'm grateful for being secure for the night. I'm weary of sleeping with one eye open at least a little!" although he tried to smile, he knew it didn't go further than the corners of his lips. His whole face was just too tired to join in.

Jameisaan rang for the footman, who appeared instantly, and Prince Kezele rose unsteadily to his feet, bowed to the king, and followed the servant from the room.

Chapter Twenty-nine

So, *This* Is Renthenn
7th Day of Beltane, 2448

Even though they'd taken an extra day on the journey, the jouncing involved in riding a horse had been very hard on Jornn's ankle. Unable to elevate the limb during the day, the swelling had returned, and with it, the nearly sickening pain. Jornn was very glad they reined their horses to a halt for the night in front of the Swan's Head Inn in Renthenn.

Jornn watched with envy and frustration as Torresson easily swung down from his saddle. He'd love to be well enough to do the same, and with the same ease. A young boy of about eleven years hurriedly came to take their horses. He smiled a welcome to the courier, calling him by name with a familiarity which spoke of good friendship. The lad then stepped close to hold both mounts securely.

Torresson assisted Jornn to dismount, helping him to balance against the pain of his landing. Torresson supported Jornn into the common room and sat him as near the door as possible. The burly innkeeper bustled over to them.

"Fredrick!" Torresson greeted his friend enthusiastically.

"How've you been, Torresson? Haven't seen you around for a good while!" He reached forward and clasped the courier's hand in a hearty grip.

"I've been well, and off on business, as usual. I'm to be stationed here under this new courier system, though, so I'll not be going far for awhile. I've an apprentice to train, too." He grinned as they broke their hand shake and Torresson gestured in Jornn's direction.

Fredrick, a quick look in Jornn's direction, nodded. "Well, you'll be looking for a good meal, unless I miss my guess, and to find out where you'll be sleeping, usually the first two things on a traveling man's mind!"

Torresson laughed. "You should know, you, who serves the traveling man the best. You're exactly right, too!"

Fredrick scratched his head. "Well, much as I hate to lose the trade," he cocked his head sideways, squinting at Torresson with mischief glinting from his eyes, and then rubbed his jaw slowly. Torresson's smile slipped a little as he watched the innkeeper. Jornn wondered if the man was going to lead them astray for the sake of making a few coins.

Fredrick grinned openly, "I'll tell you anyway, as you've always been a good customer, when you're in town." His eyes sparkled merrily.

"You know I always stay here, Fredrick! You have the best beer in the Ten, ah, Nine Kingdoms!"

Fredrick laughed, his eyes twinkling with his merriment. "The couriers are eating and sleeping at the palace, so they can be grabbed out of their beds if young Fergan needs them. So I'll have your horses fetched again, and you'll both be there in plenty of time for your supper." He reached out his hand again in friendship, acknowledging the seated Jornn with a nod of his head.

Torresson clasped Fredrick's hand. "And I'll be back here again later for beer and news, of course." The sparkle in his eyes answered Fredrick's, both smiles stretching wide.

"Of course; I'll pour you one myself!"

"I'll count on it, Fredrick!" Torresson turned and stepped to Jornn once more, gathering him for the final ride this night. When he returned later, Torresson would be alone and Jornn would be in the hands of a capable healer.

Jornn wished more than ever he'd be back here tonight with Torresson, but a small scraping of his ankle against Torresson's leg as he was lifted back on his horse reminded him that the best place for him for the next several days would be in a soft bed somewhere with his leg propped on a pillow and a kind person to fetch food and fresh water for him.

There was no waiting at the estate gates, as the gatekeeper had known Torresson for years and opened the way as they were still approaching. They rode around to the back of the large manor home and gladly turned their mounts over to the stablemen. Jornn found it hard to believe that this simple building was the ruling seat of the kingdom. It was much smaller than the palace in Jurisse.

Torresson unstrapped their small bags from behind the saddles, and tossed both his and Jornn's over one shoulder.

"That should be my job," Jornn protested, reaching for the saddlebags.

Torresson slapped his hands away, his blow more playful than painful. "It will be your job, once you've healed. Right now, you've all you can do just to move yourself." He grabbed the shoulder of one of the passing stable boys. "Where have they got the couriers billeted?"

The stable boy pointed toward a two-story building attached to the main house by a long hallway. "They got the couriers in the men's room of the servant's wing."

Torresson nodded, and then offered a supporting arm to Jornn. Jornn sighed. He eyed the distance to the building the boy had indicated, and knew he'd never make it there under his own power. Leaning on his master, he began the long, slow hobble toward the door embedded in the corner of the building.

They entered and found themselves in an antechamber. A flight of stairs led upward, a long hall on their left led off toward the main house, and a door on their right opened into a large room filled with beds. There was an outsized fireplace at each end. Each bed had a small cabinet next to the head, and a trunk at the foot, as well as pegs on the wall for hanging clothing on.

Torresson eased him onto the nearest bed and dropped the saddlebags at the foot. "Wait here for me, Jornn. I'll go find someone who can assign us a place, and also ask for the healer to be sent."

Jornn nodded, and Torresson vanished down the hall, returning in about fifteen minutes with a woman who could only be the housekeeper. She directed them to a pair of beds in the far corner, explaining that the entire corner had been given over to the lodging of whichever couriers were currently in residence.

She bustled off, returning in moments with fresh blankets, and making up a pair of un-claimed beds. Torresson helped Jornn to lie down, and tossed their travel bags onto their trunks, asking for and receiving directions on such things as the location of the bath house, the hours it was reserved for men and for women, how and when meals could be obtained, and how to go about getting their laundry taken care of. The housekeeper bustled off again, with an in-junction to Torresson that if he was late for sup-per, he would get only scraps.

"Your ankle hurting?" Torresson asked.

Jornn shook his head. "No more than ex-pected. She got us two blankets apiece. We're nearly to Midsummer. How bad will it be in the depths of winter?"

Torresson laughed. "You'll get used to it. For now, it will be pleasantly warm in the days, but it does cool at night. I'll wager you won't be using all the blankets at once."

The healer entered, and unwrapped Jornn's ankle, then set about berating them both soundly for traveling from Jurisse before it had healed. He produced smelly salves and wrappings, muttering dark imprecations at both their heads the full while as he ministered and rewrapped the foot.

"Thar be no circ'mstances dire 'nough to merit yer goin' further than th' chamber pot, Young Jornn, until I, meself, pronounce ye fit. The full healing process must be observed properly or it'll end by ye bein' a-crippled fer th' rest o' yer days. Not thet it matters a fig to *me* feet and *me* own ability to walk as a natch'ral man, ye unnerstand. It's jist that them imbeciles in town'ud lay th' fault o' the inefficient healing at *me* own door 'stead o' endertainin' th' notion thet ye two couriers simply dinn't follow me instructions to the finite letter! I'll be hanged afore thet happens, an' I won't countenance thet happ'nin' in th' least degree! Me entire reputation as a good healer is at stake here, an' I'll tolerate no change ter me 'structions. D' ye unnerstan' everythin' I've said to ye?" He glared at them both as if expecting them to argue.

The couriers kept silent and both nodded their understanding of his minute injunctions. Torresson winked at Jornn behind the healer's back. Jornn forced a smile to his lips, figuring the man's rantings were hiding a deep concern for his patient. He was hoping neither would notice the blood in his mouth as he bit his inner cheek to keep from screaming from the pain of the treatment he was receiving. At the moment, the pain was so bad, he didn't think he'd even need the chamber pot for hours and hours, unless it was for catching the meal he had not yet eaten.

As the healer finished the wrapping, he growled at Torresson to tuck a pillow beneath the injured ankle while he gently lifted the member high enough to enable the act to be completed. He lightly laid the foot and ankle on the soft nest of pillow, and then glanced at Jornn's face.

A grimace slid across his features and he dug in his bag for a packet of powder. He carefully opened it, sprinkling some into a glass on a nearby table. Lifting the jug of water beside the glass, he poured some of the liquid into the glass, stirred it, and then passed it to Jornn, watching carefully to see he drained the whole of it. "It'll help ye ter sleep lad, and thet's th' best thing fer ye just now. You, Torresson, be orf wit' ye, an' doann' hurry back. Give th' lad some time ter mend. I don't know what ye be a-thinkin' of, bringing him here 'stead of waiting fer him to get well afore ye set orf ter come here, an' 'at's the truth!"

He then motioned it was time for them to leave, telling Torresson he was to go up to the hall to eat with the masses. Food would be sent to Jornn so that when he woke later, it would be there for him. Torresson, after a last look at Jornn, left with the medical man.

Jornn lay, listening to their receding footsteps, perceiving the pain in his ankle was abating now the man had let go of it, and was thankful for the respite. He looked around him, grateful the room was warm, and very pleased he wasn't still mounted on the horse, feeling new pain with every step of the animal.

He took a deep breath and realized he was extremely hungry and very alone. He tried to guess what they might be eating in the big hall right now, and so great was his imagination, he could almost smell the food.

Actually, he thought, sniffing deeply and appreciatively, he *could* smell the food, and it was heavenly. His mouth watered in anticipation until his brain reminded him bitterly that an invalid was likely to be given a restorative broth or some such nonsense. He made a distasteful moue, a low sound stealing from his throat. He wondered how long it would be before anyone would be sent with even a thin gruel for him to sup. If someone came by, maybe he could ask them to get him something to eat soon.

A movement at the door caught his eye, and Jornn looked up. An angel had entered the chamber, quietly bearing a tray from which delicious smells were wafting. It wasn't his imagination after all! Praises be to the heavens above!

Her light yellow hair hung in a neat plait, gleaming like golden sunshine, but her grey eyes were somber and seemed too old for her beautiful face.

She wore about her left arm a band of deep blood red; the sign throughout the Kingdoms of mourning the loss of a loved one. A small flower woven of blond hair was pinned to the band. Doubtless the hair had once adorned the head of whoever she mourned. This sorrow went far to explain the age in her eyes.

The young woman had a smile for him which didn't reach her eyes, but she greeted him with a soft, pleasant voice. "Good even, Master Courier, I've brought you some supper, if ye be hungry."

"Not Master Courier, but an apprentice only. My name is Jornn. I'd be pleased if you'd use it?" He let his voice trail off in an invitation for her to give her name in return.

Without looking directly at him, she said quietly, "My name is Polly, sir; Polly the Dairymaid. They asked me to keep you fed and cared for while you recover."

She set his tray on the table next to his bed. "I'll be back later for the dishes."

With these few words, the angel departed and took the sun with her when she left, the room suddenly becoming cold.

Chapter Thirty

Weighty Matters
7th Day of Beltaine, 2448

His Highness Prince Liammial skillfully guided his galloping mount between the trees. There was nothing to do here in this backwoods pit other than ride, so ride he did. The speed he travelled at gave him a bit of a thrill, forcing him to use his greatest skill in order to avoid colliding with the trees.

He'd tried several of the women from the estate, and found all of them wanting. Even the baron's wife had not been entertaining enough in bed to warrant a second trial. No matter, it would not be long before he'd be with Lady Autrancia again. Rocnar would return soon with news from

Jurisse, and the final choices could be made as to which plan of attack would be used.

He spurred the horse on faster as he emerged from the trees and onto the road, and his horse collided with a large black mount which had been galloping swiftly down the roadway. Both riders and their horses fell to the ground.

Liammial's horse lay upon his right leg, pinning him securely in place. The scrawny thing thrashed about and screamed, though whether in fright or pain, Liammial didn't know.

The other rider, a man dressed in dusty black clothing, had rolled clear of the tangle of horses, and now jumped to his feet.

"Are you mad? Whatever did you come pelting outta the woods like that for?"

His face was florid with his anger as he retrieved his courier's pouch and resettled it on his shoulder, the strap cutting crossways over his chest.

"Get this horse off me, you incompetent lout! You should watch where you're going. How dare you come so swiftly down the road that you couldn't see the intersecting path? You ought to be more careful. Accidents of this sort will cost you a lot more than you're prepared to pay."

The man hardly listened to Liammial; he was too busy sorting out the reins and saddles, and the horses themselves.

His large black mount was quickly back on its feet again, and just as quickly tethered to a small bush at the edge of the road.

Liammial's stupid brown horse continued its screaming, becoming, if anything, louder and more annoying.

"What do you mean I shoulda been watching where I'm going? First, I was on the road, and that gives me the right of way. Secondly, I'm on a very urgent and important assignment, and there'll be worse payment for you when my master finds out you've stalled my progress."

He ran his hands over the screaming horse's body, then its legs, looking for injuries.

A sudden liquid warmth enveloped Liammial's pinned leg, and he wondered if it was the horse's blood or his own. The crushing weight of the horse had numbed his leg, and Liammial couldn't tell whether or not he had been injured. The pungent smell of urine assured Liammial that he was not, after all, bleeding, but that he would have need of a long bath upon his return to the manor.

He raised his voice in curses, raining them down upon both the courier and his stupid horse, as well as the horse Liammial had been riding. The black horse at the edge of the road shifted its weight, pulling away from the sounds of the screaming horse and rider. Liammial had a flash of satisfaction that he could cow the animal with naught but his voice.

The courier finished his inspection and reappeared in Liammial's line of sight. "I'm sorry, sir, but your horse's leg's broken. There's naught to do but put it down."

"And then how are you going to lift the dead beast off me, you idiot?"

"Nay, for I can't lift it, and the poor beastie t'aint gonna be moving its own self off, neither. Best I kin do is ride on. I'll stop at the nearest place and send help for ye. I'm sure they've men and tackle what can lift the horse off. I'll just put this poor beast out of his misery afore I go."

"Be careful where you point your pistol, you dunce. Don't point it anywhere near my direction."

"Don't worry, sir, I won't be hitting yourself. I haven't got a pistol, so the poor thing'll have to suffer just a bit longer than I'd like."

He drew his dagger, and slit the large vein at the base of the horse's neck.

The horse's screams grew louder, and he thrashed considerably, flinging blood everywhere, even as a large pool of it collected under the animal and was soaked up by Liammial's pants. His clothing would be ruined. Finally, silence fell as the horse expired. The weight of the dead animal pressed even heavier on Liammial's leg.

The courier hastily wiped his knife clean on the horse's shoulder and re-sheathed it, then retrieved his own animal from the side of the road and mounted.

"I'll send help from the first place I come across, sir, I promise. It shan't be too much of a wait."

Liammial watched the courier clatter off down the road in a haze of dust which slowly settled on the prince. He sneezed twice, biting the side of his tongue on the second violent outburst. The taste of his own blood was sharp.

The day grew warmer, and Liammial began to sweat heavily in the jacket he'd been wearing. How much longer did he have to wait for this promised help to arrive? The shock was wearing off, and his leg hurt abominably. He prayed it wasn't broken. He didn't have time to deal with a broken leg.

He wondered where the courier was, and whether he had even found the estate yet. He knew the gates could be hard to spot; they were so covered with vines that they blended right in with the hedges along that part of the road.

What if the courier had not spotted the gates? He might just keep riding until he came to the nearest village. Liammial tried to think of where that would be, how far away it was, and failed. He did not know the roads well enough in this area; that was Rocnar's duty. For all he knew, the courier might not find help to send back until he reached his destination this evening.

Perhaps he shouldn't have called the man an idiot. What if the courier was angry for that and never told anyone where he was? He wouldn't be missed at the estate until supper, and that was hours away. He should have made that idiot use his own horse to drag the dead beast from Liammial's royal body.

His leg hurt, the pain was nearly unbearable. The sun's warmth heated the horse, and the dung that had been expelled on the death of the beast. The aroma of the heated dung spread in all directions, and Liammial found breathing difficult.

Finally, he heard voices and hoof beats coming down the road toward him. At last, help had come. How long had he lain here, waiting, alone?

When the men arrived, Liammial recognized them as those who worked in the stables of Baron

Mallorry, his host. Apparently the courier had found the overgrown gates of the estate after all.

The head stableman slid from his mount and secured him to a handy bush. Two other men dismounted, and the fourth clambered down from the small, two-wheeled cart he was driving. The headman hastened to the beast's side and inspected the dead animal from one end to the other, while his three younger helpers stood about in a semicircle and watched.

"Aye, off foreleg's broke, an broke bad."

"Then he did right, slaughtering the beast?"

"Aye, he did. Nothing to be done, other than killing to put him from the pain."

The four men returned to their mounts, quietly conferring in voices so low Liammial couldn't hear what they were saying. This was the outside of enough! How dare they be more concerned for the dead horse than they were for a living, innocent victim of the accident?

"The horse is dead. I demand you get the thing off me; it's crushing my leg."

"Aye, Majesty, betide a moment or three while we figure the best way to do just that."

The consultation continued, and then a pair of the men vanished into the forest. The two remaining men started uncoiling ropes, and threading them through a pair of large blocks, each containing a couple of wheels.

Liammial gritted his teeth against the pain.

"This dilly-dallying is too much. Tie a rope around the horse and drag it off me and have done with it."

The eldest of the stablemen peered over the bulk of the horse at Liammial, his blue eyes twinkling.

"Cain't be doing that, Majesty. If yer leg be broke, then draggin the horse off it might mess it up so bad the healer'll have to take your own leg off. We don't be a-wanting that. We gots to lift the horse up, just enough to drag ye out from under. Then we can drag the horse up onto the wagon we brought, and take the meat home fer the dogs. "

He gestured into the forest.

"Jemm and Hamm went to find the wood we need fer the lifting. Sorry, Majesty, but you'll hafta wait a bit longer."

He returned to his business of tying a harness around the body of the dead horse, and attaching it to one end of the rope that was threaded through the blocks.

Time dragged before the men finally returned with a trio of long logs. The men quickly lashed them together at the top, and set them upright, with one of the blocks tied firmly to the lashing. The second block was tied to the small wagon, now lying at a slant, as the horse which had pulled it here had been unhitched from it. The wheels of the wagon were blocked to keep it from rolling.

The rope threaded through the arrangements of wheels was tied to two of the horses. They were encouraged to pull, and as they moved forward, the strain increased on the ropes.

The logs bent a little, and Liammial worried that the entire thing was going to collapse on top of him. Then slowly, he felt the burden of the horse's weight lifting from his leg, and as soon as it was off him, the stable master's hands grasped him firmly beneath the armpits and dragged him swiftly from beneath the horse.

He was peremptorily laid in the dirt of the road and told to remain there. The dead animal was laid back in the roadway, and the arrangement of the ropes altered. The pair of horses then made short work of dragging the dead animal into the back of the wagon. They righted the wagon and re-hitched the horse to it.

The stable master returned to Liammial's side with some short planks, and bound them to his leg.

"Just until the healer can get a good look at ya, and decide what's ta be done with yer leg."

The four men rolled Liammial painfully onto a blanket, then picked it up by its corners and transferred him to the wagon, where he was forced to lay next to the dead horse for the slow and careful journey back to Baron Mallorry's estate.

Once there, they carefully carried him into the house and up to his bedchamber, where his borrowed valet stripped the filthy clothing from his body.

"I'll have these cleaned immediately, Majesty."

"Burn them. And bring me bathwater. And where's the healer who's supposed to check my leg and tell me if it's broken?"

"The healer is on his way, Majesty."

Clean, dry, and comfortable, Liammial lay in his bed waiting for the servant to come take the supper tray away. The healer had pronounced his leg to be whole of bone, though badly bruised. He'd left some vile tasting concoction to dull the pain, and an admonition that Liammial was not to use alcohol for that function.

A tap at the door heralded the arrival of the man to take the tray.

"Bring me a bottle of brandy."

"Sorry, Majesty, the healer said not to. Is your leg paining? I can give you some more of the potion he left. Also, there is a courier here with a message for you; urgent he said it was, and he has not been pleased about waiting for you to be wakened and fed."

"Send me the courier. And a bottle of brandy. I will not take more of that vile potion. It makes me sleep, and gives me horrible dreams."

The servant left in silence, and in a few minutes a second tap on the door heralded the entrance of the courier.

"You!"

The courier took one look at Liammial and collapsed in laughter until he took a second look at the rage on Liammail's face.

"If I had known who you were, Majesty," he said apologetically, letting the rest of his sentence dwindle to nothing, but offering his hands palms up, a slight shrug to his shoulders.

"Give me your scroll. And bring me some brandy."

The courier handed over a scroll, and left the room.

Liammial read through the contents of it quickly, then a second time more slowly. The message came from the Squire of County Cran, one of the Barons in his secret kingdom. It contained Fergasse's defense plans, which had been distributed throughout the kingdom. The scroll also reaffirmed the squire's loyalty to Liammial, and asked where and when his troops should meet Liammial's forces to better give aid to his true liege.

It was a long time before Liammial realized that neither the courier nor the servant had returned with a bottle of brandy to soothe his pains.

Chapter Thirty-one

A Secret Courier Leaves
7th Day of Beltaine, 2448

The plate of untouched food lay before King Fergasse, growing colder by the moment. His full attention, however, was not on his plate but on his friend, King Jameisaan. He listened raptly as the essence of the interview with the self-proclaimed Prince Kezele was laid before him. Jameisaan's words ended and silence stole around the room in waves.

Jameisaan sat quietly as he waited for Fergasse to assimilate all he'd imparted. At last, with a deep sigh, Fergasse spoke.

"What was your feeling about the lad? Do you feel he's sincere about being the prince?"

His eyes keenly watched his friend as, without hesitation, Jameisaan answered him.

"Yes, I do, but it has to do more with instinct and study of human nature than whether he knew the lineage of Anthonny's genealogy. I wish we had some way of actually proving it, though. These times seem to bring out the best thespians, and the more they personally have to lose, the better they can spin a tale." Closing his eyes wearily, he shook his head slowly, his lean fingers rubbing his unshaven jaw, nearly unaware of the day's stubbling growth rasping his fingertips.

"There is a way this time, Jameisaan." Fergasse leaned forward in his chair and laid his palm on the table before them. Jameisaan's eyes popped open, the weariness instantly dropping away.

"How?" His voice betrayed his eagerness.

"I have never met the lad, but Fergan has. They are of an age, and used to visit back and forth between Havenhill and Anthonny's summer palace in northern Shuell. There must be some incident that only the two of them know about. We can dispatch a courier to Fergan tonight and have an answer back within a few days." He smiled. "At least *something* can move in our favor for a change!"

Jameisaan answered his smile, nodding, before his face became serious once more. "If he and his information prove true, then Milord's Army is as deadly as our own informants have given reports on. We must proceed quickly with our plans to protect our people." His look was particularly grim as he shifted restlessly in his chair.

"I agree. Also, if Kezele is the prince, then he's actually the king."

"You're quite right." Their looks said much more than their words conveyed.

"Even though he hasn't anything to rule just now, he'll still know much more about the lay of the land, and how we can set up defenses. We must impress the courier to the highest speed possible. We need to have Kezele in on our war councils, but only after we've had the assurance."

"Precisely."

Fergasse pushed the still-untouched plate of food aside and stood. "Let's get the courier on his way, and then we can concentrate on the home-front plans. Being out with the people through the evacuation process has given me a few ideas." He walked to the bell-pull to summon a courier.

Jameisaan, his plate also untouched, drained his goblet of cool lemonade, glad of the moisture his throat needed after so much talking. As he set the goblet down, he watched Fergasse rummaging for parchment and quill in the desk in the corner of the room.

"You know," he said slowly, "Kezele's observation of how the army swept so quickly through his country and then stopped so completely on the border raises my own curiosity as well, not to mention that's a very imperial viewpoint. It's one of the factors which causes me believe him, actually."

Fergasse straightened from his task and looked across the room at Jameisaan. "Yes, and the thought which haunts me about that very fact is the possibility my highly ambitious brother may be involved in this whole mess in some way."

Even from the room's distance, Jameisaan saw the pain in Fergasse's very stance. "A distinct possibility, I'm afraid. But come, let's get the messenger on his way and find some facts we can work with, instead of some worry we can do nothing about."

With a sigh, Fergasse turned back to his task as a knock was heard upon the door, followed by the courier's entrance.

Chapter Thirty-two

Turncoat!
7th Day of Beltaine, 2448

Rocnar rode through the dim streets of Jurisse, the early evening breeze stirring branches on the trees he passed. Something was amiss and he strove to identify what was troubling him.

His horse's hooves clipped sharply in the quiet street, and suddenly it dawned on him the street was as empty as it should be only late at night.

The marketplace, too, was deserted, save for a small dog snuffling through piles of trash looking for its supper.

The evening torches hadn't been lit, either. Rocnar hurried his weary horse. He felt as though he was riding through a dead city. He urged his horse into a gallop, only slowing as he came within a street or two of the palace.

Here, there were lights in the windows of some of the homes, and the torches had been kindled in the street lamps, sending small glimmers into the gathering darkness and leaving dark pools between them. The silence was still unsettling, but at least the lights were familiar and comforting.

He rode boldly up to the palace gates, as though it wasn't an unusual occurrence for the prince's valet to arrive a full moonatt after he and his master had crept from the palace in disgrace and possibly carrying the label of traitor to the crown.

As it was not yet full dark, the palace gates had not been closed, and none challenged his right to enter, nor his errand.

Rocnar left his horse at the stable, then proceeded to the servant's entrance and sought the kitchens. Not only was he in need of sustenance for himself, but he had need to speak to Lexander, the middle butler, and arrange an audience with the king.

He only prayed they would listen to him before they had him hung for treachery.

Rocnar was able to join the queue of servants awaiting their turn to dip out their supper from the pots on the hearth. Talk was quiet, and none looked askance at the extra person in line. He looked for those he knew, but didn't see any he recognized. He wasn't sure, either, but the ranks of servants seemed a lot thinner than usual.

Much as the city itself was thin. Had the fevers come to Jurisse? Or was this because of something Milord's Army had done? He shivered as he thought of what they were capable of. Where had everyone gone? Rocnar bit his lip as he worried about the problem. Until he talked with Lexander, he dared not ask anyone; his ignorance of recent happenings would only point out his absence He didn't think even his usually discerning abilities of getting people to talk easily to him covered this situation, and he preferred to keep silent and a little apart from the bulk of the servants until he found someone he knew.

He dished up his food and sat in his customary place, warily wolfing his food down as quickly as possible, his eyes darting around the room as he looked for Lexander.

A hand fell heavily on his shoulder, and Rocnar looked up. Lexander stood above and behind him. He cowered out of instinct, but only for a moment.

Lexander gestured for Rocnar to follow him, and then silently left the room. Rocnar rose with haste from his place and set his dishes near the scrubbing tub before following Lexander from the room.

As soon as the kitchen door shut behind him, Rocnar realized he may have just made a fatal mistake.

Two of the largest men-at-arms he'd ever seen stood in the passage with Lexander.

"Why did you return?" Lexander's voice was deadly quiet. Rocnar knew he had only this one chance to get his message across, and he'd better not muddle the meaning.

"Prince Liammial sent me with a message to deliver, but I've an even more important message for the King, one not from Liammial. I've got to tell him the prince's life is in danger."

Rocnar spoke quickly, his words tumbling over one another.

"As I thought," Lexander said. Turning to the men-at-arms, he spoke. "Take him away and put him somewhere safe."

The men laid hold of Rocnar and he struggled against their firm grip.

"Lexander, you've got to believe me! The prince's life is in danger. We have to act, to warn him!"

Lexander sneered. "Oh, yes, Liammial's life is in great danger, Rocnar. The king already knows that. His life is forfeit if he ever returns to Jurisse!"

Rocnar was so stunned by this pronouncement he quit struggling, and the men dragged him off easily, opening a door which let to descending steps. The open door emitted only darkness and a musty odor.

Rocnar only regained the use of his wits as the iron door swung closed behind him and the men-at-arms to scream with all his strength, "Not Liammial, you idiot! Fergan!"

Chapter Thirty-three

Out of Darkness
8th Day of Beltaine, 2448

Rocnar sat quietly, his eyes useless in the totality of the darkness which surrounded him. His ears were more useful, though the sounds they brought were not comforting. Soft chitterings and assorted squeaks and scufflings told him he was not alone. The rodents and insects he heard appeared to be his only companions in the dungeon, for there were none of the groans, whispers, or chain rattling which might indicate a human presence.

Rocnar had no idea how much time had passed since Lexander's men-at-arms had dragged him down the steps and into the darkness. Without striking a light, they had taken him down several passages before thrusting him into a cell.

The clanging of the door and the snick of the key in its well-oiled lock had sounded a final death-knell on his hope.

Rocnar had spent the first part of his imprisonment investigating his surroundings by touch. He'd found a pile of last year's straw molding in one corner of the stone room. Walls and floor were of rough stone with only the cold iron of the door to divide the stone. There were chains bolted to three of the walls; enough to secure half a dozen men, though there was little enough space in the room.

He'd discovered a small wood chest in the center of the floor. When opened, there had been a loaf of stale bread, a slimy water skin, and a chunk of cheese, well molded. He'd been able to eat enough at the servant's table to stave off being hungry enough to eat when he'd found it in the chest. A small bowl for slops adorned one corner, and, though it was wooden, it was chipped along the top edge, as though it had been scraped along the uneven masonry floor.

Time passed slowly for Rocnar, but how quickly it passed in the world of light, he could not say. He slept, and awoke hungry. He ate some of the tasteless food, but not all, not knowing when, or if, more would be provided. As he chewed at the slightly crumbly, dry bread, he reflected the food must have been placed in the cell fairly recently, perhaps within the past three or four days, as the bread had not yet disintegrated to dust. The outer skin of the cheese, though well covered in mold, was not yet hardened to where he could not rip it open with his fingernails and gnaw at the somewhat fresher interior. The water bag was saturated and the water itself a bit slimy, tasting of the leather hide and the tanner's not-well-finished work, but the water was wet and a bit cool, having lain on the cold stone for quite some time. Surprisingly, the leather skin was still intact, given the scratchings of tiny feet nearby. It was all Rocnar could do to keep his meager meal down.

Rocnar slept again and awoke to eat more of his precious, nearly rotten stores. He held out no hope for life and no thought of release. He pleaded within his skull he might be able to see the sun once more before he died, but very much doubted the wish would be granted. He groaned with the deepest despair.

From far away, he heard the distant slam of a door. Unbidden, hope sprang anew in his breast. Heavy footsteps clumped across a stone floor and echoed throughout the dungeon.

Rocnar leapt to his feet and hurried to the small grating in the door.

"Hey!" He yelled as loud as he could, his voice echoing off the damp walls. "I have to see the King! Prince Fergan's life is in danger!"

The booted feet came closer, bringing the light of a torch with them.

"Hey!" he shouted again, his voice growing stronger with his hope.

"Shut yer mouth, or we'll shut it fer ye," a voice growled back at him through the grate.

"Please," Rocnar made himself speak in a more reasonable tone, pleading with the unseen speaker. "Please tell the King that Fergan's in great danger."

Suddenly the bolt on the door was thrown free. The door was shoved open, striking Rocnar's leg and causing him to fall to the stone floor, adding more scrapes and bruises to his current collection. A large hand grasped his arm firmly, pulling him to his feet and dragging him ignominiously from the cell.

"Tell him yerse'f," the voice growled, unpleasantly. "He wants ta see yer."

"N-now?" Rocnar gasped. With the dust of travel still upon him and the smell of his own fear coupled with the odor of other bodily functions he'd picked up in the dungeon, Rocnar had a keen awareness of being extremely unprepared to enter the royal presence.

"Now." There was no kindness in the tones.

"May I clean up a little first? Surely His Majesty doesn't want to see me like this." he stammered to a halt, his filthy hand gesturing to his person.

"Now is what he said, and now is what he gets. And yer just lucky he didn't leave ye in the dungeon a week instead of on'y overnight." The man's voice sounded disgruntled now, instead of threatening.

Rocnar swallowed hard. He'd only been in the dungeon overnight? It had felt like at least half a week. He determined he would never return to the dungeon. Even death would be better than wasting away in the timeless dark with rodents and vermin for roommates.

The man-at-arms guided Rocnar to the door of the king's study and thrust him through it. He took up a watchful position just inside the portal, making it clear he thought Rocnar was quite likely here with orders to kill the king.

Rocnar studied the man behind the desk. King Jameisaan finished reading the paper in his hand, put it away in a drawer, and then looked up at Rocnar with a serious and impassive face.

The king examined him from head to toe, as though he could look into Rocnar's soul and see the guilt he had tried to bury within his heart. Rocnar tried to scrub the filth from the dungeon on the seat of his trousers. As his trousers were every bit as filthy as his hands, this accomplished nothing.

Finally, the king spoke. "I am King Jameisaan. King Fergasse is busy this morning with other tasks and asked me to see to you. I have little time for you myself, so I'll be blunt. You're Liammial's man and I have no reason to trust you." He stared unblinkingly into Rocnar's eyes.

"First I want you to tell me the message you've been sent to deliver. Then I want to hear everything you know about Liammial's plans. Lastly, you can *try* to convince me to trust you. The longer you talk, the longer you stay out of the dungeon and alive. If I find you're lying, or if your information isn't useful, back you go. Personally, I think the world would be safer without you loose in it and I'd just as soon see you hang as rot in the dungeon . Start talking."

Rocnar nodded, and then swallowed. His throat was suddenly dry.

"Could I have a drink of water, Your Majesty?" he asked hoarsely, bowing in a manner at once both courtly and servile.

Jameisaan waved at a sideboard. "Help yourself."

Rocnar nearly ran to the table, gratefully poured a glass of clear water and drank it greedily. He poured a second glass, lingering a little longer over it, then a third, though he did not drink from this one. Finally, he turned back to the room, walked to the center and faced King Jameisaan. With a bow of his head to show respect to the man seated before him, he took a deep and ragged breath, and then froze in place. Where should he begin?

Chapter Thirty-four

A Rat's Tale
8th Day of Beltaine, 2448

What had the king meant when he'd said Fergasse had asked him to 'take care of him'? Were those the exact words he'd used, or was Rocnar putting his own meaning to the words he'd heard, or thought he'd heard? The meaning had been there, he knew, even if the actual words had been different. He was full of dread and panic. Would this king order him to be reimprisoned, or killed outright? He'd done nothing of his own will which warranted death. There *was* the matter of the Kwennish courier, though, and he stood now before Kwenn's own king, a man who was not likely to lightly dismiss his own man's death, should he know of it. Rocnar tried to swallow in his throat without much success; despite the water he'd just consumed, his throat was totally dry.

He could read nothing from the face of the man who silently regarded him; the man who, with one word or flick of a finger could cause life to end, painfully or quickly, for any who crossed him. His personal guilt over the courier's death pressed upon him as though a giant hand were crushing down upon his chest.

The king stayed quiet, just watching him. As the silence stretched, so did Rocnar's guilt-laden nerves, finally reaching the breaking point. He couldn't keep his body from shaking with fear; moisture seeping from the corners of his eyes. Still the king sat, saying nothing. Rocnar's panic caused his breath to come only in desperate gasps now, and his terror, rapidly expanding in his mind, was so great he began to sob aloud, his whole body quaking with the depth of his emotions despite his efforts to hold it inside of himself and keep still. The water goblet slipped from his fingers and smashed on the floor, splashing his feet with its contents. What was to become of him? What would happen to his sisters if he were killed?

"Rocnar," the word was quietly spoken, but made him jump as though his name were shouted across the room.

"There is much I would learn this day," the king said. "I want you to start at the beginning of your association with Prince Liammial and tell me all you know of Liammial's dealings, his plans, and his whereabouts. How did you come to be in his service?"

Rocnar's eyes flew to the king's face in surprise and wonder. The voice didn't sound angry like he expected, but gentle. The blue eyes, though kind, still seemed to pierce right through to his very soul. He felt somewhat calmed, and managed to quiet his sobs, though he continued to draw great shuddering breaths as he spoke. His voice was the servile whine he used in Liammial's presence, wanting to placate the king sitting before him.

"I came to P-prince Liammial's service a hand of years ago, after an *accident* took my Da, my father," he began, holding out his hand with all five fingers extended in demonstration.

"Tell me about the accident, please," he said. Rocnar swallowed, a distant look coming into his eyes, as though he were there, seeing the incident afresh.

"My father, you see, my Da was a tenant on Prince Liammial's estate, Royalhaven. My family had been farming in Dell Hollow since my thrice great grandfather's time. Da was in the field, him and me. The prince came riding out of the woods next to the field with some of his hunting friends. He, I mean they, all of them, jumped their horses over the fence and galloped into the field, riding up and down the rows, trampling all over the vegetables growing there. They had been drinking and were laughing, and my Da was running around, waving the hoe as he tried to save the food, but they just dodged out of his way. Then he tripped and fell. They all jumped their horses over him, but when Liammial's horse was in the middle of jumping over him, my Da moved a little. The hoe came up and caught the rear legs of the horse. The horse stumbled and fell on top of my Da, breaking the horse's leg. The horse had to be put down. Prince Liammial blamed my Da; he said it was my Da's fault the horse was dead, and told him Da had to pay for it.

"My Da's leg was broken, too, from the horse. The bones were sticking out of the leg. We got the healer in. She bound him up, with sticks and sweet herbs, and told my Da he had to stay abed for a moonatt and half a moonatt more."

Rocnar again swiped his hand across his face, his thoughts on his injured father.

"Da did what the healer told him but the leg festered anyway. The healer did what she could, but my Da died." He took several deep, steadying breaths.

"I was just fifteen then, but I was working in the fields with Da from the time I was seven. My father had taught me well, and I kept working the fields alone from the time he got hurt, because we all knew that if we didn't have the rent price for the prince at harvest reckoning time, the prince would turn us all out, and my mother with three little ones to care for.

"When it came time for the rents to be paid, we didn't have quite enough. I didn't know what to do with Mother and the three little girls to feed. If I'd paid the full rent, we wouldn't have enough for eating in the winter, nor for seeding in the spring." Fear began to creep into his voice.

"Prince Liammial, told my mother if she'd come serve in the manor, he'd let us stay on in the cottage. Mother had little choice, we'd no money and nowhere else to go, so she went to be a servant.

"Me, I stayed at the cottage during that winter, caring for the young ones and teaching them their letters, same's my mother taught me. When spring came, I started the planting, as we always did, but one day a man came and took me off to see the prince." Rocnar shuddered.

"Prince Liammial told me my mother was too ill to work, that she'd called for me. I was taken in to see her." Rocnar broke off, a sob wracking his body with the sharpness of his memories.

"My mother was in a tiny room in the attics. Her bed was wet with blood and there wasn't a place on her which wasn't bruised. She'd been cut up a fair bit. I wanted to ask for the healer, but she shushed me, said it was too late for her and to listen as she hadn't long. I grabbed a toweling piece near to hand and tried to stop the bleeding, but there was too much already gone." Rocnar stopped, swallowing until he had gained control of his voice.

"She told me she'd been punished because she refused to do as the prince wanted. When I asked what it was, she merely said he wanted of her things not his to have."

Several minutes passed before the king's quiet voice brought Rocnar back to the present. "Did your mother die, Rocnar?"

"Mother made me promise to obey the prince in all things so as to spare my sisters the same treatment she'd received. She said she'd be glad of death's release, and then kissed my cheek. She gave me one last smile and died in my arms." His head still bowed, he took one hand, balling it into a fist, and then carefully set it within the other palm, the outer hand squeezing the fist tightly.

"The prince's man didn't allow me to linger with Mother, but took me back into the chamber where the prince was. He, Prince Liammial, told me it was my choice to keep my sisters from being thrown out of the cottage. I asked him to explain it to me because I didn't understand what he meant by 'my choice'.

"He told me I would have to serve him, to pay for everything. He'd send a woman who'd care for my sisters in the cottage until they were old enough to serve at Royalhaven. Food would be delivered to them. The prince would pay the death taxes for my mother and I could work for him to pay it off. My work would also pay the rents for my sisters, for their food and the care-woman. He said I also still had to pay the price of the horse my father had killed. I told him I didn't think the farm could bring in that much money. He laughed, then told me I wouldn't be working the farm, but I'd become his valet. If I didn't choose to serve him as valet, he'd throw us all out of the cottage before the end of the day. We had nowhere to go. I wasn't sure where my mother's cousin lived exactly, nor if he were still alive. With no money of my own, I had no choice but to enter his service and he knew it."

Rocnar was silent for long moments before he wiped his eyes with the back of his hand, and then looked at King Jameisaan. He took a deep breath, and let it out in a rush. Drawing in another breath, he spoke, still in that flat tone.

"He called me his valet but others cared for him and his clothes for quite some time until I was trained for it. What he mainly wanted me to do, he said, was get things for him. When I asked what he meant, he told me he'd heard I was good at ferreting out information. That's what he wanted. He would tell me what information he needed, and I would get it. He never told me why he needed the details, and I didn't dare ask." He continued looking at the king, but was silent now.

"I'm sorry you've had these terrible things happen to you, Rocnar. It can't be easy to serve such a one as he." The king's piercing blue eyes were on Rocnar's face, kindness there.

Rocnar shrugged his shoulders, his lip trembling a little. "It keeps my sisters safe, Sire. That's what's important."

"Tell me what you know of the past two or three years. Are you aware of his plans, his accomplices?"

"In the last three years, I've found out bits and pieces. I've made arrangements for travel for some of the prince's couriers. He uses other king's men, mostly, several of yours and a few of King Fergasse's, but he has a whole slew of men who are loyal to him only. He says there's lords who've sworn their loyalty to him. He's told me that much; he says he's the king of a secret realm. He boasts that someday his realm will no longer be secret and he will be declared king openly, but until just four days ago, I didn't realize it was more than bragging." He swallowed hard, but kept his eyes on the king.

"What happened four days ago that changed your mind?" King Jameisaan sat a little straighter in his chair, his unwavering gaze on Rocnar's face. Rocnar squirmed uncomfortably.

"Prince Liammial's been sending messengers to that army for nearly a year now. He helped them to get ships to come north. I saw that letter before the courier left with it." Rocnar cleared his throat and continued. "Then, four days ago, he ordered me," Rocnar's voice trailed off into silence, and his gaze dropped to his boot tops.

King Jameisaan waited for him to begin again. Several long moments passed in tense silence. Rocnar's lower lip trembled, his face taking on a greenish hue. Tears were streaming down his cheeks again before he continued. He cleared his throat and then spoke in a rush.

"Please understand something first, Your Highness. I had never hurt anyone before." He choked, coughing for a few moments before he could go on. Finally he gained control again and spoke.

"He, Prince Liammial, last month, he ordered me to k-kill your courier, the young lad from K-Kwenn. Crispin, I think his name was, in the note he was carrying. He told me to make it look like it was done by highwaymen, so I also had to rob him. I didn't want to do it, but he said if I didn't, he'd have my sisters brought to his house in Jurisse. He told me he'd make me watch what he did to them. I'm sorry for the courier, Your Majesty, but I had no choice. I had to do what he told me.

"The prince takes every penny of my wages to pay my debts to him. I've been saving the coins I get sometimes for delivering messages and the like, but I don't have enough yet to get me and my sisters away." He bowed his head in shame, his hands made a small gesture, palms up, but he knew his efforts to free his family were hopeless; knew he'd run out of time for all of them. He continued.

222

"I killed the courier, but I was always a good shot, hunting for dinner and such so I did my best to make it so he didn't suffer when he died. But now, I can't do what he's asking me now. Please, I beg you, send someone to Royalhaven and have my sisters killed, merciful and quick, so Prince Liammial can't get his filthy hands on them. When I don't go back to him with the information he wants and do what he wants me to do, he'll send for them, I'm sure." His voice broke on a sob. Rocnar stood, shudders racking his slender body; he kept his gaze steadily on his feet, his whole being radiating the despair of his life; there wasn't even a gleam of hope anywhere within him.

Jameisaan was quiet for a time, then spoke, a raspy note in his voice. "I am appalled what some men can do to others, especially ones who have been brought up to care for and protect people." Jameisaan stopped for a moment, and then continued.

"Rocnar, war makes monsters of us all, especially those who start the war for what they perceive as their personal gain. I regret with the deepest part of my heart that you and your family have suffered so, especially at the hands of one with royal blood in his veins." He stopped again, as if considering options.

"During wartime conditions, as we are in right now, Rocnar, we sometimes don't have the freedom to do things in a way we normally would. I'm not sure we can move your sisters right now, because we have to see to the best good of the most people and not tip our hand to the enemy just yet. What we need are more facts to complete the picture, and then we'll be able to best decide what our course of action must be." The king sighed, the sound reaching Rocnar's ears with the sound of a death knell to his hopes for sparing his sisters. His shoulders slumped, his head dropping another inch toward the floor.

"What I need you to tell me, no matter how painful you perceive the consequences to be, is what information Liammial sent you for. What, exactly and explicitly as you can tell me, is your mission here?" A harder note had crept into the king's voice now.

Rocnar, keeping his eyes on the floor, spoke clearly.

"He gave me a sealed scroll I was to deliver to the Lady Autrancia. I was to bring him a reply. He said I was to find out if any dispatches had arrived from Shuell; they would be bearing ribbons of black and flame red. He wanted to know when King Fergasse would be returning from the wedding but he said the most important thing was to find out where the prince and princess would be living, when they'd be traveling, and on what roads." He stopped and swallowed hard, then went on.

"I asked if he meant to kill them. He said he meant to see that he was the only living heir to the throne. He's worried the princess will get with child, and wants to see her dead before that happens." He choked on the words, swallowed again, and proceeded.

"I knew I couldn't help him kill any more innocent people. The one was enough; that poor courier boy. I brought grief to the girl whose hair lock he carried. But I also knew if I didn't do what he bade me, Prince Liammial would kill me. He'll torture me first, though. He's told me often enough what will come before my death, both to me and to my sisters." He choked to a stop once again, finally raising his tear-wetted eyes to the king seated before him.

"He terrifies me, Sire, but I knew I had to warn the prince, Prince Fergan, that is, and please," he raised his hands in supplication, "my sisters, if there is any way to safeguard them, I'll do whatever you want me to do to protect them!" Tears were now pouring unheeded down his cheeks as he made his final plea to King Jameisaan, sobs bringing him to incoherency.

225

King Jameisaan looked at the man before him for long moments before answering Rocnar. "Please know, Rocnar, I must discuss all of this with King Fergasse before we can decide on a course of action. If there is a way we can protect your sisters without causing danger to the greater number, we'll do our best." His voice was soothing, but sounded full of strength to Rocnar. The king went on.

"It will be several hours before King Fergasse returns to the palace. In the meanwhile, I must ask you to remain our guest. You will not be in the exact room you left to come here, but it won't be where you can leave at your will, either. Remember, we are at war, and you have been known to be in the employ of the enemy." He signaled the guard to remove the valet, but before they had reached the outer doors, he halted them for a last word.

"Thank you for being as merciful as you could be with my courier under your circumstances. I'll let his people know he didn't suffer."

Rocnar bowed his head and the guard led him from the room.

Chapter Thirty-five

Delightful Interlude
8th Day of Beltaine, 2448

Lady Autrancia went to the ladies parlor, off the throne room. The room was empty. She seated herself in her favorite chair, pulling her embroidery from the box where she'd left it before they'd gone to Kwenn for the wedding. Some women actually enjoyed the pursuit, but for her, embroidery had only one purpose, to make her appear profitably engaged while she listened to the court gossip, seeking new information to report to the prince. None were here now, but she needed to keep up the pretense that she enjoyed the stupid stitching.

A footman entered and bowed before her, handing her a small scroll. She took it from his hand. He bowed again and withdrew. Autrancia looked at the scroll, her heart skipping a beat. It was tied with the black and flame ribbon of Prince Liammial's Jurat, yet there was no wax seal on the ribbon's knot. Her tongue wet just the corner of her flame-rouged lips as she carefully pulled the ribbon from the scroll and tucked it into her bosom where it would be safe from prying eyes. Prince Liammial had specific plans for his new kingdom, and she meant to rule it at his side.

Unrolling the scroll, she was disappointed and a bit suspicious to see it was not written in Liammial's own hand. The sparse words were merely a request to meet with Rocnar in Liammial's sitting room, at her earliest convenience.

Autrancia frowned, a small line puckering the skin between her finely plucked brows. Most unusual. Of course she would go. Liammial had no doubt sent word by Rocnar, as he was not able to come to the palace himself. However, she must by no means accrue suspicions to herself. Therefore, she tucked the note away and returned to her stitching for another quarter of an hour before arising and leaving the room.

Knowing several different ways to Liammial's suite by long practice, she took one of the least obvious routes, climbing a narrow servant's stairway which coiled so tightly upon itself it was positively dizzying. She quietly crept along the small passage used by ladies maids and valets to serve their masters while not being visible to the guests of the king, and arrived shortly at an unremarkable door. She pulled a small golden key from her bodice, kept there more from habit than hope it would be of use to her in Liammial's absence, and unlocked the portal, closing it carefully and locking it behind her before returning the key to its hiding place.

Quietly gliding through the cupboard Rocnar had called home, she passed on through the great bedchamber where she had spent the most delectable hours, and thence into the sitting room, where a startled Rocnar jumped from the settee as if she'd scared the living daylights out of him.

Chest heaving, he stared back at her, and it suddenly occurred to Autrancia just how young and handsome Rocnar was. Now this could be entertaining, not to mention interesting. She wondered, from the way the young man had jumped, if Liammial had been teaching Rocnar anything other than fear.

"I have a message for you, Lady Autrancia," the servant stammered, still staring at her as if she'd suddenly grown three heads, "and Prince Liammial bid me give it to you in private." Rocnar swallowed before continuing. "He said there would be an answer for him and I was to wait for it." He held out a scroll to her, his hand shaking.

Autrancia smiled at the young man, tilting her head and looking at him through her long and carefully though artificially darkened lashes, but not taking the scroll just yet. Really, he was delectable, and who knew how much longer it would be before she saw Liammial again?

"Well, this is hardly private," she purred, waving her hand to indicate the room, "here in the Prince's public sitting room. Anyone could walk in at any moment and see us together. They might draw the wrong conclusion about what we're doing, together, too." She smiled widely at him.

Rocnar looked at the closed door, and then back at her. "I couldn't think of any other private place, milady, but I thought no one would be likely to enter the prince's room while he's not in residence, 'twas the best I could think of." His voice was full of apology, his wide eyes still fixed on her person, but not necessarily just on her face.

Autrancia slowly slid her tongue along the bottom edge of her top lip and watched Rocnar swallow convulsively. She smiled at him again. She caught Rocnar's eye and was surprised to see him blush. Was Rocnar truly that innocent? It was definitely time to see to his education. Liammial was wonderful, but still, one man would never be enough for her.

Autrancia shrugged her shoulders expressively, allowing her gown to gape away from her bosom slightly. She was pleased to note that Rocnar's eyes appeared to be glued to the small gap. Her decision made, the lady strolled back toward Liammial's bedchamber.

"They might enter his sitting room, but, knowing your master, no one would enter his bedchamber without his leave. Bring the scroll in here. I will read it at his desk." She turned her back to Rocnar and swayed her way into the bedchamber, seating herself on the very edge of the chair at Liammial's desk.

Rocnar followed her into the chamber, bowing low to hand her the scroll once she'd seated herself. Autrancia took the scroll from his hand and allowed the parchment to brush the skin of her bosom before she opened it. Rocnar's eyes followed every movement, and she exulted in her heart that she had his full attention.

The parchment contained little in the way of endearments, but it was no more than she expected. There was a plea from Liammial that he be allowed to stay for a season at a certain cottage they had employed in the past for trysts, and which stood in a forgotten corner of Collwiin's estate.

Liammial also asked if she would join with him in celebrating the Beltaine Festival. Autrancia frowned. Beltaine was three days of celebration at solstice, just two weeks away. It involved a lot of public drunkenness, loud and rowdy partying, and many earthy fertility rites. The festival was one which was celebrated publicly, not by a tryst in a small cottage in a swamp. She could not possibly be away from Jurisse during Beltaine. Liammial knew this, and knew that she knew it as well.

She considered the note's contents again. The only thing she could understand from that part of the missive was that if Liammial expected to see her and celebrate certain fertility rites with her, then what he was really telling her was he expected to be in Jurisse himself on that day.

Autrancia widened her smile, looking up into Rocnar's eyes. "Yes," she said softly, "of course there will be a reply. If you'll wait just a moment or two longer, I'll pen it for you." Her voice was smooth and silky. She noted he was breathing rapidly and had not yet removed his eyes from her carefully exposed bosom.

She leaned forward to procure parchment and pen from the bottom-most drawer of Liammial's desk and quite purposely fell off the chair, landing in an undignified heap on the floor. Rocnar gasped and leaned over to help her arise. With a practiced movement, Autrancia knocked his feet from beneath him.

Some time later, she left Liammial's suite the way she had entered it, through the servant's passages. She left behind her a dazed valet and a sealed scroll addressed to Liammial giving him permission to use the cottage and expressing the fondest hope she would be able to celebrate Beltaine with him.

Chapter Thirty-six

Self-Incrimination
9th Day of Beltaine, 2448

The beautiful Lady Autrancia opened her eyes and greeted another day. She stretched languidly in the warm morning air and let her gaze wander over her sleeping husband, who lay beside her, snoring gently into his pillow.

Autrancia indulged herself in a vision of pressing that pillow tight against his face, and felt the tremor of anticipatory joy she always had in the pit of her stomach as she contemplated a killing. She had long been at court as the wife of Ambassador Collwiin of Verr. King Zeraff of Verr knew of her other function, as spy and occasional assassin, when his Majesty Zeraff commanded, but not even Liammial knew that of her.

This thought changed the direction of Autrancia's thinking, and the contents of the letter Rocnar had given her yesterday came to her mind. She thought about the reference regarding the cottage on her husband's estate in a forgotten corner of Verr. That was very irregular, even for Liammial, because they'd never been together in Verr. Liammial never traveled that far from Jurisse if he could help it, so why would he have mentioned a cottage on their estate?

Several different scenarios came to the forefront of her mind only to be discarded as quickly because they'd never been together outside of Jurisse, and then she remembered a small cottage just two days from the castle, and on the road leading to Verr. They'd only met there one time, which is why it took her so long to think of the slightly shabby, old-fashioned little house.

Surely he couldn't expect her to up and leave Jurisse during the height of the festivities just to meet with him in that dank little shack for a quiet interval of passion? There was nothing in the furnishings there which were in the least either comfortable or fashionable. Her absence from the capital at that time would be very visible and highly remarked upon, which Liammial also knew. What must he really be saying?

Suddenly the meaning of Liammial's letter dropped into place. He wasn't asking her to leave the capital to meet him. He was telling her what direction he was coming from, and that he'd be joining her in Jurisse and how soon he'd be there. Of course; it had to be that!

Her husband made a little snorting sound as he shifted his position on the bed next to her, and she looked at him, a moue of distaste twisting her beautiful lips. Someday, soon, she'd be done with being the wife of an ambassador and take her place alongside King Liammial, as Queen of Jurat. He'd as good as promised it to her. That day was not yet here, so, almost reluctantly, she suffered her husband to live another day in the world.

Autrancia rose from her bed and poured herself a glass of wine. She carefully sipped it, checking both smell and taste for purity and freedom from any of the numerous poisons she'd learned to recognize. She carefully added the bitter powder which enabled her to pursue court 'politics' without conceiving, then drank the wine in a single gulp. She rinsed the glass, then refilled it and washed the bitter taste from her mouth with a fresh draught.

She knew Collwiin was well aware she dallied among the court, but she'd always been discreet when taking a lover and brought no public shame upon his head. He enjoyed seeing the family coffers increase from time to time with expensive jewels and other worthy gifts she brought to them with her activities, sometimes commenting or comparing them with others she'd already received.

He privately crowed with delight in the fact his wife had costlier clothing and better jewels than most queens had, and it hadn't cost him anything more than turning a blind eye from time to time. He'd told her more than once he realized he couldn't have given her one tenth of what she wore from his own pockets. Because of her talents, she enhanced his career as ambassador by not only helping them both dress better than most others, but by associating with the highest connected men in the Ten Kingdoms. This conversation usually came as she was adding yet another priceless necklace to the strong box of her jewelry collection. Biding her time, she'd never corrected his thinking that these were *her* jewels, not his nor 'the family's' possessions. He'd find out soon enough; if she told him at all before she snuffed his life, that is.

Now, Liammial; there was a man! She'd rarely had so satisfying a partner, even though she was the more physical of the two; the rich gifts he gave her from time to time were exquisite and well worth her tricks.

She vividly recalled the last time they'd been together. The blood-red rubies he'd given her had glinted in the candlelight, gleaming against her pale skin. It had been the night of culmination in several ways. The two years she'd invested in him had paid off, and Liammial had pledged to her she should be his queen.

It would be only a short time, now, before their plans came to fruition. She wished Liammial were at court still. She couldn't understand, at first, why he'd left so suddenly and without even a note to her, until they'd heard the news a courier of Kwenn had been killed by highwaymen only a day's travel from Jurisse.

Recognizing Liammial's hand in the matter made everything clear to her. She would be content to wait; after all, he was in hiding, and not free to move around as easily as he was used to doing. As ambassadors to Jurat's court, she and her husband had travelled to Kwenn to attend the wedding of Prince Fergan and the brat from Kwenn.

Following the wedding, of course, nothing would do but to travel back to the fens of Verr and bring news of the wedding to their own king. There had really been no question which of the two ambassadors would be chosen to represent Verr's interests in Kwennjurat, the very idea was ludicrous. Ambassador Jordonn who had been assigned to Kwenn's court didn't have a king's assassin as his wife, so he would be finding other employment. In all, Autrancia had been away from Jurat's court for just over two weeks. Even without Liammial in residence, it had felt good to be back within the castle and court of Jurisse; like coming home.

Autrancia smirked at the thought as her maid finished dressing her, then proceeded into the sitting room of their suite and seated herself at the desk, looking among the missives which had collected in their absence. Nothing of any import here worth considering; unless she counted the other, hand-delivered note of yesterday from her liege, her secretly betrothed, King-to-be Liammial, given to her by the very delicious Rocnar. She idly wondered where he'd spent the night, and what his dreams had been made of. Maybe she'd ask him next time they were alone.

Autrancia rose from the desk and left the suite to her husband and her maid. If her husband looked no higher than a lady's maid for entertainment and had no higher ambitions than an embassy for himself, let him. She'd better herself. She would be queen and the son she would bear to Liammial would be king.

Chapter Thirty-seven

A Rat Resolute
10th Day of Beltaine, 2448

His mind still full of his meeting with the Lady Autrancia, Rocnar hastily washed and dressed in preparation for his early morning appointment with the kings. He knew the lady did not love him. His mind told him any thought of experiencing such bliss again was folly. His senses, however, were still drugged with her beauty, desiring her company, and determined to do anything she asked of him, if only she would favor him with the smallest bit of her affection once more before he died.

Rocnar shook his head and firmly put thoughts of Autrancia away. She was a traitor to the kingdom. Associating himself with her would only result in death for himself, and worse than death for his sisters.

Fully dressed, he poked his head out the door of Liammial's old suite, and let the guard there know he was ready to see their majesties at any time they should summon him. The summons didn't arrive until well after the dinner hour, when Rocnar had eaten all of the wonderful food on the tray the rather attractive young serving girl brought him.

Two large guards accompanied him to the door of the king's office, and Rocnar grimaced. If he was in their shoes, he wouldn't trust him either.

Smiling at the convolutedness of his last thought, Rocnar stepped through the door and bowed low enough that he was practically groveling on the floor at the king's feet. His face turned toward the floor, Rocnar wasn't even certain which king he was paying obeisance to, but as they co-ruled a single kingdom, it hardly mattered. He'd made his choice. His fealty belonged to the king, and he would do all in his power to stop Liammial.

"Rise."

Rocnar scrambled back to his feet, still keeping his eyes lowered in humility.

"Report to me everything that happened when you delivered the message to Lady Autrancia."

Rocnar took a deep breath, then began, outlining each happening, every word spoken, and even the shameful happenings afterward, in complete detail. Fearing this was a test, and the kings had other spies watching the happenings, Rocnar left nothing out of his account, even though he felt his face grow hot during parts of the telling, and knew he was blushing.

"Very well; she will, of course, be watched. Do you know the contents of the scroll you delivered to her?"

Rocnar shook his head, his eyes still examining his shoe tops.

"Where is the message she wrote for you to carry back to my brother?"

Rocnar pulled it from his purse and proffered it to King Fergasse; at least now he was sure of which king he stood before, and then realized he'd known that from the first word, simply by recognizing the voice he'd heard since he'd come to the castle as Liammial's valet. Mentally he gave a shrug, knowing this last bit didn't matter; however, he now had the courage to properly face his monarch.

He raised his head and watched as the king carried the message to his desk, and sat. On the desk was a candle, a thin-bladed knife, and a small wax stick in the green color of Verr.

"Please, Majesty, be careful," he begged, knowing that to speak without being given leave to do so was practically an act of treason, but he wanted to live, even if it was only to continue to protect his sisters from Liammial. "I cannot deliver an unsealed message to Prince Liammial and live to make mention of it."

"Have no fear, Rocnar, Liammial will have no idea it has been opened and read. I know exactly what I'm doing."

The king picked up the thin bladed knife and heated the blade just a bit in the flame of the candle, then deftly slid the warmed blade under Autrancia's wax seal, popping it up from the round surface of the small scroll.

Carefully, he unrolled the parchment and silently read the writing thereon.

Just as silently, he carefully rolled the scroll up, to exactly the same thickness and tightness it had been rolled originally, taking care to make sure the wax seal lined up perfectly with the shadowy outline it had left behind on the back of the scroll.

With a smile, Fergasse heated the knife once more. He set the hot blade against the green wax on the desk, and gathered a bit of molten wax on the blade of the knife. Quickly, he wiped the blade against the back of the seal, and then stuck it down against the scroll, using the new bit of wet wax to remoisten the back of the seal, and affix it to the scroll.

With delicate movements, he put the small knife down and pinched the seal tightly to the scroll, holding it securely in place while the wax had time to cool and harden in place.

Silently, the scroll was passed back across the desk into Rocnar's shaking hands. He examined the scroll carefully, but could not tell it had been opened, or sealed more than once.

"Well," asked the king, "are you satisfied the sealing is secure?"

"If I had not watched you accomplish that, Your Majesty, I never would be able to guess. How did you learn to do such a thing?"

King Fergasse chuckled. "I learned that particular trick from Liammial."

His laughter died.

"I want you to return to Liammial, to deliver this message, and I am going to ask you to be my spy. He'll never believe you'd have the courage to do such a thing."

"Not with my sisters securely in his keeping."

"I sent a courier to Royalhaven this morning ."

"To free my sisters?" Hope burgeoned within his heart and he held his breath for the answer.

"No, I daren't free them yet, for he might hear of it and know you're my man now. His instructions are to watch over them, and remove them from the estate only if they are in danger of being harmed."

Rocnar let out his breath, a small smile stretching his lips. "That's good enough for me. If he doesn't realize I'm working against him, he won't move against them; and if he finds out I've taken a new master, then your man will be in place to rescue them. What would you have me find out for you, Your Majesty?" he asked as he straightened his shoulders, standing a little taller.

"We would very much like to know the exact nature of Liammial's connection to Milord's Divine Army. We also would be interested in learning anything you can discover about the timing and manner of the attack which will be made. This conflict has gone on too long now to be resolved in any manner other than open warfare. The more we know of his plans, the better we can prepare for them, and counter them."

Rocnar nodded and bowed again, deeply.

"When would you have me leave, Your Majesty?"

"As soon as you gather the necessities of travel; I'll send word to the stable that your horse should be prepared, and to the kitchen that some travel rations be readied for you."

He rose from his seat at the desk, turned his back to Rocnar, and settled himself in one of the comfortable chairs near the fire.

Rocnar knew a dismissal when he saw one, and quietly let himself from the room. The guards accompanied him back to his lonely suite of rooms.

Chapter Thirty-eight

Questioned Trust
10th Day of Beltaine, 2448

The door closed behind Rocnar, and silence reigned long in the room while Fergasse contemplated the flames jumping about in the fireplace as they eagerly consumed the wood.

"Do you think we can trust him, Fergasse?"

Jameisaan lifted the goblet beside his chair and took a sip of the cool lemonade.

"I don't know. I hope so. He seemed truly remorseful on the count of Crispin's death, and determined to prevent any more deaths."

"He's been through a lot, and I don't feel he's very emotionally stable."

Fergasse took a drink from his own goblet with a matching beverage and burrowed his shoulders deeper into his own chair.

"Perhaps, but only time will tell."

Chapter Thirty-nine

The Blackberry Patch
13th Day of Beltaine, 2448

Prince Kezele checked his reflection in the glass and concluded his appearance was the best it could be, considering the ill-fitting borrowed clothing he was wearing. Since his first interview with the king six days ago, he had been well fed and given clothing and make-work projects which were supposedly in the best interests of the kingdom as they prepared for this war.

Any of these projects could have been carried out just as competently by any of the servants in the palace, and he knew it. He was certain the kings disbelieved his tale, and thought him a spy. Hoping to find some way to prove his claim, he never complained, but faithfully executed the duties and chores assigned to him on a daily basis. Tonight a summons had been given him to come to the kings' office, and he was delighted to obey this order.

On arriving at the office door, he was admitted without delay. King Jameisaan sat alone at the desk, and Kezele bowed before him as the king waved him to a seat.

"By all reports, you've been carrying out your assignments with a high degree of excellence. Thank you for all your efforts."

"You're most welcome, Sire, but truly, it was work anyone could have accomplished."

"Yes, so it was, but the aspect I delight in was that you neither had to be instructed, nor did you complain. You simply set to the task and completed it, no matter the obstacles."

Kezele nodded, wondering where this conversation was leading.

"I'm told you spent part of at least two summers visiting at Havenhill with Prince Fergan."

"Yes, they were very enjoyable times. However I've discovered he is unable to be reached in order to confirm my identity to your majesties."

Jameisaan chuckled.

"So you've seen to the heart of our dilemma, have you?"

"It's just how I'd have treated me, were I in your position. I haven't been able to come up with any way I can prove my identity to you, though."

"What can you tell me of blackberry juice tattoos?"

Kezele burst out laughing. It was a few minutes before he was able to continue speaking.

"The last summer we were together at Havenhill. We were both eleven, and we knew our childhoods were coming to an end, that we'd both become more a part of doings at court on our twelfth birthdays. We'd become such good friends, we wanted to share some mark of our friendship, something lasting.

"It was late in the summer, we were eating wild blackberries in the woods, and laughing about how badly the juice stained our skin. 'Twas Fergan's idea, actually; he'd heard of sailors marking themselves with ink and needles, making a permanent mark on their skin.

"We decided we'd do the same, but the mark would have to be where it wouldn't show, for it wouldn't do to have permanent and visible marks on the precious body of a king's son.

"We each tattooed the other with our initials, high on the right hip. We used blackberry thorns for our needles, and crushed the berries into the pricks so the juice would be our ink.

Mine was still sore when I rode home. The mark has long faded; I expect blackberry juice is able to be absorbed by the body, where ink is not, but the memories are still fresh."

King Jameisaan nodded, and then looked behind the chair where Kezele sat.

"Well?"

"That's just about the way Prince Fergan told it to me, Majesty."

The courier dressed in Kwenn's blue and gold moved forward into the light.

Happiness burst in Kezele's chest.

"Now that we know for a certainty who you are, Your Highness, we have some different assignments for you. What do you know of the drilling of soldiers, and the stratagems of war?"

Prince Kezele smiled with the knowledge of his exoneration.

Chapter Forty

The Wrong Image Fostered
17th Day of Beltaine, 2448

Tanella emerged from the inner dressing room wiping her perspiring face with a small, dampened cloth. She took three deep breaths to steady herself and to settle her stomach. Walking to the window, she moved the draperies aside and opened the tall windowed door onto her shallow balcony. Dawn's pinky gold rays were just beginning to stretch thin fingerlets of radiance across the barely lightening sky.

She looked over the city spread below her, where the shadows were still deep with the night's darkness. A few of the taller rooftops caught the slender light edging the birth of the day. She drank deeply of the clean morning air, and thought of the itinerary of this day's work. It was full enough for two days and a bit more. She'd need to be on her way rapidly or she'd be caught up in the rigors facing her and miss this chance for answers.

Taking one last, deep breath, she moved back into the room and slipped into her closet. It only took her moments to find the box which held her peasant dress and its accouterments. Quickly slipping into the skirt and top, she fidgeted with the layers of fabric, twitching them into place. Plain cotton stockings and small slippers completed the outfit. Looking at her reflection in the silvered looking glass, she thought she looked fine for a quick traverse into the city to the healer and back to Kwenndara Castle before any palace people knew she was even awake.

Brushing the tangles from her long red hair and quickly plaiting the tresses into one piece, the princess took a smallish triangular piece of cloth and tied it over her hair. She went to the door and listened, but heard nothing.

Opening the door, she slipped out into the empty hallway, quietly making her way down the back stairways and out the back door, taking only a small candle with her to light the way once she reached the interior of the animals' quarters. Being much practiced in this type of activity gave her the advantage of stealth and silence as she skimmed the edge of the grounds and slipped into the dark stables.

Lighting the candle's wick, she looked guardedly around. Halters and small saddles were in their usual places, and she gathered what she required as quietly as she could before going down the row to select a mount.

"May I help ye, my lady?" inquired one of the main grooms, stepping from a cubicle partway down the main row between the stalls.

Tanella jumped and turned almost guiltily to face him. Remembering her disguise, she gulped and spluttered as she tried to spit out the excuse she'd made up for being here.

"I need a horse saddled so I may complete a task for Her Highness," she said.

"At this time of day?" he asked, looking at her with disbelief marking his face.

"She asked if I could do a small service for her before she got caught up in the cares of helping the refugees and aiding the regular citizens for the day."

"Could I go for ye, my lady, and serve my princess?"

"No, but thank you; it's just a small thing of slight consequence to any but herself. 'Twill take very little time to accomplish, and she wanted none other to be taxed with its commission."

"Very well, my lady, but who is riding as yer escort?"

Tanella ground her teeth in frustration. Eminently glad she'd been raised in Renthenn, where the rules were more relaxed, she smiled her best smile at the groom before speaking.

"What is your name, please?"

"I be Gibbonns, my lady, Head Groom ter His Majesty's stable." He straightened just a bit as he gave his name and rank, the pride of generations who served in the same capacity subconsciously adding to his stature.

"On any other day, Gibbonns, I'd probably ask you to attend me, because of your devotion to the princess and your thoroughness in obeying the rules of the castle. Today, however, with this small duty Her Highness has given me, I'll just go quickly by myself and be back nearly before you can get a second mount saddled."

She turned and continued to walk down the stalls, inspecting horses as she went, looking for one she'd brought with her from Renthenn; one who was familiar with her and would do her bidding the easiest.

"But, my lady," Gibbonns said as he hurried after her, "'tisn't safe fer ye to be out in the city on yer own, even this early."

"I've told you, I'm not going far, and Her Highness will expect me to complete this and be back within her chambers ere she awakens. Please, Gibbonns, don't get me into trouble with the princess. Allow me to be on my way, and quickly, or I shan't be back in time."

Reaching the stall of one of her favorite horses, she stopped beside it and set the small saddle at the edge of the door.

"If you'd like to help by saddling this horse for me, I'd appreciate it. Otherwise, please move so I may do it and serve my princess."

"But, but," Gibbonns began to splutter.

"Gibbonns," Tanella said, her voice becoming cold and more commanding. "Please believe me in this. I'm a cousin to the princess, so I've known her a long time. Let me be about her business and you won't run the risk of getting on her bad side. Trust me; she can be as fiery as her red hair. You never, *ever* want to be on the wrong side of her when she's angry. I've been there more than once. I know. Now; either saddle this horse or get out of my way. I've *got* to be back by the time she expects me, or *I'll* be in trouble.

Getting flogged isn't my favorite pastime, so I'd be much obliged if you'd saddle the horse."

Gibbonns stood indecisive, biting his lip.

"Now, Gibbonns!"

He jumped just a notch, his eyes wide. Blinking several times, he came to a decision.

"Would she really flog you?" he asked, reaching for the saddle blanket.

"You have no idea what she'd do, Gibbonns, but I'd advise you to do exactly what she says, when she says, and do it without question, no matter how bizarre it sounds to you. She once brought her nanny into high court and accused her of treason, just for giving her a much-deserved walloping. Obeying her bidding is the best way to keep your head attached to your neck!"

He reached for the saddle and laid it atop the blanket, pulling the cinch into place. As she watched him work quickly and efficiently, a small part of her heart was pleased she had such steadfast people surrounding her. She vowed to get to know them all better and quickly. With the war on the edges of their country, this was the type of person she needed to depend upon.

Finished, he helped her up into the saddle and led the horse and rider out into the nearly fully sunlit sky.

Looking down at him as he handed her the reins, she nodded her head, not allowing herself a smile, but she did give him a small 'thank you' as she grasped the leather lines.

"When you know her better," she said briskly, "you'll understand why I'm doing this little errand on my own, and this early in the morning!"

With that, she touched a heel to a flank, and not looking behind her at the groom left in her wake, she trotted the horse out the gate.

Well, she thought with just a sliver of guilt as she guided the horse toward the city center, *when he comes to know me better, he* will *know why I'm doing what I'm doing!*

With that thought giving a small comfort, she nudged the horse on to a higher speed, not regretting for an instant the lamentable reputation of Ogre she had just given to herself. Hopefully, there would be time enough for the truth of it to surface later.

Chapter Forty-one

A Welcome Surprise
17th Day of Beltaine, 2448

Tanella guided her horse into the area occupied by the healer, a short distance from the city's center. She had to find out why she'd not been able to sustain the energy she'd enjoyed all her life, and to discover why her stomach was so touchy these days. She needed to know if it was some sort of fever she'd gotten as she'd traveled through the villages between Renthenn and Kwenndara and if so, she'd need to prepare the entire city for a fever season, as the refugees from Jurisse would come through the same villages.

Tanella and Janna had been throughout the capital city appraising the assets available to them. As they readied her people to receive the evacuees from Jurisse, she'd come to know where most things were; millinery, apothecary, cooper, miller, glass blower and tin smith, among others. She knew where the mayor and others of the town council resided. She'd made a special note of where the healers could be found, for when the refugees arrived, many might need the attention of a healer after such a long journey.

As she rode in this bright new day, she felt the bile begin to rise, but knew she was but one street from her destination now. Hellenne was one of the few female healers in the city, and had seemed to have a kind eye when Tanella had met her.

Tanella swallowed repeatedly and guided her horse into the side yard of the healer's cottage next to small bushes, sliding from the saddle and stepping to those bushes before the retching began. There was nothing in her stomach so nothing came up, but the heaving, gagging response was as vile as if she'd let fly an entire banquet.

At last the spasms subsided, and she straightened, brushing the back of her hand across her forehead.

"This should be better, Highness," said a quiet voice as a cool cloth was thrust into her shaking hands.

Tanella jumped at the sound and spun to see who was speaking. It was the healer, a kind smile on her lined face.

At the nod from the healer, Tanella wiped the sweat from her forehead and cheeks, then swiped the cloth across the front of her throat. A second pass over her forehead, and Tanella was ready to speak.

A thankful smile tilted her lips as she began to form her words. Only a croaking sound could be heard instead of her voice when she tried to pass the words across her tongue. She tried to clear her throat for a second attempt at speech, but it was painful. She swallowed, and tried again.

The healer, Hellenne, made a quick curtsey and gestured toward her small cottage as she addressed Tanella.

"Highness, come into my home, if it pleases you. I've a pitcher of cool water if you wish it, or even better, I've some refreshing peppermint tea to which we could add a spoonful or two of sweetening and that should help even more. I'd recommend the tea, were I to be asked, and perhaps a bite or two of a biscuit with no butter or jam upon it to settle your innards just a bit. You can sit for a spell by my kitchen table until you're feeling more the thing."

Tanella nodded, not wanting to try to speak without adding at least some moisture to her throat first, and gestured for Hellenne to lead the way.

A quick bob of a curtsey and Hellenne walked into the small home, holding the door open. She ushered the princess to the tiny kitchen table set in front of the small window, pulling out the wooden chair for her. She set a saucer and cup in front of Tanella.

Hellenne stepped to a corner of the kitchen where a small stone box, nearly covered with wet rough cloths, was balanced on two ropes over a hole in the floor. Tanella could hear the unmistakable sounds of a running stream coming from the hole.

Sitting on top of the wet cloths on the box's top was a stone the size of a fist. Hellenne picked it up and set it aside; she moved the cloth and pulled a linen-covered pitcher from within the box. This she carried to the little table where she removed the linen and poured some of the contents of the pitcher into the cup.

Setting the pitcher on the table, the healer then plucked a spoon from the nearby sideboard along with a petite jar of something and brought them to the table. Dumping two heaping spoonfuls from the jar into the cup of liquid, she stirred it for a few moments before setting the spoon beside the saucer in front of Tanella.

"Here you are, Highness, a cup of cold peppermint tea with extra sweetening in it to soothe your throat and becalm your stomach. Take just a sip, and tell me if I need to add more sweetening to it."

Tanella looked at the cup, then the box, then the jar of sweetening, then up at the healer. She tried to speak, but again only a raspy croak came from her throat made raw by the retching. The healer nodded encouragingly and gestured for Tanella to drink. She did.

The tea was more than simply cool, it was downright cold, and felt wonderful to her throat. She took another swallow, and felt the healing effects of the sweetening coat the back of her throat; she felt her stomach cease its roiling sensation.

This time when she tried to speak, her words came easily.

"That coldness is wonderful! It feels soothing to my throat as well as my stomach, just as you said. Usually we only have cold things to drink during the winter months when we can chip the ice from the blocks we've cut from the frozen pond. It's much too late in the year for this cold of drink. Tell me if that really is a brook below

265

that hole that I'm hearing and how does that give you cold water?"

"Well, Highness,"

"Please, Hellenne, will you refer to me as Lady Tanella or simply as My Lady and drop the 'Highness' part? I fear I'm not used to the formality shown to me here! In Renthenn, we were much more casual, and the difference between the two is almost disquieting. Also, please sit at the table with me. Otherwise, I'll get a crick in my neck from looking up!"

The healer's wide smile greeted this confession, and Tanella breathed a sigh of relief as Hellenne pulled up a chair and sat at the table with her.

"Thank you, Your...My Lady. I'll honor your wishes, mostly, I think, because of my own preferences. When you see people as I do, hurting, or ill like you just were, you realize that people are people, and are the same beneath the titles as the servants are. Each person has feelings and needs understanding and sympathy along with their healing. As a matter of fact, my worst patient is really a huge baby when it comes to illness or pain. He's a prominent citizen, who I won't name to you, and if you guess who it is, I'll deny it."

They both laughed, in full charity with each other.

"Now, My Lady, besides a soothing tea, how may I serve you?"

Tanella spoke of her concerns of picking up a fever or other type of illness during her traveling, and how she wanted to keep the evacuees and others from contracting it and spreading it further.

"When does the illness come upon you?"

"Usually first thing in the morning, as you just saw, or if I go a long time without a meal. Actually, though, this is the first time I've vomited. Up until this morning, I was simply queasy."

"If you eat something really greasy, does that also turn your stomach?"

Tanella had to swallow a couple of times before she could answer Hellenne. "As a matter of fact, when you simply asked the question about the greasy food, I thought I was going to retch." She gave the healer a small smile.

Hellenne handed Tanella a dry biscuit to nibble on, and Tanella took a small bite.

"Thank you, this helps." She took another small bite, and followed it with a drink of the cold tea.

"Am I going to be giving anyone this illness as I meet with them?" Tanella asked, her eyes steady on Hellenne's face.

"Oh, My Lady, I don't think you're about to give this illness to anyone else at all."

"Well," Tanella said, expelling a huge sigh, "that's most comforting to know. What have I picked up along the way?"

"How long have you been married?"

Tanella sat up a little straighter and was sure her face reflected the surprise she felt, because the healer smiled broadly.

"We married on the 16th of Corith; why?"

"Did you have any sort of a honeymoon before you were packed off here?"

"Yes, we had a week together before we had to come back to Renthenn and then became involved in the preparations for the war. Again, why?"

"One more question before I answer yours, I think, My Lady. Have you missed your womanly season at all?"

Tanella thought, nibbling on the biscuit as she cast about in her mind for the answer.

"I don't think I had it, but I've been on the road travelling so much in the last couple of months that I've set my whole system off balance. Does it make a difference?"

"Well, it's only been just over a moonatt so it's a bit early to be really sure, but if any were to ask my thoughts on the matter, I'd say the next heir to the throne of Kwennjurat is on the way."

Tanella sat and stared at the healer. She realized her mouth was hanging open and shut it. She shook her head trying to clear what felt like newly-developed cobwebs from her brain. "Excuse me, but I thought I heard you say...did you say...am I...oh, goodness!" Tanella put two fingers to her lips and pressed them gently there. Hellenne said nothing, just sat smiling.

Tanella took a deep breath and squealed a delighted 'yes!' and then promptly burst into tears.

"There, there," soothed Hellenne. "It's all right. It's a perfectly natural thing, My Lady; perfectly natural. You'll see; you'll be all right."

Hellenne patted Tanella's shoulder, then got up and got another cloth damp with cool water and handed it to Tanella to mop up her face.

"With this war, I don't know when I'll be able to see Fergan and tell him, or Papa, either," she wailed, hiccupping.

It took a huge effort, but Tanella gathered herself together and wiped her face clear of her tears. She took another deep breath and looked at Hellenne. She searched the healer's face for a long moment before she nodded.

"Hellenne, for now, this must be our secret. Swear it." She looked steadily at the healer.

Solemnly the healer swore an oath to keep the child a secret for as long as possible.

"Thank you, Hellenne. As the princess, I must attend to certain things until we can be as prepared for war as we may possibly be. It won't do anyone any good to be worried about my health as we move through the next moonatt or two. How do I manage this? I surely miss not having a mother at a time like this, especially with Aunt RaeLee clear in Renthenn! How long will it be before I start showing my condition to the world?"

"It depends on your body, and your clothing. The looser you can wear your clothing the better. You must also guard against missing meals, and if you had some plain buns or biscuits in your room which you could nibble on before rising in the mornings, you shouldn't be as ill as you would be if you didn't take those precautions.

"Peppermint tea, either hot or cold is helpful. Listen to your body and try to figure out what it needs. Find the things you can eat without causing upset, and then stick to those foods, whatever they are. Make sure you have plenty of rest. See if you can take a nap during the afternoon each day, but especially if there is a night meeting or evening court dealings you must attend. Instead of riding horses, take your carriage. Other than that, only time will tell.

"Some women get big enough to show the world they are with child within three moonatts, while others only begin to exhibit their condition by the sixth or seventh moonatt. As far as anything else, is there someone you trust that you can send for me if you need to? Too many visits to or from me will put paid to our secret right away."

"My cousin will keep my secret, and is my Lady-in-waiting. The problem there is that we look so much alike we can pass for each other. I'll have to think about it. Maybe I can send to Havenhill and get Maggie to come be my maid. I'll have to see. I don't want to hurt my current maid's feelings, but I'd feel much better having someone nearby that I know more closely. I'll see what Janna can help me devise."

"You can pass for each other?" Hellenne asked, her eyebrows reaching for her hairline. Tanella nodded. "Is that why you're dressed in peasant clothing, My Lady?" the healer asked, placing much emphasis on the last two words, her smile full and knowing.

Tanella nodded once more, an answering smile on her own face. "Actually," she said, "I was surprised you recognized me. Hmmm, I'll have to remember that. Most would not have been able to tell. There's one servant in Renthenn my cousins and I could never fool. That makes two of you. We could even fool our fathers, but not Quins."

Hellenne laughed out loud. "You naughty girl! I think you'll turn this new country of ours on its ear, but I also think it's time we have your kind of energy and youth in charge of our country; then we won't be such rut-seekers!"

"Rut-seekers?"

"Rut-seekers; people who are so complacent and comfortable that we'd stay walking in a wagon rut rather than challenge the conventions and actually get out onto the edge of the road where the grass and flowers are and really accomplish things with our lives!"

Tanella laughed. "Rut-seekers. I understand your implications, and know people just like that; people similar to the mayor and his council, you mean. They don't want to change because 'it's been done this way from time out of mind'!"

"You'll never hear me admit to that, My Lady!" Hellenne's smile was wider than ever.

"Neither will I, and I'll deny I actually said it to my dying day!" Tanella giggled.

"Drink up your tea, My Lady, and then you'd best be leaving, as people will be up and about soon, and we don't want to give them something to talk about this morning or everyone in Kwenndara will know your secret before the nooning hour!"

"Yes, Ma'am!" she said, pretending to be cowed by the older woman's council. The very docile manner made Hellenne laugh out loud once more.

A few minutes later Tanella left on her horse, feeling she'd made a friend at last in this city. As she rode toward the palace, her feelings took turns at spiraling up and then down. She felt at peace with the world and full of the joy from having Fergan's baby growing just below her heart; then her emotions crashed to the darkest despair for fear something would happen to her precious Fergan before the war was over and she would be a widow and he'd never know his child. Her papa would be very happy, though, and this was the cheering thought she concentrated on as she rode through the back gate of the mews and into the stable yard.

Gibbonns came rushing forward to help her with the horse, and she schooled her face into seriousness so he'd never guess at her commission from the wretched and volatile princess.

As she walked into the back hallways and started up the servant's staircase, she realized they'd never gotten back to discussing the box over the stream. The thought of the contraption still intrigued her. If she could have access to something like that during the summer months, the icy cold tea could help her keep common knowledge of her condition quiet much longer; a worthy goal to pursue. She didn't want to take the risk of Milord's army using her condition as a pawn against either her husband or their fathers. She had to keep it quiet for as long as possible.

She slipped down the hallway and back into her own suite unnoticed. Thankful she'd learned the nature of her infirmity, glad that she didn't need to worry about spreading illness among her subjects, Tanella pulled off the peasant dress and slipped back into her voluminous nightdress and wearily climbed back into bed. If she could just get an hour's rest before she had to face the rest of her day....

Chapter Forty-two

Milady Poison
20th Day of Beltaine, 2448

Liammial was coming! Autrancia lay in bed in the golden glow of dawn and hugged that thought to her for a few precious moments before she tucked it into the deepest, darkest recesses of her heart. Liammial was coming. His army would be assembling near the cottage where they'd rendezvoused and by Beltaine, he would be here.

She must prepare for his coming. One way or another, she would be Queen of Jurat, and rule at Liammial's side. And then, who knew? If anything happened to her husband the king, she would just have to rule their kingdom alone. Especially if all of the other blood heirs were deceased. Something would have to be done about that brat Fergan and his new wife, and quickly, but first, the way must be paved for her to become Queen. These things must be taken one step at a time.

Autrancia rose and stretched, then walked languidly over to her private bottle of wine. She quickly downed her own potion, washing it down as usual with a chalice of undoctored drink. Rinsing the cup, she prepared another for her husband. As she did every morning, she filled the cup with the sweet, dark berry wine her husband preferred.

Today, she knowingly committed treason against King Zeraff of Verr. She was about to murder one of his ambassadors. She carefully poured the packet of poison she'd been feeding her husband on a daily basis into his wine, and stirred it until it was completely dissolved.

Then, her hand trembling slightly, she opened a second packet, and then a third. If anyone discovered today's work, her life would be forfeit. Assassins were forbidden to murder for their own ends; they must only kill at the behest of their liege. As she watched the powder soak into the fluid, she noticed her hand trembling again; she didn't know, however, if she trembled out of fear of discovery or joyous celebration of finally being free of the encumbrance of a husband hanging around her neck.

She stirred again until the wine was clear, and added yet two more packets to the drink. When the wine was clear a third time, Lady Autrancia took a deep breath to calm her agitation; fear of discovery was uppermost in her mind at this moment.

For the last time, she carried the cup to her marital bed, and set it within easy reach of the occupant. For the last time, she roused her husband to passion, and pretended he was able to bring her satisfaction. And for the last time, she handed him the cup and watched while he drained it.

She rose then from the bed, and called her maid to her, dressing as usual for the day, and leaving the apartment to her indolent husband. She rather hoped he was actually dallying with her maid; the physical activity would allow his heart to speed the poison through his veins. Also, she'd have an excuse to turn the slut out, if Collwiin died while they were intimately engaged.

Autrancia made her way to the ladies parlor off the throne room, where the wives of the other ambassadors daily met together to gossip and work their embroidery. The preparations of war had changed the customary usages of court. The ambassadors all awaited instructions from their own kings at home, and the kings here in Jurisse.

Within an hour, a messenger burst into the ladies parlor with the terrible news; Lady Autrancia's maid had found Lord Collwiin dead in his bed. Lady Autrancia did her very best to look shocked, even going so far as to slide to the floor in a credible approximation of a faint.

Chapter Forty-three

Army of Rats
24th day of Beltaine, 2448

Dremmin shifted his weight to the other foot and peeked out from behind the bushes once again. Nothing about the city had changed since the last time he'd looked five minutes ago, although the growing light of dawn gave a slightly better view.

He stretched the cramped muscled in his back, then immediately regretted the action. There were a couple of slices of flesh that were still tender after the flogging he'd received for allowing the stupid princess to escape. He devoutly wished he could locate Tomas, who'd actively aided the girl. He'd take more than a few stripes of skin from *his* back in fair payment.

He peeked through the bushes again and eyed the city walls, some two miles distant; still no changes. He wondered what Milord was waiting for. There'd been a lot of conferencing when the new commander, King Liammial, had arrived in camp. Milord's Divine Army had been marching by night for the last two nights, and marching quickly to cover an entire day's worth of travel in the shortest nights of the year. Just as he'd been ready to tumble into sleep, his group leader had grabbed him and sent him off with a different commander.

He didn't understand why, with an entire army, they didn't just lay siege to the city and get it over with. They outnumbered those on the wall by at least four to one. They were experienced mercenaries, as opposed to the farmers manning the walls who were likely to run at the first volley of fire.

This was without doubt the strangest campaign he'd been on. They hadn't even built any of the usual siege engines, and having gotten a good look at the target city, he knew there was no way they were going to be able to reduce the walls, farmers or no farmers, without heavy casualties and quite a few catapults and assault towers. They hadn't even been gathering rocks to throw in the catapults they hadn't built. Strange ideas, their client had, but as long as he paid their fee, Dremmin didn't really care what he was told to do.

The group leader motioned them all into a small conference circle, and proceeded to brief them using the silent hand language the troop had perfected. It was excellent for communicating over a distance, or on a noisy battlefield, and none of the opponents they'd yet been up against had been able to break their code. Swiftly and silently, the leader gave them their assignment then tossed each of the men a packet.

Dremmin opened his and found a complete change of clothing that would closely match the peasant clothing the farmers manning the wall were wearing. Each man also had a red cloth to tie about his left arm, so they could tell their own men from the peasant army after the troops mixed. They were told to secure the clothing in a small bundle on their backs; they would be changing later.

There was a pounding behind them, of feet on the dusty road, and the army made itself known, marching out into view at the appointed hour.

A few hand gestures and Dremmin's group leader set off in a different direction, toward the River Jurat. They waited a long while under cover of bushes along the river bank while their leader found whatever it was he was looking for.

The river itself tumbled along, passing out of the city through a gap in the walls which was secured by means of a grate. Small branches and other bits of flotsam caught against the rods showed the grate was sunk clear to the bottom of the streambed.

Their leader disappeared downstream, rounding a corner, and did not reappear for a long while. Finally, the distant whistle of a bird native to their homeland floated above the rushing sounds of the water, and the group cautiously moved out in the direction of the bird's cry.

The group leader stood at the outflow end of a pipe, roughly three feet across, where stinking muck oozed into the main flow of the river. A few minutes work, and the grate covering the pipe was removed and tossed into the main channel of the river. Dremmin swallowed convulsively. They were going to have to crawl through this sewage-filled pipe all the way to the interior of the city. He hoped there were no insects in the tunnel. He'd always hated them, and in the darkness that would exist there, he wouldn't be able to see them coming.

One by one, the men slung their swords across their backs to keep them out of the putrid filth, and secured the small bundles of clothing, before dropping to their hands and knees and crawling into the pipe after their group leader. When his turn came, Dremmin took a deep breath and followed his assigned partner, Timmone, into the gaping maw.

There was moss under the goo; Dremmin could feel it giving and springing back under his hands and knees as he moved. He held his breath for as long as he could, then when he could hold it no longer, he breathed through his mouth, as shallowly as possible. He quickly changed to nose breathing, though once he experienced the sharp, acidic taste of the air. Surely the smell would not be as bad. He'd never *tasted* air before.

The small circle of daylight receded behind them as they crawled around a small bend, and were left alone in the dark. They crawled ever onward, without guide. There were no side passages, and this alone kept them from getting lost.

From time to time, his hand or knee would crush some juicy insect, the hard body giving a little crunching sound as it gave way. Some of the insects scuttled over his hands, and each time, Dremmin would shudder and continue on. The only thing that kept him moving was the knowledge that for him, there was only one way out of this hellish place; forward. Dremmin was certain several of the bugs had crept inside his shirt. He couldn't just be imagining their feet on the bare skin of his back.

The men crawled onward, the distance to the city seeming a lot longer than it actually was. Dremmin wondered if that was because they were crawling, or because of the dark pressing in on them from all directions.

There was a sudden exclamation from their group leader. Dremmin ran into Timmone's hindquarters and stopped, wondering what the problem was. Sounds of a scuffle came from somewhere ahead, and Dremmin could hear the grunting of men, and a high-pitched squeaking. There must be some rats in the tunnel.

Timmone's feet started twitching, then furry bodies and slashing teeth engulfed him. In the darkness, Dremmin didn't know how many were attacking, but it felt like at least three or four. He grabbed at one and came up empty. He felt feet on his arm and grabbed again, catching the thing just as it sank its teeth in him. He ripped it off him, and drew his knife, killing it while he had hold of the nasty creature

For what seemed like an eternity, Dremmin was busy grabbing at rats and killing all he could get his hands on. Just as suddenly as they appeared, they were gone. He wondered if they'd killed them all or if the rats had given up and left.

Dremmin was bleeding from so many places he couldn't count them all. He hoped the blood would wash out any contamination from the rats. He felt around him in the darkness for the rats he'd killed, and moved them one at a time to the side of the tunnel so the men behind him wouldn't have to crawl through them. Out of curiosity, he counted them as he moved them. He was surprised when the tally stopped at fifteen. He hadn't thought it was that many.

Finally, the line started moving again. The ooze in the tunnel was deeper now, and Dremmin no longer wondered how far they had come. He simply prayed they would arrive soon. So gradually that he didn't notice it at first, the tunnel was lightening. He could suddenly see the bricks beside him, and the long brown insects they were crawling on. Timmone's back was so covered with the bugs it looked like he was wearing them for a shirt. Dremmin shuddered. His own back was probably similarly covered, and he didn't really want to think about that.

The conduit continued to grow both lighter and wetter, and with a startling suddenness, Timmone was no longer crawling in front of him. Then Dremmin, too, was being assisted to stand,

and encouraged to move out of the way. He joined the other men in slapping the insects from their bodies.

Once cleared of insects, Dremmin looked around. They were standing ankle deep in liquids in what looked like the bottom of a well. There were several openings in the walls above their heads, and a ladder up one side leading to a metal grate. Dremmin's spirits sank. Had they come all this way only to be foiled by a grate? Would they be punished for failing to achieve their objective? Worse yet, would they have to crawl back out through that horrible tunnel again?

A sudden stream of water and other offal showered down upon their heads, gushing out of one of the openings above. With muttered curses, the men moved about, trying to avoid getting the gunk on them as much as possible.

When all the men in their small group were as de-bugged as possible, their group leader started up the ladder. He stopped at the top for a very long time. Something dark and heavy dropped with a splash in the water, and then the group leader suddenly swung a portion of the grate open, and climbed out into the open space above. When he got to the top, Dremmin found he was in a small building. There was a tank of water nearby, and the team stripped off their stinking clothing.

They tossed their black uniforms down into the bottom of the pit, and made use of the water from the tank to clean themselves, before getting dressed in the peasant clothing they'd carried through the tunnel. Some of the smell still remained, but by and large, they were presentable.

Dremmin made certain he washed his rat bites as thoroughly as he could without having soap. He hoped it would be enough to keep them from festering.

Ready for the next phase of their operation, the team left the small building and hurried down the street, blinking in the bright sunlight.

Chapter Forty-four

Traitors at the Gate
24th Day of Beltaine, 2448

The small party of men slipped down the street, following their group leader. Dremmin didn't see anyone; the place looked deserted. Of course, most of the men would be on the walls fighting the first battle against Milord's Divine Army, but Dremmin had been in many captured cities, and this one didn't feel right. There should have been dogs, women and children. An uneasy feeling crept over him that these people were more prepared for them than they were expecting.

He wondered what other surprises were in store.

They made their way through the city, swiftly and unchallenged, until they reached the west gate. Judging from the number of men lying in the road next to the wall, the Army's archers were doing a fair job. Dremmin watched with glee as another man fell from the wall, an arrow embedded in his throat. He loved battle, and even more, he loved the looting and raping after a battle was over.

Their group leader walked up to the men at the gate and yelled in his most commanding voice.

"All right; you men are relieved," he said pointing to the men on the wall. "We've been sent to take care of the gate." He turned to some farmers at the base of the gates, pointing at them in an all-encompassing way. "You men get up on the wall."

The group of men who'd been busy piling bags full of sand at the base of the gates nodded and moved out, climbing the walls with alacrity. Dremmin saw one of them fall a victim of the Army's archers the instant he reached the top of the wall and poked his head over the top of the battlements.

Dremmin's group milled around at the base of the gate for a few minutes, pretending they were adjusting the sandbags, but in fact, removing them. When they were certain the men on the wall were fully occupied with the fighting on the outside of the walls and paying no attention to them at all, they quickly and efficiently removed the remaining sand bags.

Dremmin saw his group leader look upward to the walls again. He checked the walls himself. No one was paying the least bit of attention to the small group of so-called defenders at the gate. Dremmin chuckled as his group leader gave the sign. He and Timmone removed the bar from the gate and swung it open to admit the army. Jurisse was theirs.

The farmers manning the walls were quickly taken into custody, wisely surrendering to the vastly greater force. The main body of the army moved on to the walls surrounding the palace.

The palace gates were only made of widely spaced metal bars, and a massive volley of arrows combined with a small battering ram expertly wielded by eight men combined to give them access to the castle itself.

The door of the keep also yielded swiftly to the battering ram, and according to the instructions they'd been given, the main body of the army halted.

The new commander, King Liammial, and a select body of troops entered the castle. Dremmin and Timmone settled down to wait for their next orders.

Chapter Forty-five

A Royal Dungeon
24th Day of Beltaine, 2448

King Jameisaan the Good was awakened at dawn when a servant rushed into his bedchamber and shook him awake.

"Your Majesty, sorry to bother you, but the walls are under attack!"

Jameisaan groaned, but opened his eyes.

"What? There's been an attack?"

The servant nodded, grabbing up the clothing Jameisaan had been wearing last night and throwing it at him.

"Yes, Sire, an enormous army just walked up to the west gate, and there's fighting there now."

Jameisaan hastily began donning his clothing, with the help of the anxious servant.

"At the west gate, you say?"

"Yes, a massive army. Ten or twelve times the people we have behind the walls, or so I've been given to understand."

"What about the other three gates?"

"Haven't heard no word from any of them, Sire, but I come to get you as soon as I heard about the west gate, so I don't know more than what I just told you."

"All right; we'll find out soon enough, I imagine. Has King Fergasse been summoned as well?"

"Think so, leastways there was two of us who jumped and ran when the first news come in."

"I'll head for his office then. Should you see him, tell him where I'll be, or send word to me if I should be elsewhere."

Jameisaan pulled his final boot on with a grunt, and headed for the door as quickly as he could move.

He was slightly amused that he and Fergasse arrived at the office door at the precise same moment.

Two servants jumped to their feet at their approach.

"What news?" Fergasse's voice was a low growl.

Both servants commenced bowing.

"Quit that bobbing up and down nonsense, and tell me what you came to report."

"They've breached the city gates, Majesty. I heard there were traitors that opened the gates to them."

"Traitors?"

Fergasse's face paled. The servant nodded his head vigorously.

"Traitors, or else who was it what opened the gates to the army?"

"They're at the palace gates now, Sire."

There was a loud crashing sound from the direction of the main entrance to the castle.

"I imagine they've arrived." Jameisaan was amazed at how even his voice sounded, considering the dryness of his throat and the taste of fear on his tongue.

A score of men dressed in black poured into the corridor where they stood.

The two servants hastily grabbed up pikes from antique suits of armor displayed in niches nearby. Jameisaan armed himself with a sword, while Fergasse laid hold of a long-handled, two-headed war axe.

Hefting their weapons, they waited the on-slaught of the troops.

The men from the black army advanced with implacable force, their confidence in their victory a palpable thing. A single swipe of their modern steel swords served to halve the rotted antique wood handle of the pikes. The servants still tried to use the handles remaining in their grasp as weapons, but were quickly cut down, valiant defenders of the crown.

With equal dispatch, the kings were disarmed, but just before the killing blows could fall, a familiar voice rang through the hall.

"Hold! Capture but do not kill those men!"

Liammial had returned to Jurisse.

"Bring them this way." His voice was brisk, commanding. Liammial walked past the pair of kings as though he really couldn't see them, and opened a secreted door in the corridor wall. The men from the army followed, hands firmly grasping Fergasse's and Jameisaan's arms and forcing them down the stairs and into the dungeon.

The black uniformed men left Jameisaan no choice. Their tight grasp on his arms was already turning his fingers numb. They followed Liammial through several twists and turns in the torch-lit darkness, and were finally thrust into a small, damp cell. The door was locked behind them, and the footsteps retreated until silence fell.

Jameisaan looked around, assessing the situation. "We're in an inside cell," he said calmly.

"Why do you say that?" Fergasse's voice reached out in the near pitch darkness.

"No windows in the walls," was the answer.

"None of the cells have windows, as they're all underground. We could be anywhere."

"Oh."

"We're lucky in one respect," Fergasse said, as calmly as Jameisaan had been speaking.

"What's that?"

"They didn't chain us to the walls." Fergasse held up a set of manacles bolted to the wall.

"That was nice of them," came the acerbic reply.

"Very nice. The manacles are measured so you can't sit or lie down."

"I see. In that case, I'm really glad they decided to forgo the formality."

"Absolutely," Fergasse agreed.

Jameisaan walked over to the door and peered out the small window.

"There's a torch burning in the hallway. I hope that means they intend to come back soon. Do you think they'll feed us? I didn't get breakfast this morning."

Fergasse chuckled.

"One thing I can say about my brother, he's an excellent strategist; however I'd love to know how he had people inside Jurisse willing to open the gates to the army. I hate the thought that my kingdom was so filled with traitors that any of the men would welcome captors. We can ask Liammial when he comes back."

"What makes you sure he'll come back here in person?"

"He didn't speak to us when he had them capture us. He'll come back to gloat."

"I noticed he didn't tell the soldiers who we were when he had us captured. Why do you think that is?"

"I don't know, but if I were to guess, I would think it was because he doesn't want anyone to know where we are, or who we are. He is now free to put out the story that we were killed in the attack. He'll probably be able to produce suitably dressed bodies, with unrecognizable faces. The men who captured us know where we are, but not who. They won't be able to refute his claim that the king is dead, which will pave the way for him to have what he wants; the throne of Kwennjurat. It's always been his aim and greatest desire, I'm afraid. We may as well settle in for a long stay."

He scraped some moldering straw together in a corner with one toe and sat on it, settling his shoulders into the corner.

Jameisaan did the same thing in a second corner.

"Do you have any rats in here?"

"What?"

"Rats in the dungeon. It's in all the stories, you know, the rat-filled dungeon, watching the prisoners with their beady red eyes."

Fergasse laughed.

"I doubt it; the dungeons haven't been used in so long there's nothing for them to eat here. Most of the rats in Jurisse live in the sewer or in the warehouses."

"Good."

"Why?"

"Because I hate rats."

Chapter Forty-six

First Day at Court
25th Day of Beltaine, 2448

Liammial checked the mirror to be certain his clothing was perfect. The black velvet tunic was a good fit, and the silver trim had a way of making his body look sleeker than it actually was. Some of that was the cut of the tunic, he was certain. Pity he didn't know which tailor his brother had purchased this particular tunic from. The black hose hid the bruising on his leg, and the soft black slippers were perfect for wearing at court.

He gestured toward the servants. They picked up the heavy purple robe only the king was allowed to wear. Fergasse had only worn it at the most formal of occasions, but Liammial felt the announcements he was about to make at court constituted a formal occasion.

He stood patiently while they draped the robe around his shoulders and fastened the silver strap across his chest that served to keep the heavy garment from sliding off whenever he moved. As soon as their work was completed, he moved toward the door. A man leaped to open it for him, and hold it for as long as it took for him to pass through. This is what he had waited for all these years, the respect that came with the crown.

These men served him because the crown was his; they didn't have to be beaten, threatened, or cowed into giving him the respect that was due him by virtue of his birth. Soon enough word would come from the men he'd sent to Renthenn and Kwenndara telling him Fergan and his wife, that sassy little red-headed troublemaker, were both dead.

He walked slowly to the throne room, dragging the long and heavy robes behind him. In truth, he didn't think he could move any faster. The sheer weight of the robe seemed to pin him down and hold him back; almost as though it knew he did not yet have the legal right to wear it.

The ambassadors and their wives had all better be in attendance at court as he'd ordered. He had phrased the order that 'the king wished to meet with the entire complement of the court.' He would allow his mere presence in the royal robe to make the announcement for him.

Again, lackeys jumped to open the door of the throne room for him. The doors swung open, and all eyes turned toward the portal. Conversations broke off, and stillness reigned. Then one after the other, every knee bent to the floor as the assemblage honored him, Liammial, as the undisputed king of Jurat.

He made his stately way to the dais and turned. Two servants stepped unobtrusively to his side to assist in settling the robe so he could sit in the throne and not choke himself. His eyes took in the assemblage, counting the diplomats and their wives, enjoying this time of power when all persons present concentrated on him alone, kneeling in silent obeisance.

By his count, several were missing. Well Fergan, of course, and there would only be eight, not nine sets of ambassadors, since Kwenn had already been added to his kingdom. But still, he didn't see Collwiin; had Verr sent someone else? No, Autrancia was here. Hmmm. Autrancia was here and Collwiin was not. This could be rather interesting. He allowed just the slightest hint of a smile to rest upon his features, and waved his hand, allowing the court toadies to rise to their feet and begin the dealings of the day.

He motioned one of the servants to his side, and whispered in his ear. The servant nodded and turned to address the open court in a loud, declamatory voice.

"Liammial the Strong, King of Jurat, has a few things he wishes to say to you all, and bids you come close enough to hear."

The ambassadors all moved nearer the throne and remained silent, waiting to hear his pronouncements.

"First, I must announce the unfortunate deaths of my brother, Fergasse, and his co-ruler Jameisaan. They were killed during fighting in the halls of the palace yesterday. Unfortunately, their bodies are not fit for viewing, so there will be no lying in state. The remains have already been disposed of."

There was a little surprised murmuring, and Liammial allowed it to continue for a few moments, letting them bury the dead in their own minds.

"Second, although the Black Army has been repulsed, they still lay siege to our town. I swear to you that my first act as King will be to do all in my power to disperse this rabble and bring peace to our homes."

There was more murmuring, and Liammial relaxed a fraction. The army had, on his orders, withdrawn to a besieging stance beyond the walls as soon as the two kings were locked into the dungeon. The necessity of a few mock battles before the city fell again would cement the ambassadors into his loyal service. As soon as Jurisse fell, the army would loot the town, take their pay and leave, according to the arrangement he had made with Milord.

"Finally, I have had word that there was an uprising in what used to be Kwenn. Prince Fergan and Princess Tanella are, unfortunately, deceased."

There was decidedly more murmuring this time, as the ambassadors realized there was now only one remaining individual with the requisite heritage to assume the throne of Jurat.

"Because we need immediate leadership during this time of war, I have decided that my coronation will take place this afternoon. I assure you that as soon as this army here has been dispersed, I will deal with the uprising in the northern provinces of Jurat. I'd offer you the use of couriers to send this latest news to your kings at home, but unfortunately, for the moment at least, we seem to be besieged. As Ambassadors, I realize you are not my subjects, but if any of you would care to volunteer to help the few citizens who remain here to strengthen our defenses, any help you could offer would be greatly appreciated."

He waved them to be about their business, and then turned to the servant again, murmuring instrucions. The servant quickly left the dais and made his way through the room to where the Lady Autrancia sat, plying her needlework.

The servant whispered in her ear, and she approached the throne with outward calm. The depth of her curtsey caused the black gown she wore to gap away from her marvelous bosom, exposing most of it to his view. She wore the red band of mourning on her left arm, and the rubies Liammial had given her around her neck.

He still recalled how they had looked against her pale skin on the night he had given them to her. His loins tightened in memory. He had been too long without the sort of lover he appreciated.

"Rise."

She stood, and he motioned for her to draw near to his throne. She climbed the three steps of the small platform, and seated herself on the floor at his feet. This was fitting, as he had provided no other chair, and it was not seemly for her to stand taller than he was. Besides, it gave him another excellent view of the treasures within her gown.

"Why is Lord Collwiin not in attendance? Is he ill?"

Autrancia bowed her head as though in grief.

"He is dead, Your Majesty, and I am acting in his stead as Verr's ambassador until such time as King Zeraff sees fit to assign someone else."

"That's a pity. How did he die?"

"No one knows, Your Majesty. He was found dead in his bed by my dressing maid. He was certainly in fine health when last I saw him."

"No one had any suspicions as to how or why he died?"

"No, Your Majesty; the healer said it appeared that his heart gave out. I suppose I should have expected it, having married someone so much older than myself."

"Yes, I suppose you should have. Is it your desire to return to Verr?"

"No, Your Majesty. My desire is to remain here in Jurisse, and to serve you in any way I can."

She leaned toward him a little as she spoke, and bowed her shoulders. Liammial knew her body language would seem to the rest of the room as though she were expressing grief over Collwiin's demise. In reality, she was blatantly showing him that she wore nothing beneath her gown, and was inviting him to share in all he glimpsed.

"Are you prepared to openly disassociate yourself with the kingdom of Verr?"

"I await only your orders, Your Majesty."

"Then I name you as my consort, and I will openly acknowledge our relationship to all who dare inquire."

Lady Autrancia smiled and, despite her seated position, managed to curtsy deeply to him. Liammial's loins tightened again, and he found himself wishing he could just whisk her away to a private chamber somewhere. Ah! He could!

He gestured the servant to his side again, and Autrancia straightened, covering her assets. Good. She reserved them for him alone.

He whispered in the servant's ear, and was assisted to rise, then offered his hand to Autrancia, helping her to regain her feet. There would be nothing said about him taking an ambassador into the private sitting room, Fergasse had done so on many occasions.

As he proceeded from the room, with both Autrancia and the servant in his wake, he felt the gaze of every eye in the room, and reveled in the feeling.

He gestured for Autrancia to precede him through the door, as it was fitting for a lady to do so. He gave some more instructions to the servant, and closed the door.

Immediately, Autrancia's fingers were at the fastening of the heavy cloak, and it fell to the floor. Liammial swept the paperwork from the desk and together the lovers draped the soft, thick, fur-lined robe across the desk as a makeshift location for their reunion.

Much later in the afternoon, Liammial rose from the purple robe, and stretched himself. He had really needed this time together, and judging from Autrancia's reactions, so had she. She really was the perfect match for him, no other woman possessed the savage ardor he so enjoyed. One slim, white hand reached out for him, to draw him back down to where they had rested on the floor before the fireplace, but he pulled away.

"I really can't be late for my own coronation, my dear."

Chapter Forty-seven

Life Sentence
25th Day of Beltaine, 2448

Liammial waited until he was certain Lady Autrancia was truly sleeping, and crept from his bed. He wrapped his dressing gown tightly around him, then pulled on a pair of long woolen socks for warmth and thrust his feet into his slippers.

It was not his usual style, he knew, going abroad at this time of the night, but some things are best accomplished in the dark hours. He lit a candle from the embers in the fireplace and crept through the large dressing room. He woke Rocnar, ordering him to accompany his liege through the darkened castle.

Rocnar followed, his head still hanging sleepily from his shoulders. They passed into the servant's back staircase, and quickly navigated to the kitchen. Liammial directed Rocnar to carry two loaves of left-over bread, and a half-empty skin of warmish water, then made his way to the hidden door in the downstairs corridor that led to the dungeons.

Liammial took the direct path to the cell where he'd left his two prisoners, rather than the roundabout path he'd led the guards on yesterday morning. He shoved the bread and water skin through the small opening at the bottom of the door. His brother would be able to find the rations when he awoke. The twin sounds of snoring from within the cell assured him that both of his prisoners yet lived.

He directed Rocnar to the cell across the corridor where there was a pile of squarish stones that matched the walls of the dungeons. He set Rocnar to moving the stones into the corridor, while he took the bucket of powder and the bucket of water from the same cell, and commenced mixing the mortar.

Liammial began by laying mortar across the floor, save in the center where the feeding hole was. He directed Rocnar to lay the stones in the mortar, and he then pressed them firmly into place. He laid the mortar and stones for the second course, and then the third. A long, thin stone functioned as a lintel over the top of the feeding hole.

Rocnar worked in silence, his head drooping further with each stone. Perhaps he was weakened from his previous injuries, or his recent travels, but Liammial would have no other help him. He could depend on Rocnar's silence; after all, he still held the man's sisters in his power.

It took several hours to complete the wall. Liammial looked at it by the light of the candle, and knew it to be an adequate job. It could have been done better, perhaps, by experienced stonemasons, but he would not have had their guarantee of silence, as he held Rocnar's.

As they climbed the servant's stairs toward their beds, Rocnar asked him who was in that cell. Liammial continued up the stairs as though he hadn't heard the query. No one but he knew where the kings were. The soldiers who'd put them in the cell had been led around in circles before they were deposited within. They didn't know the identity of the prisoners.

Rocnar knew there was a newly bricked up cell, but not the identity of the prisoners within it. And he wouldn't know his way to and from the cell. Liammial had long wondered how long it would take someone to die of starvation. He made a vow to himself to visit his brother daily, so he could discover the exact course starvation took. After all, he had Jurat now, he probably owed his dear brother that much gratitude; a daily visit seemed like it would be exactly the thing to do.

Chapter Forty-eight

Hen Pecking
26th Day of Beltaine, 2448

"I heard them whispering again, the women at court. They all think I'm just a whore!"

"You're not a whore; you are the king's consort."

Lady Autrancia paced across the room, displaying her naked body to her lover. She could feel Liammial's eyes on her, watching every move. She counted on that, knowing that with her body she could get any man to do anything she wanted. She paused near the window, and twisted around to look at him over one shoulder.

"You could do something about it, you know."

"There's nothing I could do. It would make me appear foolish if I forbade my people from talking about my consort. And it would make it appear that it was true; which it's not. Even if I did give the command, it would only stop them from talking about you in public. Even a king can't control what people talk about in private."

Autrancia strutted over to the bed, standing next to Liammial. Liammial suddenly grabbed her around the waist and pulled her down onto the bed, rolling over and pinning her down with his body. Autrancia lay quiet and unresponsive. She blinked several times, and allowed her eyes to fill with faux tears.

Liammial continued his efforts to arouse her, and Autrancia fought her body's desire to respond. This was her single most powerful weapon against men. She was relieved when Liammial ceased his efforts. She had nearly given in.

"What's wrong, Autrancia?"

She blinked once more, allowing the tears to flow.

"You know what's wrong! You just don't *want* to fix it!"

Autrancia bit her lip, and turned her face away from Liammial.

"It's not that I don't want to fix it, it's that there is nothing I can do to stop them talking! What do you want me to do?"

"You *can* do something about it. You could marry me and make me your queen! As your wife, they wouldn't be able to call me a whore."

Liammial pulled away from her and stared at her rather like she imagined he would stare at a poisonous serpent he found in his bed.

"*Marry* you?"

"Yes, marry me! The day you gave me the rubies, you promised me you would make me your queen! You've broken that promise to me; instead you've just made me your whore!"

Autrancia began sobbing, allowing the motions to shake her entire body. Liammial put his arm around her. She drew him close, snuggling against him. She could feel his arousal, and knew that eventually she would win.

With a sudden viciousness, Autrancia pushed Liammial away from her. He was taken by surprise, overbalanced, and fell off the end of the bed, striking the hard wooden floor with a splatting sound. He rose to his feet with a growl. He stalked around to her side of the bed, and she rolled across it, fleeing, with a sheet wrapped around her body. Autrancia stopped on the far side of the room, and looked at him.

"I never said I would marry you!" he growled.

"Yes, you did; you promised! You said the rubies were your betrothal gift to me! If you never intended to marry me, then the women at court are right! And I won't be any man's whore!"

Autrancia ran out of the room clad only in her sheet, and slammed the door of the dressing room, barring it against the king.

Chapter Forty-nine

Double Agents
26th Day of Beltaine, 2448

"Hold up!"

Kiim reined his horse slightly, allowing his two companions to catch up. It had been a long time since they'd stayed in a good inn, and they were all looking forward to reaching Jurisse tonight.

They'd been on the road a long time, ferreting out information for King Jameisaan. They'd discovered the easiest way to have complete freedom of movement in lands controlled by the black army was to appear as the army's couriers. They'd lost no time in procuring proper clothing and mounts, and no one had questioned their business. Furthermore, they'd been asked by some group leaders to carry additional dispatches, and in this way gained even more knowledge. The group leaders spoke freely with them, as did the common soldiers. The three of them had gained the information their King had sent them after, and were now nearly to Jurisse, well on the way home.

"What?"

"I was wondering if it would be a good time to change into our own clothing. Couriers from the black army are probably not going to be openly welcomed in Jurisse."

"Good point, Kympokk. Let's find a place to change."

"I saw a goodly-sized barn not ten minutes back."

Issak pointed over his shoulder, back the way they had come. As one, the three men turned their mounts and returned to the barn. On arrival, they checked that no one was about, and then dug the blue and gold uniforms they'd not worn for nearly two months out of the very bottom of their bedrolls. They were badly creased, but the clothing still proclaimed their true identity as king's couriers on the business of Jameisaan of Kwenn.

They swung back into the saddles of their black horses, and continued down the road toward Jurisse. Kiim sent Issak to take the lead. By habit, they rode spaced out. Couriers bunched together looked suspicious. He left Kympokk to ride in the center, and he himself lagged behind the group. They were often out of sight, but not sound of each other, and all knew how to both yell and whistle loudly if occasion demanded.

Kiim surveyed the country around him, looking for clues that would tell him exactly how far away from Jurisse they were. He tensed as he heard oncoming hoof beats ahead of him, wondering who was in such a hurry to be leaving the city at this time of day, nearing evening.

The makers of the hoof beats appeared; Kympokk and Issak were riding, hard, toward him. Issak made a hand gesture that they should flee, and without pausing to ask why, Kiim had turned his horse and retreated up the road at a gallop. He saw a side road, more of a trail, and turned his horse sharply onto it, plunging into a small copse of woods between farm fields. His two companions followed. When he could see he was running out of trees, Kiim reined to a halt, both waiting for his companions, and checking for other signs of pursuit.

Kympokk and Issak were shortly reined in beside him, Issak checking the trail behind them suspiciously. Silence reigned. The men and horses kept that stillness, till the birds resumed their callings from their nests.

Issak took a deep breath, before he began his report.

"Came out of the trees and I could see Jurisse out ahead of me, to the north, just where it should be."

"And?"

"What looks like the entire Black Army is camped around the walls."

Kiim cursed. Kympokk looked worried.

"What do we do?"

Kiim smiled, suddenly.

"Did any of them see you?"

Issak shook his head.

"I turned around smart and got outta there, quick as I could. I didn't hear any of them chasing us, so it's a fair bet none of them saw me."

Kiim's smile broadened.

"In that case, we change back into our black clothing. We come out of the woods separately, and lodge ourselves in different parts of the army for tonight. Kympokk, you take the south side, I'll take the east, and Issak, you can have the north. Find out everything you can, and meet me tomorrow at the old well on the Renthenn road for our nooning meal."

The men hastened to change their clothing, and put Kiim's plan into action. Much information for King Jameisaan could be gained this night.

Chapter Fifty

Enlightening News
29th Day of Beltaine, 2448

"Thank you for your report, Kiim, you've given me a lot to think about."

"You've given me much to think about too, Highness, and thank you for setting us straight on who is where and what has happened. Seems the whole world's fallen apart and been put back together again while we were gone to Shuell."

Fergan laughed.

"I can see how you might feel that way, yes. Now, I want the three of you to rest a bit, and when you're ready, we'll find posts for you. Rest well, you've done excellently, and I thank you. I'm certain King Jameisaan, were he here, would be very pleased with your findings."

Kiim bowed, and left the prince, intending to return to the fine quarters they had for the couriers hereabouts, and garner just a bit more sleep.

Fergan paced the length of the office twice, and then turned to Tinne.

"I'll need you to draft a couple of letters for me, and post them off as soon as may be. I intend to call a meeting of the king's council, and also the mayor's council from Kwenndara. Send letters to all the appropriate people. Make sure Tanella is specifically invited to the meeting also, she has a penchant for devious thinking, and I'll need her advice. We're up against a tricky opponent."

"When shall we call the meeting for, Highness?

Fergan stared at the map of Kwenn, figuring travel times and weighing possibilities against the necessity of haste.

"First thing in the morning on the Third of Monleth, at whatever place would hold the assemblage, halfway between here and Kwenndara. Is there such a place in that area, or is it just an inn in the middle of nowhere?"

Tinne chuckled.

"The Orchard House is very nearly halfway betwixt here and Kwenndara, and would be big enough for a meeting, though putting up every-one…well, some might have to use the inn, also."

Fergan nodded.

"The Orchard House it is, then. See the messages get out immediately."

He left the office and took himself off to the stables. There was a massive black stallion there, which the stable hands said belonged to Tanella. He hoped a wild ride atop the beast would be a refreshing way to clear his head, and settle himself for a bout of good, hard thinking.

Chapter Fifty-one

Rational Pilfering
29th Day of Beltaine, 2448

Rocnar crept silently through the dark passage that led to the wall he had assisted Liammial in making. He didn't know who had been sealed in, but he had his suspicions.

Liammial had kept him so busy running meaningless errands here, there, and everywhere to all parts of Jurisse that he hadn't had time to come back and check on the prisoners. Liammial himself had remained closeted with advisors whenever he wasn't with Lady Autrancia, trying to buy his way back into her heart. Rocnar hadn't a clue what they'd quarreled over, but whatever it was the Lady was holding over Liammial's head,

Rocnar was certain things would be resolved soon, to the lady's complete satisfaction.

Rocnar had been watching the two of them since their falling out, and Liammial had become steadily more ragged in temperament and appearance, while Autrancia had an air about her of a cat who'd gotten into the cream and gotten away with it.

Rocnar's hand brushed against the new stonework, and he halted. He was at least reasonably certain he was in the right place, as the mortar was still cold, and a little damp. He knelt on the floor, placing his face near the small opening Liammial had left for feeding the prisoners.

"Hello? Who's in there?"

There was a scrambling sound inside, then a small thunk, as of knees landing near the other side of the opening.

"Who's there? Liammial, is that you?"

"No, I'm Rocnar."

"Rocnar! I hoped you would find us!"

"Who are you?"

"Fergasse, and Jameisaan. Tell us what's been happening."

"We're besieged by the black army, but we're managing to fight off their frequent attacks. I don't think we can hold out much longer, though, they've just announced rationing to the soldiers, and our numbers are getting thin. Liammial's crowned himself king, and taken Lady Autrancia as his consort. Has he sent you any food? Can I bring you anything?"

An explosive sigh came from the other side of the wall.

"We need food, and water, if you can manage it. Water alone would be most welcome, if you can't manage any food. Even stale bread would be an improvement over the nothing we've had."

Rocnar nodded in the darkness before he realized he couldn't possibly be seen.

"I'll see what I can do, Majesty, and I'll be quick about it."

He leapt to his feet and headed for the kitchen.

Rocnar entered cautiously, and seeing no one around, quietly slipped into the pantry. He took several water skins and filled them, slinging them on his back. He cut a large piece of cheese, and turned the gap in the wheel to the back so the theft wouldn't be noticed for a while. He wrapped the cheese in a napkin and tucked it inside his shirt. A little more searching turned up a couple of loaves of bread. Moments later, one loaf resided within his shirt as well.

Peering around the corner, Rocnar saw no one about and quietly made his way across the kitchen and back to the hidden staircase. Navigating again by the touch of his fingertips against the wall, Rocnar was soon sliding the stolen bounty through the small hole.

"Rocnar, you've saved our lives."

King Fergasse's voice was cracked and broken. There was a pause, and it returned again, stronger.

"If we should survive this, it will be because of you, and your reward will be great."

"I don't feel I've done any great service. I wish there was more I could do."

"The only thing we could hope for is that you could carry a message to Fergan, in Renthenn, for us."

Carry a message to Renthenn? If he did so, he would never be able to be in the vicinity of Liammial again and remain among the living. But his king had commanded it.

"I know it's a lot to ask. Remember, the courier we sent will be watching over your sisters; he will not allow them to come to harm."

"I will leave in the morning. Can you give me a token, so Prince Fergan won't just have me locked up on sight?"

A low chuckle emanated from the opening.

"As you might have opportunity to steal a Jurat signet from Liammial, or be given it as spurious proof, my ring won't do, but King Jameisaan has offered his."

Rocnar put his hands into the small space, and found his hands gripped by a pair much weaker than his own. A ring was pressed into his palm, and the unknown hands closed his fingers over it.

Rocnar left the dungeon cautiously, feeling keenly the need for protecting the secret he now carried. He paused on the stairs and removed his shoes and hose. Though he knew it wasn't respectful to the token he carried, he felt hidden was better than discovery. He slid the ring onto the longest toe of his right foot and then replaced his hose and shoes. Liammial had never had him stripped before a beating, other than occasionally requiring him to remove his tunic so it wouldn't be torn by the lash or stained by the blood.

Rocnar left the dungeon entrance, and quietly closed it behind him. He turned back to the hallway, and his heart sank clear to the ring on his toe. Liammial stood not a dozen feet away, watching him secure the panel.

Liammial grabbed his shoulder, squeezing it painfully. Rocnar felt the bones compressing beneath that steely grip, and he felt they would snap at any moment.

"Come with me. Now."

Liammial turned and walked away, leading Rocnar to his apartments. No sooner had the door closed behind him when the usurper turned on him and struck him, hard, across the mouth. Rocnar tasted the blood as his teeth tore his inner lip open yet again.

"What do you think you were doing down there?"

"I was looking for that cell."

The hand returned again, striking his ear. Rocnar felt another warm trickle, and knew one of Liammial's heavy rings had split his ear open. That lobe had been cut by Liammial's signet often enough that the skin remained delicate and easy to damage.

"Exactly what were you going to do if you found it?"

"I was going to see if they needed any water, Majesty. That's all, just a little water."

"Did you find it?"

Rocnar curled his toes around the ring, and looked into the face of his tormentor.

"No, I couldn't find it again. I was wandering for the longest time, and when I stumbled on the bottom step, I gave it up for a bad business, and came back abovestairs."

"Liar!"

Liammial snarled and struck Rocnar across the face with his fist, barely missing his eyes with the sharp-edged ring. Another warm trickling told Rocnar he'd drawn blood once more.

"I watched you carry water skins into that passage. When you returned, your tunic was flatter, and you had no skins. Where did you leave the food? What food did you steal?"

"I...I did find the hole again, Majesty, and I pushed the water and food through it. A piece of cheese, and a bit of bread, that's all, and a little water."

"Did you speak to the prisoners?"

Rocnar shook his head violently, feeling great satisfaction that some stray droplets of his life's blood flew across the intervening space and stained Liammial's white satin tunic. One drop landed in Liammial's eye, and remained there for several seconds before he blinked it away.

"No, I didn't say anything. I heard them snoring, like we heard when we were there before."

"Them?"

"Well, yes, Majesty, I heard at least two snoring, so it must be there's more than one in there."

Liammial punched him in the stomach, and Rocnar folded in half. Unlike the other beatings he'd endured, this time he allowed himself to retch, the remains of his breakfast spewing across

Liammial's slippered feet and bare ankles. A giggle sounded from the direction of the dressing room, and Rocnar wondered through the haze of pain who would dare to spy on Liammial.

Liammial kicked him, and turned away toward the window. He paced about the room, and then pulled savagely at the bell rope.

A servant immediately entered, bowing himself before the usurper. Liammial gestured toward Rocnar's still form on the floor.

"He's been caught stealing food from the kitchens. Strip his tunic from him and place him in the stocks for four days; nothing but water in that time. Ten lashes to be given each day at noon."

He turned back toward the window. The servant roughly grabbed Rocnar's arm and tried to force him to rise. Rocnar's legs were unsteady because of his pain, and the servant settled for dragging him through the palace corridors by one arm. The servant repeated his orders to one of the men from the army, who gleefully carried them out. Rocnar curled his toes tightly around the ring while his tunic was stripped from him and he was fastened in the stocks, but no one thought to remove his hose or shoes.

He breathed a sigh of relief. Though his mission would be unavoidably delayed, his secret was still safe.

Chapter Fifty-two

The Fall of Jurisse
30th Day of Beltaine, 2448

The gates creaked, the timbers weakening. There were no defenders in position to pour the hot water from the parapet. They had run out of oil and anything else really useful during the attack yesterday.

The battering ram struck the gates again, and Tarryl could see a crack forming in the massive bar that held them closed against the Black Army. He threw rocks down on the heads of those men wielding the device, but they were not large rocks, and did not hamper the men in the slightest.

They hit the gates again, and the crack widened. One of the lower hinges burst, its bolts popping from the abused wood of the gate. The massive portal shifted, hanging slightly askew now. Cheers came from the men in the Black Army.

They hit the gate one last time, and it fell upon them. Tarryl prayed it had killed those it fell upon. The Black Army rushed into the streets of Jurisse for the second time, but now there were too few to even attempt a defense. The siege of Kwennjurat was over. The Black Army had triumphed.

Still at his place on the wall, Tarryl watched as his commander knelt in the roadway before Milord and his Black Army. He felt the tears wash over his cheeks, as he wondered if he would ever see his parents again. At least they were safe in Kwenn, with the rest of his family. They would never know how it had happened here in Jurisse.

The Black Army formed up and made a parade, all the way to the King's palace. Tarryl watched them go, half-hoping they'd kill King Liammial as they'd killed Jameisaan and Fergasse when they'd broken through the first time. At least the Kings had done what they could to protect the people.

All he'd heard of King Liammial was that he stayed in the palace and gave banquets for the ambassadors. Then they'd announced there wasn't enough food to go around, and had cut the soldiers rations by half. Twice. While the banquets for the King and his guests had continued. Yes, he mightily hoped the Black Army would take this king like they had the first two, and that a life of slavery under their rule wouldn't be too difficult to endure.

Chapter Fifty-three

The Harlot Queen
1st Day of Monleth, 2448

Autrancia was furious. Liammial had finally acquiesced; in just under an hour she would be married and crowned Queen of Jurat. However, because of the recent loss of her previous husband, and the stupid army still roaming the streets of Jurisse, she was not allowed the full festivities of a grand wedding.

Only the ambassadors and their gossiping wives would be in attendance, and she wasn't even able to have a new wedding gown made...then again, she'd had new gowns made for her first two weddings, so the gown itself wasn't especially exciting, though the admiring looks it would garner her would have been wonderful.

She had to admit she'd played her cards well in the last few days, making certain she was bathing or dressing at any time Liammial was in the room, yet keeping her new maid close, and not allowing Liammial to so much as touch her hand. In public, she smiled sweetly and often caressed him in passing. She touched his hand or arm as often as possible, and even occasionally ran her fingers across the back of his neck as she passed behind his chair at supper.

It had been a long five days for the king, besieged from within and without, and she could see his passion rising when she looked at his eyes. The wedding night should be spectacular.

She watched in the mirror as the girl carefully curled her hair. She could see the process was nearly complete. Good. It was almost time for her to go to her marriage, and her own coronation. It was about time Jurisse had a queen again, and Autrancia couldn't think of anyone better suited for the role than she herself.

Finally the girl finished, curtsied, and left. Autrancia rose and moved to the tall looking glass. She inspected herself carefully and found no imperfection. There was a tap at the door, and her footman entered. Autrancia pulled him close to her, kissing him most thoroughly. A long while later, Autrancia checked the glass again, to ensure her appearance was unchanged. With her favorite footman still lying across her bed, she left the room to make her way down the stairs to her wedding and coronation.

Chapter Fifty-four

The King's Mouse
3rd Day of Monleth, 2448

Her Royal Majesty, Autrancia, Queen of Jurat, rose from her marital bed. She lifted a goblet from the bedside table, and handed it to her liege-lord and husband, King Liammial.

Autrancia smiled. This was the first of many cups she hoped to present to her husband and the first step toward becoming sole monarch of the now very wealthy kingdom of Jurat, thanks to the diamond mines Kwenn had brought to the marriage of the countries.

"Here you go, my love, you look hot and thirsty."

Liammial smiled as he took the glass from his bride's hand.

"Thank you my dear, it was very thoughtful of you to prepare this drink for me."

"Oh, it was no trouble at all." Autrancia did her best to blush as an acceptance of his compliment.

He raised the glass in her direction.

"Would you care to join me in a drink, my sweet?"

"No, thank you, my dear, I'm not thirsty," Autrancia lied through her suddenly dry lips. There was absolutely no way she was going to take even one sip of the potion she'd put in that cup. If she started that tradition now, she'd either be drinking her own poison, or she'd have to abandon that avenue of administration. Neither one was a good option, as far as she was concerned. It might be months before she could find another way to get Liammial to ingest her... additives.

Liammial rose smoothly from the bed, without spilling a drop. Autrancia bit the inside of her cheek. Why hadn't he drunk any of it?

Liammial rang the bell pull to summon a servant, then carried the crystal goblet carefully across the room and set it down on the mantelpiece.

"What's wrong, my love?"

"With Milord staying here in the palace with us this last week, I've been extremely careful of my health. Had you not noticed I've been eating privately? Until they're gone I dare not eat or drink anything that hasn't been tested for poisoning."

Autrancia gasped.

"You don't think anyone would want to harm you, surely?"

She opened her eyes wide, putting on the sweet and innocent look that served her so well with the many lovers she'd taken over the years. Maybe the women of the court were right; maybe she was a harlot. But then, she mused as she stroked the luxurious furs on the bed, harlotry paid well if you ran with the right crowd.

"I think any mercenary would love to have his client die in a situation such as we're in. Think on it; here sits this entire city, with only Milord in a position to take total control of it should something happen to me. In fact, he could proclaim himself king of Jurat, and who would be able to gainsay him?"

"I don't want to think of things like that. They're too horrible to contemplate."

"You don't want to think of my death, or you don't want to think of someone else owning the diamond mines in the northern province of Jurat?"

Autrancia laughed to bring his attention back to where it should be.

"Why, both, of course. I love you, and wish you a long and healthy reign, and I want to see you adorning my body with a goodly number of those diamonds."

Liammial ran his eyes over her appreciatively, the flames of passion leaping anew in his eyes.

Autrancia laughed again, and let herself fall to the bed, in a manner that should clearly invite her Lord to join her there. She'd deal with the wine in the glass later.

The servant tapped on the door and entered the room, carrying a small wire cage. Autrancia wrapped a bed fur around her body and rose from the bed, wanting a closer look at the cage. It contained a small, brown mouse.

Heedless of his nudity, Liammial took the small, hollow bit of straw the servant held out to him, and used his finger to remove a bit of the wine from the glass.

He poked the straw into the cage. The mouse scampered quickly to the straw, drinking the wine it held. Autrancia bit the inner part of her cheek again.

The amount of poison she'd put in the glass wasn't enough to make a man even slightly ill, until he'd absorbed enough of it, over time. Then he would become gradually more and more ill, until it surprised no one that he died. She had no idea what that amount of poison would do to a creature this small.

She watched as Liammial fed three full straws of the poisoned wine to his mouse. He then took the cage and the wineglass back to the bed, and placed them gently on the small table near his pillows.

Scrambling back onto the bed, Liammial grinned and flung his arms wide.

"Come to me, Wife, I desire to get thirsty again!"

Autrancia forced herself to laugh as she would have even an hour ago, and acted eager as she crawled into her husband's bed. Only this morning the circle of his arms was a place of warm contentment and safety, but now they felt as prison bars when they encircled her.

At the end of an hour, Liammial cast his eyes to the small wire cage where the scrap of brown fur lay, very obviously dead.

"My mouse has died. I'll have to obtain another one."

Autrancia shivered in Liammial's suddenly cold embrace.

"Do you think Milord has the power to reach into your own chambers? How do you suppose he got the poison into the wine?"

Liammial's embrace tightened, prisoning her arms between their bodies. Autrancia squirmed in his grasp, but was powerless to escape. Every move she made was met by a powerful tightening of his arms around her, squeezing her, crushing the very breath out of her body.

She was on the threshold of unconsciousness when she saw Liammial reach to the bedside table for the knife he kept always there. Such was her need for oxygen that she scarcely felt the first slice as Liammial drew the knife down her arm, disabling it at the same time he began the spilling of her life's blood which she knew would end only with her death.

The knife danced its way down her other arm, before Liammial released his hold on her, allowing her to draw breath again.

"One sound, one cry, and you will truly wish that I would simply slit your throat."

His voice was a harsh whisper filled with pain, but tinged with excitement at a level she'd never been able to rouse him to. Suddenly, she realized that he'd known all along she had poisoned Collwiin, and that she'd try to poison him. He'd been waiting for her to hand him the cup.

She also realized the rest of her life was going to be a very long and painful interval.

Chapter Fifty-five

Stock Answer
4th – 6th Days of Monleth, 2448

The summer afternoon sun beat down upon
Rocnar's aching back. The warmth was soothing
to the stiffened muscles and the lash marks he
knew crossed each other striping his flesh. It
wasn't the first time he'd been flogged, though
having his punishment in public was a novel experience. Each day at the nooning hour, many of
Milord's soldiers came to jeer at him as Liammial himself gave the ten lashes decreed by his punishment. Sometimes Rocnar wondered if Liammial garnered his only real pleasure through the
pain he caused others.

The position he was forced into was uncomfortable, and the whipping was painful, certainly,

although he'd endured worse. The thirst was the hardest part of enduring his time in the stocks.

Each day at evening, he was brought the tail ends of hard bread, and a small amount of slimy water to drink. The soldier who had that assignment always pointed out the small mold spots on the bread, and made sure to pour the water in such a manner that Rocnar wasn't able to actually drink most of it. The greater part spilled across his face and body, and sank into the cracks between the cobbles. Sometimes he poured the water so fast that Rocnar was concerned he'd drown trying to drink what he could from the stream hitting his face.

As the sun sank behind the walls of the castle, and the evening shadows brought the beginnings of the evening chill to Rocnar's back, three large soldiers emerged from the castle. They walked toward where Rocnar sat chained, and he feared they meant to kill him. It would be the most convenient way for Liammial to be rid of him, and prevent him from telling anyone where the kings were being held.

He had no doubt Liammial meant to let the kings die of thirst and starvation. If he tried to aid them again, Rocnar knew Liammial would have him killed outright. He must take the first opportunity to leave Jurisse and get his message to

Prince Fergan in Kwenn. There was no other solution.

The three soldiers reached him, and one of them produced the key to the large iron locks that held the stocks closed around his ankles and wrists.

"I bet you're wanting to see this, huh?"

Rocnar said nothing, having learned that was the best response to their goading. Not gaining any satisfaction, they would leave off that much sooner.

The soldier grunted, then waved the key tantalizingly before Rocnar's prisoned wrist. Rocnar ignored it. Even if he could get hold of the key, he couldn't reach the lock to loose himself. The second soldier did make a grab for the key, and knocked it to the ground where it landed very close to a grating in the courtyard. Rocnar didn't know what might lie under that grate, but he feared for his life; should the key fall down the hole, Liammial might decide to just let him stay in the stocks until he died.

The two soldiers scuffled with one another, while the third man quietly retrieved the key and made short work of unlocking the locks. The soldier opened the stocks, but to Rocnar's surprise, his limbs were too stiff to move, and he was unable to rise.

The soldier grabbed him by one arm, and pulled him to his feet, where Rocnar swayed unsteadily, grasping the man's shoulder for support. The pair of brawlers were now rolling about in the dust of the pavement.

"Stop that, both of you! King Liammial asked to see this man immediately, and if we don't get him upstairs right smart, we'll be next in the stocks, mark my words. Now help me carry the poor sot; he can't walk yet."

The speed with which the two men broke off their fighting and scrambled to help him made Rocnar wonder what Liammial had been doing to so completely terrorize these hardened soldiers.

It wasn't long before Rocnar had been brought into the king's chambers, and, by Liammial's orders, chained to the bed in the dressing room for the night. At least he was given food and water, and allowed to feed himself.

The next morning, Rocnar was violently shaken awake and ordered to bathe and dress. He was given bread and cheese for breakfast, and taken down to the kitchen, where he was put to work in the scullery, "to pay for the rations ya stole". He was assigned the most menial tasks the cook could devise for him and allowed no nooning meal. Bread and cheese made up his supper, and once it was eaten, he was returned to the servant's bed in Liammial's dressing room and chained to it for the night. Clearly Liammial was taking no chances on his being able to sneak away and offer aid which might save the kings' lives.

The pattern continued the next day. Rocnar's only consolation was the king's ring still residing on his toe. He still looked daily for an opportunity to escape to Renthenn. As he fell asleep, chained once more to his cot, he conceived a plan. It would take a great deal of daring, but he thought it might just succeed, if he was extremely lucky. He would put it into action on the morrow.

Chapter Fifty-six

The Death of Hope
6th Day of Monleth, 2448

"Jameisaan?"

There was no answer for a long while. Fergasse knew Jameisaan's throat was likely as dry as his own, that his co-ruler must be as weak as he was from lack of water.

"Jameisaan? Are you still alive?"

A rustling in the filthy straw covering the floor was his only answer.

"Jameisaan, I don't think he's bringing help."

"Help will come."

Even as near to death as he, himself, felt, the weakness in Jameisaan's voice frightened Fergasse.

"It's been a week. Even if he left for Ren-thenn, there's no promise he'll bring help back."

Silence.

"I'm afraid he's returned to his service at Liammial's side."

"He wouldn't. I believe in Rocnar. Have faith, Fergasse, help will come."

"In time?"

"Not for us. Even food and water won't re-vive me now. But in time for our people, yes. And the children will do well. We've taught them right."

"Have we done right, Jameisaan? Bringing our people to war?"

"Liammial brought the war. We died in our duty, defending our people. No better end."

A longer pause ensued.

"Jameisaan?"

"Yes?"

"They won't find our bodies here."

"Hand...out...door...ring."

A small thump sounded in the cell. Fergasse knew Jameisaan had died, or at least lapsed into a sleep from which he would not awaken. He felt very near that point himself, but first, he would honor his friend's request. With all the strength remaining in his body, he pulled himself painful-ly across the stone floor to the small hole in the bottom of the doorway. The uneven stone floor opened wounds on his legs, but Fergasse didn't care. The pain helped him focus his mind on his goal, and if he bled to death, it couldn't hurt any more than he did now.

Liammial had left the hole to taunt them, to give them false hope. He had never even come to gloat. He hadn't known his brother as well as he thought he had. He really hadn't known Liammial at all. The full extent of his crimes would probably never be known. Fergasse devoutly hoped some day they would meet again before their maker, and Liammial would meet his just reward.

Finally, the goal was attained. Fergasse realized he could hear only his own labored breathing. Jameisaan was gone, then. Fergasse laid his body on the floor for the last time, stretching his hand out through the hole. The signet ring would serve to identify him, and to point any searchers to his remains, if any ever came searching.

It was a good thing Jameisaan hadn't been the one to crawl to the hole. He didn't have his ring. Fergasse found himself chuckling at the absurdity of that thought, even as he felt the last shreds of life slipping from his body.

Chapter Fifty-seven

The Cornered Rat
7th Day of Monleth, 2448

Rocnar was awakened by his usual guard, who watched him while he dressed. He pulled his tunic on over the hose he'd slept in, and thrust his feet into his boots. He hastily dragged a comb through his unruly hair. The guard laughed when Rocnar winced as the comb caught in a particularly vicious snarl.

Once ready for his work in the scullery, the guard took Rocnar by the arm and dragged him into the hall. As they hastened down the back stairs leading toward the kitchen, Rocnar stumbled and fell, sliding down three or four steps before his grasping hands managed to halt his progress. The guard laughed.

"Get up. I don't got time to mess with you. I gotta get ya to the kitchen before I get to me own duties, an' I don't dare be late again. You make me late again, you're gonna pay for it."

Rocnar pulled his feet up underneath himself, preparatory to standing up, and, out of sight of the guard, drew the dagger he had kept in his boot for so long that he'd almost forgotten it was there. He came to his feet with a sudden lunge up the steps, burying the knife to the hilt in the guard's chest, and catching the man as he collapsed.

It had been a long time since Liammial had carefully taught Rocnar exactly where to stab a man so that your blade would reach his heart with the first thrust, ensuring a silent kill. It was ironic that Rocnar would now use this knowledge to escape from the man who had given it to him.

Rocnar's fall had been carefully timed, so the guard was standing near a seldom used door. Rocnar now wrenched this door open, and gagged as the stench of long dead sewage emanated from it. No one had used the old garderobe in decades; certainly not in his memory. He pushed the man into the small closet, folding the body so it was kneeling in the tiny space, with the fatal wound near the hole that had been historically used as an outlet for sewage.

Carefully, yet swiftly, Rocnar pulled his blade from the man's chest. Blood poured out in great quantities, as he had known it would, and he channeled most of it into the disposal hole. The longer he could delay the body's discovery, the longer he would have to make his escape. The last thing he needed was for some kitchen maid to see a pool of blood on the stairs and start screaming.

Rocnar wiped his blade clean on the dead man's clothing and resheathed it in his boot top. He took the man's belt and knife also, wrapping the belt firmly about his waist and sheathing the long, wicked looking blade neatly in place. It was a strange blade, longer than a dagger, yet too short to properly be called a sword.

The blade itself curved, snake-like, and at the inside of each curve was a nasty hooked barb. Rocnar could see the knife wouldn't make much damage going in, but the hooks would wreak havoc as the thrust was reversed, particularly if the stab was to the soft tissues of the belly. He rather thought he shouldn't risk having those barbs hang up on ribs. Still, it could be a useful tool, if it became necessary for him to use it.

He slipped through the back hallways into one of the several entrances to the dungeons, and set about finding his way to the king's cell. He wanted to let them know that although he had been delayed, he would be leaving immediately for Renthenn, and would return with help.

In the darkness, he trod on something that had a bit of give to it, and immediately stopped his footfall, reaching down to find out what it was. His discovery chilled him to the bone. It was a hand; a human hand, wearing a large ring on one emaciated finger. The hand was as cold as the stones on which it lay. Further investigation revealed it was sticking out through a small hole in the bricked up door of a cell.

Hot tears flooded his eyes and spilled unheeded down his cheeks. It was too late. The kings had died while he labored at scrubbing pots in the scullery. Rocnar gently laid the hand back on the floor, a grisly marker of their resting place. He stood, his heart filling with great resolve, and a righteous wrath. He could not go to Renthenn and bring help for his king, but he could certainly avenge his death.

What he was about to do would cost him his life, and he did not want King Jamiesaan's ring to simply vanish while he was the custodian of it. He removed the ring from his toe, and, reaching as far as he could through the hole in the masonry, placed it near King Fergasse's body where it would be found, when their bodies were eventually discovered.

Now knowing exactly where in the dungeon he was, Rocnar made for the exit in the hallway near the king's office. He listened long at that portal before daring to open it. Once in the corridor, he made his way swiftly to Liammial's suite. He entered, but Liammial was not in evidence. Liammial's valet entered; presumably he heard the door open and wanted to know if anything was needed.

Rocnar seized the man and held him against the wall, his fury lending his frame strength he'd never before possessed. He drew the serpentine knife and allowed the valet to see it up close.

"Where is Liammial?"

"His Majesty has gone belowstairs for court."

Not wanting to kill the man, and not daring to allow him to raise the alarm, Rocnar reversed his grip on the blade and thwacked the heavy pommel against the side of the valet's head, rendering him instantly unconscious, and therefore harmless.

He exited the suite of rooms and made his way through the back corridors to the throne room, quietly entering through a side door.

Liammial sat on the throne, watching the ambassadors as they circulated and spoke to one another. He was again wearing the heavy royal robe, and the profusion of purple velvet and white fur spilled from the sides of the throne, flowing down the stairs beyond his feet.

Rocnar walked quickly toward the throne at an angle that ensured Liammial would not see him. The guardsmen who served here were accustomed to thinking of him as Liammial's personal servant, and none of them should have occasion to pay any attention to him until it was far too late. Rocnar tried to walk as though he had legitimate business with the king, perhaps as if he had a message to deliver.

His only regret was that, here in the throne room and before so great an audience, he would not be able to give Liammial the time and attention he deserved for the loss of his mother, that poor courier, and the kings. The death would have to be swift, or he would be stopped before he'd completed his task.

Knowing full well his own miserable life would be forfeit for his actions, Rocnar leaned over Liammial's shoulder and whispered in his ear.

"They're dead."

Faster than eye could follow, he plunged the serpentine sword into Liammial's guts, and the knife acted as he had imagined it would. A gaping wound opened in the wake of the blade, and all things once held prisoner burst out of Liammial's midsection and slithered down across the purple robe and onto the cold stone floor.

Rocnar's voice rose to a shriek.

"Did you ever go back and look? They're both dead, both of the kings are dead in the cell where you bricked them up! They're dead, and the courier is dead, and my mother is dead, and all at your hands."

He jerked the knife from his boot top and slit Liammial's throat, watching the blood stream down the king's chest and soak into the white fur. He looked up and out across the throne room. All conversation had stopped. All eyes were on him. The ambassadors and their wives stood immobile, pale and shocked at the violence which had occurred before them. A few guards were in the same condition, but most of them were heading rapidly in his direction.

Long association with Liammial had made Rocnar well aware of the many ways a body could be tortured, and how slowly a death could be accomplished. In a moment, he decided he would not allow anyone to impose their will on him ever again. Liammial had decreed how he had lived, but he, Rocnar, would decree how he died.

Before the guards could reach him, he took his own boot knife, the same one Liammial had once threatened him with, and plunged it into his own chest, directly into his heart.

Chapter Fifty-eight

Suddenly Unemployed
9th Day of Monleth, 2448

Lakota stretched the knotted muscles of his back and settled deeper into the hot water. Bathing in such luxurious surroundings was a treat. As a mercenary, he'd all too often bathed in ice cold stream water. Once he'd reached the pinnacle of his band of men, bathing had been moved inside his tent, but still the water never reached this wonderful warmth.

There was a tap at the door. Doubtless it was yet another servant, desiring to do his bidding.

"Come."

He raised himself from the tub and began to dry off, noting with amusement he'd been soaking long enough that his toes and fingers had begun to wrinkle. He looked up, and was surprised to see Skakopee, his lieutenant, standing before him.

Skakopee dropped to one knee, bowing his head nearly deep enough to touch his raised knee with his forehead.

"Milord."

Lakota laughed.

"That's good enough from everyone else in the army, but not from you, my brother.

What do you need?"

He began dressing in his customary white robes. Skakopee stood up and lounged against the mantelpiece.

"That guy that was killed day before yesterday?"

"Yeah, what about him?"

"Well, he was the one who was supposed to be paying us for this job, wasn't he?"

"Yeah; so now the men are worried about how we're gonna get paid?"

"Exactly."

"I've been thinking about that."

"And?"

"I've come up with two plans. I wanted to talk to you about which you liked best."

"So tell me these two plans."

Lakota laughed.

"You do get straight to the point, my friend."

"Always."

"Well first, we've taken on a lot of conscript labor and taught them to fight. I don't necessarily want them chasing us back to our boats in Kingsport."

"So, do we turn them loose unarmed, lock them up while we leave, or kill them?"

"We have a contest between our seasoned men and their best champions. After we kill the champions, we tell them we'll let the rest of them live and be free, so long as they don't follow us when we leave. After that, we disarm them and turn them loose just before we leave."

"Works for me."

"If we leave."

"What?"

Lakota laughed again. The look on Skakopee's face was beautiful.

"Have you considered this? There's no one to pay us. We could loot the town, but although there might be some valuables here in the palace, it won't be enough to buy supplies while we winter at home. You already know food's in short supply, and things will stay that way until the harvest starts. We need to be leaving now if we're to avoid the winter sea storms. We can't wait around until harvest."

"Yeah, I'd worked that much out myself. So your solution is?"

"What if we just settled here? Oh, some of the men won't want to, I'm sure, but the older men who've been with us a long time might find a settled life attractive. We could still work during the summer, but we'd also have income from the markets during harvest, and have a stable base to work from."

"How would you get the locals to hand over the city to us?"

"It's ours now, isn't it? Besides; the guy who was killed?"

"Yeah, what about him?"

"He was the king here. And I don't see any princes beating down the doors to take over from dear old dad. So it looks like we pretty much already own this palace, if we want to keep it."

"Interesting. I've been talking to the boys about it though, and they have other ideas."

"Such as?"

"They think we should just loot the place, kill the locals, and get outta here before the storms keep us out all winter."

Lakota snorted.

"No imagination."

"That's what we pay you for, *Milord.*"

365

"We'll lose too many men if we try killing all of them; we've got half a kingdom of them. A compromise then: spend the next three days stripping the city and taking stock of what there is of use and value. Then we'll hold that contest to scare them into submission, and we'll be on our way. We didn't do much looting on the way here; we can loot Shuell on the way back to our ships. That'll satisfy those who are more interested in rape and pillage than in working hard as a mercenary for a living. Separate out the groups now, and let our core men rest while the rest strip the city for our benefit."

He turned toward the window. He listened as his lieutenant and brother crossed the room and closed the door behind him.

Chapter Fifty-nine

The Battle of Jurisse, Act I
10th Day of Monleth, 2448

Fergan grimly smiled as he looked across the small valley. It would be perfect, as he had thought it would. The small wooded hills on either side were gently rolling, yet steep enough for their purposes.

He looked at the men gathered around him. Most of them were townsmen, servants, couriers, and anyone else he could gather up from Renthenn and press into service, but today they looked like farmers. Their small wagons were loaded with fighting men, hidden by bags of light-weight debris scraped up from the forest floor. Hopefully it would look enough like the early harvest it was supposed to represent.

Each wagon's harness was fixed so that a single knife slice would free the cart horse, enabling it to be ridden. Each man's weapons lay on the floor of the cart, at their feet. The outriders were visibly armed, but they were few in number and poorly dressed. They looked more like armed farmhands than soldiers, but in fact were King Jameisaan's personal guard. All was in readiness. At his signal, the small train of farm carts moved out on the last few miles of their travel. Their objective: the north gate of Jurisse.

As the nooning hour approached, Fergan and his troops drove their carts right up to the north gate. The wall on both sides of the gate was topped with men in black uniforms. Fergan took a deep breath.

"Hey!"

One of the soldiers, who had been watching their approach, leaned out over the battlement.

"Hey what?"

"What's the gate closed for?"

"It's closed, is all. Especially to you."

"Well, open it then."

"Can't"

"Why not?"

"Because my orders is to keep the gate shut. So if I was to open it and let you in, my boss would be plenty mad, see?"

Fergan nodded his understanding.

"Can I talk to him?"

"Who?"

"Your boss; the one who told you to keep the gate shut."

"Whaddaya wanna talk to him for?"

"Well, so's he can open the gate for me."

The soldier on the wall sighed. Some of his companions hid their smiles behind their hands. The sight cheered Fergan's heart. They thought him a farmer, and not too bright. Good.

"He's not going to open the gate for you, either. Why do you want it open, anyway?"

"Well, how am I gonna sell my goods, if I can't get them to the market?"

"The market's closed, and nobody is gonna open the gate for you."

"What sort of goods are you bringing?"

One of the other soldiers on the wall entered the conversation.

Fergan shrugged.

"Not much, but I brung the first bits of harvesting we done. Mostly vegetables, cause the grain is a bit slow this year. Not enough rain, you know. Having just the right amount of rain is very important for grain. You gotta have enough, but then again, you can't have too much, neither. Too much rain gives ya stalk rot.

369

"Stalk rot's bad; all yer grain turns black and falls over, and you'll go without bread fer the whole season. It spreads. You find stalk rot on one shoot, you rip it out, and all the ones it touches. Only way to keep it from taking yer whole field. You ever dealt with stalk rot?"

The second soldier shook his head. "I've never even heard of stalk rot."

Fergan chortled. "Where you been, if you never heard of stalk rot? It hits all the farms hereabouts in wet years, lessen you get it first. Never heard of stalk rot, humph."

He turned to the man driving the second wagon.

"Can you believe that, Lars? He's never heard of stalk rot hitting the grain fields when there's too much rain!"

The fisherman had likely just learned more about stalk rot than he'd ever known, but he played along with his prince.

"I never knew anyone could be so stupid that they never heard o' stalk rot. Why does he think grain costs more in wet years? 'Cause there's less of it, o' course, 'cause of the stalk rot."

Fergan turned back to the men on the wall.

"See, he knows all about stalk rot."

"Well he would, being a farmer, wouldn't he? But I'm not a farmer, I've been a mercenary all my days, and I never heard of the stuff."

"A mercenary!"

Fergan pretended to be shocked. "I've heard of such, but didn't know there was any in the whole of the Kingdoms, since we been at peace forever. Who would need to hire mercenaries? Say, all them men on the walls, is wearin' the same black stuff you are. Are all you mercenaries then?"

"Shaddup, Modoc."

The first man tried to take control of the conversation again.

"Shaddup yerself, Ossage. I want summa that food he's got on his wagons."

Ossage walked calmly across, over the top of the gate to where Modoc stood. Without a word, he belted Modoc in the mouth, hard enough that Modoc fell from the wall with a startled cry. His yell stopped abruptly with the sound of his body hitting the pavement. Ossage walked back to his assigned post without undue haste.

"I'll tell you what I'll do. You blokes back off from the wall a bit. You're making some of my men nervous. When you've backed off, I'll send a messenger to my boss and ask him what he wants me to do with your wagons."

"I hope he opens the gates. Matter of fact, if your boss wants the food we've got, I'd be willing to sell to him as to anyone else."

"What sorts are you carrying? My boss will want to know."

"Well, like I said, not much; mostly carrots and potatoes, a few turnips. Rooty things that don't mind much the dry summer."

"I'll tell him. You men back off now."

"How far off do you want me? And how will I know if you want to talk some more?"

"Far enough off that you're not a threat. And we'll wave a flag at you if we want you closer."

"Fair enough; but I'd have thought we're not a threat now, unless mercenaries are scared of farmers."

"Mercenaries don't like anyone blocking the gates of their cities."

"Then we move far enough off to get out of the road, is that it?"

"That'll work just fine."

Fergan motioned to his men, and they began to move away from the gate. Fergan sat with his cart, still blocking the gate, until he saw Ossage send one of the other men from the top of the wall to act as messenger to whoever his boss was. Then he took his cart off to join the other farmers in their wait.

Chapter Sixty

The Battle of Jurisse, Act II
10th Day of Monleth, 2448

Skakopee looked carefully at the group of men gathered in the throne room. These were his best men, the group leaders who represented the core of Milord's Divine Army.

"A group of farmers showed up at the north gate today, wanting to bring the early harvest to market. They're camped about a half mile from the walls, on the east side of the road. Milord wants the food they're carrying, and the wagons as well, to speed our homeward journey."

"We hafta share the food with the scabbers?"

Skakopee shook his head.

"That's why we're moving at night. Milord wants it to look like they left on their own. We're to bring the wagons and food in, and store them and the horses in the king's stable."

"And the farmers?"

"Dead. Every one. No witnesses, no escapees running off for help. Dead, and buried by morning. No traces left."

The men all nodded, showing their acceptance and understanding of their orders.

"We'll be operating in complete silence. The moon's very near full, so there should be enough light to see by. Use our signs for communication, and have your men wear their white gloves. Get your weapons and groups together and meet me at the north gate in an hour."

Skakopee spent the next five minutes detailing the overall stratagem they would use for overpowering and killing the farmers. Milord's army never went into battle, even a raid against simple farmers, without a well-made plan. This was the secret of their success. When he had finished detailing the plan, the group leaders silently dispersed.

Before the hour had expired, the greater number of Milord's regular troops were gathered near the north gate of the city, but just out of sight of both the gate guards and the farmers. Skakopee visually inspected the troops, mentally tallying their numbers. Good. Everyone was here, and they appeared to be ready.

Swords and axes hung at the men's waists. Those few who preferred to wear partial armor had it strapped on, and the sissies who liked shields were carrying them. The greater part of the men preferred to go armed, but not armored, though most wore hardened, boiled leather tied about their forearms and occasionally over their chest.

All were dressed entirely in black, rendering them nearly invisible, even in the bright moonlight. Their white gloves did stand out sharply, so the hand signs could be more easily seen and understood, and communication could be carried out swiftly, efficiently, and silently among the various soldiers and groups.

Skakopee signaled Ossage. They, with two other men to help, slunk silently to the wall. Skakopee and Ossage silently climbed to the top of the wall, where the scabbers from Shuell watched the gate. In complete silence, they slit their throats, tossing the bodies down from the wall to their waiting men. Now there would be no one who knew they had even gone on a night outing. The gates would be safe enough, unguarded for the scant hour or two it would take to overcome the farmers. There had been very little opposition to their occupation of the city, and all of those men had already been on the inside of the walls.

The bodies were swiftly disposed of, then the signal was passed back to the main body of the troops, and the gates swung silently open. Milord's Divine Army poured outward along the road toward where the poor farmers were camped.

Chapter Sixty-one

The Battle of Jurisse, Act III
10th – 11th Days of Monleth, 2448

A small figure dressed in dark brown came running into Fergan's camp, crouched low to the ground. He shook one of the apparently sleeping men laying on the ground about the bright fire.

"Highness, you were right. They've left the city, coming this way. Hordes of them."

"Steady on, Jornn. You've done well getting the news back here ahead of them. Are they mounted?"

"Nay, afoot."

"Did Tomas take his men inside the walls?"

"They were headed that way, but I didn't wait to see if they got in. He said to get back here right smart and warn you."

"Well done, Jornn. Arm yourself now."

Jornn nodded and moved off into the darkness.

Fergan reached out and tapped the foot of the man nearest him, the signal to be ready. Each man, having lain close enough to the others to be touched, passed the signal onward. Though none of his small force appeared to rouse from their pallets around the fire, Fergan could feel the tension as his men prepared to engage the enemy.

Watching the darkness intently from where he lay, Fergan could see small movements, and the occasional flash of white as their enemy surrounded them. Well, if it was the wagons and their bags of dirt they wanted, they were welcomed to them. The men who had been hiding in those wagons were already within the city, if naught had gone awry.

With a suddenness that was alarming even to those prepared and waiting for an attack, the black figures appeared out of the darkness, rushing in upon the men at the fire.

"Now!"

At Fergan's shout, his men leapt to their feet. Blades clashed, men shouted, wounds were inflicted on both sides. The army's surprise was complete. They quickly discovered the difference between a midnight attack on unarmed and sleeping farmers, and a battle against armed men alert and ready for the alarm. The first several ranks of the black army were completely decimated in their surprise.

One of Fergan's men, a hunter by profession, had clambered atop a cart and was shooting arrows at the army with devastating accuracy. Fergan wondered how he was aiming so well in the dark, and resolved to ask him later.

The difference of experience began to show, as Fergan's small force took more and more injuries.

"Retreat!"

Fergan couldn't have been more proud of his troops. Even though inexperienced as soldiers, their discipline was perfect. Each man had stayed in the fight, and immediately upon his order, each one broke off and ran, fleeing up the road to the north and away from Jurisse.

The bulk of the attacking forces followed in close pursuit, as Tomas had predicted in the planning meeting. The army had a bad habit of not allowing news to get out once they had made an attack. While the farmers, in their eyes, did not present much of a threat, the escape of farmers who might return in greater numbers was a risk they were not willing to take.

Fergan's men maintained the slowest pace that would keep them ahead of their pursuers. They had about ten miles to run to reach the safety of the small valley. About halfway there, they turned and briefly engaged the enemy again. Several of Fergan's men were killed, but a greater number of the Black Army fell to the earth.

Again, Fergan's men had the advantage of surprise. No order had been given aloud, but the plan had been made beforehand to make the second attack at a given point in their retreat. Apparently the Members of Milord's army were too accustomed to being told what to do at every step of the way, and did not react quickly or easily to surprises.

Fergan found that heartening, because the biggest surprise yet would be thrust upon the Black Army when they reached the little valley.

The sun was well up when Fergan's men reached the small valley. The road wound next to the River Jurisse, which at this point was twice as wide as a man was tall, yet only as deep as his knees. Though nearly exhausted, Fergan's men continued on, climbing halfway up the hill at the head of the valley. There they stopped, and turned as though to engage the army behind them in one final battle.

Milord's Army gave a shout of exultation. They were also tired, no doubt, and Fergan hoped they were thinking to overwhelm his small force with their sheer numbers.

The Black Army drew their weapons, advancing grimly toward Fergan's small band. Fergan stood, fearless, watching the army draw nearer, carefully gauging their position.

With a suddenness that startled even Fergan, who was expecting it, a flight of arrows rose from just behind the hill, arching and falling point first among the men of the Black Army.

The archers then appeared atop the hills on either side of the small valley, raking the ranks of the enemy with their arrows, killing and disabling many.

In a show of confusion, some of Milord's men turned to retreat, but, much to their astonishment, the way had been cut off by mounted soldiers. These men rode through the ranks. Many were wounded by the swords and axes wielded by the mounted men. Many others were trampled beneath the iron-shod hooves of the great plow-beasts that had been pressed into service as war horses.

The battle went badly for Milord's Divine Army after that. Fergan's hidden foot soldiers appeared next, and amid a hailstorm of steel, the army was pressed into an ever smaller knot of men. When few were remaining, Fergan gave the order for his men to put up their swords. Having beaten them, he intended to offer them amnesty in return for a peaceful retreat from his kingdom. Although his men tried to obey him, the Black Soldiers refused to stop fighting, and Fergan's men were forced to defend themselves. The battle ended only when every man from the Divine Army was dead.

Wearily, Fergan's men made camp. It was not yet dark, but it had been a hard-fought battle, and even those who had not run ten miles in the dead of night were tired in both body and spirit.

They would rest for what remained of the day, and make their return to Jurisse on the morrow.

Chapter Sixty-two

Bittersweet Reunion
12th Day of Monleth, 2448

Tomas climbed to the top of the wall and looked out over the terrain. His thoughts and hopes were with his prince, as he anxiously waited to find out how the sortie had fared.

He'd been flattered when Fergan had asked him to join them at the Orchard House for the planning session. Fergan's reasoning was sound; he knew Tomas had once been a conscripted member of Milord's Army, and would at least know the general practices and habits they employed. He'd spent a good deal of time telling them everything he knew about the Black Army, and now prayed that he'd learned enough about them to aid his prince.

Something moved at the furthest extent of the road that was visible from the wall, and Tomas strained his eyes, trying to discern which army was returning to Jurisse. Would they be welcoming their prince with open arms, or holding the city against Milord's Divine Army?

The small column of men came nearer, and eventually approached closely enough to be identified.

Tomas gave orders swiftly. The gates of Jurisse were flung open, and the inhabitants flowed out onto the road, engulfing the troops as they approached.

Glad cries abounded among those who recognized Prince Fergan on sight, and it was a while before Tomas could get near enough to him to speak.

"Your Majesty, I request a private audience. I have much news for you."

Fergan looked puzzled a moment, then blanched, evidently absorbing the full import of the exact words Tomas had used. He nodded.

"As soon as possible; is Jurisse secured?"

Tomas gestured with his hand toward the city wall as they entered through the gate.

"Jurisse is yours, Milord."

"Then if you will, await me in…my office? I'll join you as soon as I can."

Tomas nodded and moved off through the jubilant crowd, his mind racing quickly as he mentally assembled the report he would give his king.

Chapter Sixty-three

The Rightful King
12th Day of Monleth, 2448

Several hours later, Fergan strode wearily up to the door of the king's office. Tomas and another man awaited him there; a man who looked vaguely familiar to him.

"Gamron!"

The stranger greeted him rather more familiarly than he'd expected. He passed his hand across his brow, thinking hard. No one at court, or even anyone anywhere in Jurisse, called him by his second name. The only people who used that term for him were those of his staff and retainers who'd raised him at Havenhill, his own estate.

"You don't recognize me, do you?"

Fergan shook his head in denial. The stranger held out his hand in a greeting of equals.

"Kezele of Shuell."

Fergan's face split into a grin.

"I was hoping you were still here. Come into the office. Tomas, you, too. I think both of you have a lot of news I need to hear."

Fergan opened the door into the king's office, and entered. He shivered, but could not have said whether it was from the cool air in the perpetually chilly room, or the depths of the memories it held. The room still contained many of his father's things, and he took a deep breath. For all the time he'd spent preparing for this moment, somehow he'd never thought it would actually ever arrive.

His feet unaccountably took him away from the desk, to the more comfortable chairs near the fireplace. Though a fire had been laid, it was not yet lit. Fergan waved his guests toward the chairs, and went to the fireplace to light it.

"Allow me, Your Majesty."

Tomas quickly stepped past him, drawing flint and steel from his purse. Fergan allowed him the service, and seated himself in his father's favorite chair.

Soon the three men were comfortably warm.

"That's the second time you've called me 'Majesty', Tomas. However, I want my news chronologically, if you don't mind. I think I'll be able to absorb it better that way. So Kezele, you've been here since before the army arrived. Please catch me up on all you know of the happenings here."

Fergan settled his shoulders back into the chair to listen.

Some time later, Kezele wound down his narrative. Fergan's brow was creased in thought.

"You know for an absolute certainty that Liammial was killed?"

"Oh, yes. His servant came into the throne room and slaughtered him in front of all the ambassadors and their wives, and at least half a dozen guards. Then he took his own life. The healer was sent for at once, of course, but his wounds were too severe, and he'd bled to death before the healer had even arrived."

"And we have only Liammial's word that my father and King Jameisaan were killed?"

"I...," Kezele furrowed his brow in thought. "You're right. He told us they'd been killed near this office in the fighting, the first time the army broke through into Jurisse. He did produce bodies, but their faces were so badly mangled, they were unidentifiable. They were dressed in the clothing the kings wore most often."

"But that signifies nothing. My uncle was sly enough to think of that. I want to see the bodies, where were they buried?"

"I'm not certain; I wasn't invited to the ceremony, but I understood they were to be placed in your family crypt."

"I'll check on that at first opportunity. I will want the servants who were here in the palace at the time questioned, to see if anyone might have seen anything of significance. Also, has anyone searched the dungeons?"

"You have dungeons here?"

Fergan laughed.

"I take it no one has thought to search."

"No one thought there was a need to search for their bodies, or to question the veracity of Liammial's account."

Fergan grimaced. "I think most of the servants were aware Liammial was missing from court, but most probably did not know he'd been revealed as a traitor to the crown, and was under sentence of death for murder. We'll institute the search as soon as we're through here."

He turned to Tomas.

"Now, tell me what happened when you got here last night."

Tomas shifted in his seat, sitting well forward on the chair and leaning earnestly toward the king.

"When the army came pouring out the gate, I sent Jornn off to warn you they were on their way, then we snuck closer. They'd left the gates propped wide open, and no guards at all, although a few freshly dead bodies were on both sides of the wall. We secured the gates, and I left my men on guard there.

"I went alone to look for the barracks, and soon found them, near the palace. Nearly all of the mercenaries had gone off after you, but they'd left all of the conscript forces in the city. I talked to the group leaders, and told them this was their opportunity to retake Jurisse, if they'd fall in with me.

"The men from Shuell, as well as what was left of the original defenders of Jurisse were quick to join with me. I sent most of them to man the walls against the possible return of the mercenaries, but kept a small troop with me as we penetrated the castle itself.

"Because we were all in uniform, we met with no resistance, and were able to reach Milord's chambers unhindered. From that point, it was swift and easy work to do away with him and the guards he had kept around him.

"After that, I rejoined the men at the north gate, and waited to see which army would be returning to Jurisse."

Fergan sat for a long moment or three, absorbing everything he'd been told, and arranging it properly in his mind. He took a deep breath, preparing for what lay ahead.

"Kezele, as King of Shuell, I'd appreciate it if you would accompany me to the royal crypt. Whether those bodies do or do not belong to my father and King Jameisaan, they need to be identified properly, if possible. I will want you as my witness to whatever finds are made."

Kezele rose from his chair and stretched.

"I'm ready whenever you are."

Fergan rose also, as did Tomas.

"Do you want me to come as well?"

"No, Tomas, I want you to organize a search of the dungeons as quickly as possible. Even if there are no bodies to discover, there have been so many changes of leadership here lately that there's no telling who has put what prisoners down there, or why. At the very least, we'll need an inventory of prisoners."

"You can count on me, Majesty."

Tomas hurriedly left the room.

"There's one more thing, Gamron, before we close this meeting."

"What?" Fergan faced his friend fully.

"A goodly number of my subjects are here, as freed men, but brought here by the army. I believe my country is still suffering beneath the rule of remnants of Milord's Army, parts who have no idea the war is ended.

"As soon as the matter of your kingship has been determined, I would beg leave of you to take my men and depart, to free my own country from these men."

Fergan nodded. "I'll send as many men and as much in the way of supplies as we can give you. You've my blessing to go; and my wishes for your success, as well."

"Thank you, my friend."

They walked in silence to the royal vault, and entered quietly. Fergan lifted his lantern high as they approached the two newest arrivals, not yet interred in the cubbyholes which held the bones of his ancestors.

The bodies were already decomposing, but because of the coolness of the crypt the process had been slowed and the bodies were not yet so far gone that the two men couldn't learn more about them.

"No signet ring."

"None here either, nor any evidence he's ever worn one."

"The clothing's right. I've seen father wear this tunic often, and the last time I saw King Jameisaan, he was dressed similar to that."

Fergan pointed at the body Kezele was examining.

"No chance of identifying them by looking at their faces." Kezele's voice was soft and respectful here in this place of the dead. Fergan knew he was right. Both faces had been utterly destroyed.

"The rest of their body isn't as beat up as you'd have thought it should be, for that much damage being done to the face."

"That's very true Gamron, good eye. It's as though whoever killed them wanted to make sure the body couldn't be identified. I can't think why the army would have wanted to do that. They would want to boast that they'd killed the king, I would think."

"The hair's wrong, too, Kezele. These men were old, but their hair is not as whitened as my father and Jameisaan's."

"Did your father do his own writing?"

"Occasionally; most of the time his secretary wrote for him. Why?"

Kezele chuckled.

"Then this is definitely not your father. He's got ink stains and pen calluses on his center finger."

"So we can definitely conclude that this pair of bodies is not Kings Jameisaan and Fergasse?"

"Definitely; do you want them moved from your family vault?"

Fergan surveyed the men one last time.

"No, I think we'll leave them here. Whoever they are, they doubtlessly died in my father's defense, when the palace was breached. Let them rest here as faithful servants."

Together they left the vault, securing the door carefully behind them, and silently treading the steps back up to the small chapel which was customarily used for royal naming, weddings, and funerals.

Tomas was waiting for them in the corridor just outside the chapel.

"Majesty, would you come to the dungeon? We've discovered something there which you should see."

Fergan's heart sank. He nodded, and gestured for Tomas to lead the way.

The path through the dungeon was short. The torchlight was bright enough to illuminate the entirety of the narrow passage between the cells.

Tomas stopped, and gestured to Fergan to pass him. Fergan stepped past Tomas, and immediately saw the hand, lying on the floor, the ruby ring glistening in the fitful, spitting light of the torches.

He knelt on the stone floor, lifting the hand gently, and holding it carefully in his own. The tears ran hot down his cheeks, but he didn't care who saw them. If anyone thought him less than a man because he grieved for his father, so be it.

A sniffle behind him told him his were not the only tears being shed. Fergan slowly removed the ring from his father's hand, and placed it on his own, then stood, feeling at this moment very lost and alone in the world.

"Get this wall down; King Jameisaan is likely in there with him. They both will need to lie in state. Get them out, and prepare their bodies for a proper burial. And someone send word to Kwenndara. Tanella will need to be informed of her father's death, and tell them, too, that the battle's won, and the citizens of Jurisse are to come home with all haste. We have a city to rebuild before the harvest market opens."

He walked out of the dungeon without a backward look.

Chapter Sixty-four

Bad News is Badly Received
19th Day of Monleth, 2448

Time hung heavy on the princess's hands since she'd returned from the Orchard House. She was lonely, for one thing. Seeing her beloved Fergan for even those few short hours, and none of those hours were private, was almost more than torture for her. There'd been no time for anything personal with the black army camped around the gates of Jurisse. A kiss hello and another for goodbye were nearly more torment than no kiss at all, but those few moments had also reaffirmed to herself how much her heart and mind belonged to her husband.

Another reason time was dragging had to do with worry. Word coming back to her was very slow. She knew part of that was the distances involved, but she also knew part was the desire of her father and her husband to protect her from everything unpleasant. Tanella knew full well she was the one chosen to head up the refugee camp because her father wished her to remain safely out of harm's way. Perhaps they feared that if she was kept current on happenings, she might leave her assigned post in order to help.

The babe within her moved, and the slight flutter brought Tanella's thoughts back to the moment. She put her arms protectively over her child and wished once more she'd had a few minutes of private time to tell her sweetheart of their impending parenthood.

Looking up, she saw Janna seated by the window, an open book in her lap, but her gaze turned to outside the glass. She grinned. Her cousin was a very great help to her when they were out and about in the city, and when they were in the midst of organizing some project. But as their activities were decreasing more as Tanella's babe was increasing, Janna was becoming more and more bored with the "listless ways of the rich" as she was wont to call it when they were alone.

Used to being actively busy at the inn, the enforced leisure was wearing on her. Actually, it was wearing on Tanella as well, but there wasn't much either of them could do about it.

A brief knock on the door drew her attention, and her maid opened and slipped between the portals, a small tray in her hands.

A small curtsey bobbed in her direction, drew a silent sigh from Tanella as the girl came forward. She hadn't been able to break the girl of that habit yet, but at least she'd been able to quell the very formal 'My Princess' or 'Highness' in front of every sentence. Glinndee was speaking as she walked.

"A small snack of blackberries and cream for ye both, My Lady," she said, placing the tray on a small table next to the lounging chair Tanella was resting upon. She began fussing with napkins and silver, pouring cream from the minute silver cream pitcher over both dishes of fat black fruit.

A tightness constricted Tanella's throat, tears immediately sheening her eyes and rendering speech impossible. Janna, however, snapped the book shut and quickly rose, words of thanks flowing profusely from her lips as she neared Glinndee. It covered Tanella's lapse perfectly while she savored the memory of the blackberries growing on the grounds of Havenhill.

By the time the other two had finished exclaiming over the size of this fruit and their gratitude that it was finally the season for them, Tanella had composed herself and neither woman was aware aught was amiss.

She'd always enjoyed blackberries, but since her sojourn to Fergan's estates, they'd never been the same, nor, she thought, would they ever be just a simple fruit for her. She only wished she could be eating these across the table from her beloved right now.

She put the first spoonful into her mouth, and was enjoying their full, rich flavor, when a second knock came upon the door. Glinndee quickly went to the door and opened it a little to find who was there. The door opened wider to admit a messenger.

He was a young lad, still in his teens, were Tanella to guess, and had been in hurry enough to not wash the dirt from the roadway before he knocked upon her door. Glinndee was hissing like an angry goose about washing up before presenting himself and his message. He simply pushed past her and knelt before the princess, but was up again before any had given him leave to rise.

His chest was heaving either in agitation or with the speed of carrying the message to her.

The words he spoke, though, arrested her very breath.

"I be very sorry, Yer Majisty, but I bring ye bad news. All the kings 'ave been killed in the fightin' at Jurisse."

Tanella stood quickly, swaying a little as she did so. Janna stepped close and put a supporting arm about her waist, the other grasping her near hand to steady her. The dish of blackberries fell; the crystal bowl shattering, and the spoon clattering across the floor unheeded.

"Have you other news of the battle?" Tanella was surprised the words were recognizable, because her lips and her throat felt frozen.

"No, Yer Majisty, I doesn't. I bin workin' in me father's fields when a man came up leading 'is 'orse. It'd throwed a shoe, and he'd bin walking fer hours when he'd spotted our place. Me father said he'd help the man with 'is 'orse, but the messenger said 'twere urgent ye receive the news. Father saw the man was total spent, and sent me on while he had the man rest and eat, and while father shoed the 'orse."

"Did the messenger say anything else, give you anything to bring me or tell you who had sent the message?"

Tanella held her breath. There had to be word from Fergan. He was to lead the Kwennjurat army into battle.

"He did say the battle was somethin' fierce!"

"Who sent him with the message?"

"I doesn't know, Yer Majisty. He jist said I were to git the message to ye fast like."

Tanella heard the words, and her thoughts screamed their horror. All the kings were dead. Not both the kings, but all the kings. Fergan must also have perished in the battle. Black, swirling mists began closing in on her, smothering all light; little pinpoints of stars bursting on the outer edges of her vision. The room tilted, and she felt herself falling. One thought was uppermost in her mind, and she couldn't tell if she'd said it aloud or only in her mind. *I never even told him I was pregnant!* Darkness claimed her.

Chapter Sixty-five

Another Change of Face
20th Day of Monleth, 2448

Janna stood near the small table, ready to go and fetch anything the healer might need. The old crone was a comfortable person to be around. When she'd been sent for at Tanella's collapse yesterday, she didn't fuss over the princess or worry about her status. Instead she got right to work checking Tanella over and asking questions of the witnesses, in order to discover the problem with her Highness.

She'd determined it was merely shock at the bad news, but had warned Janna privately that such shock was not good for her, in her state of pregnancy. Janna had seen to it that every instruction of the healer had been carried out without delay.

Much to her dismay, she'd also discovered that, as her Majesty's Lady-in-waiting, the servants of the household had turned to her for every decision that must be made. To her amazement, she had had no problems in suddenly having to order the ins and outs of the household. It was rather like a larger version of her parent's inn, and she'd had plenty of training from her mother on how to be going about such matters. She thanked her maker for her years of training.

The healer had arrived first thing this morning to check on Tanella's condition, and Janna hovered anxiously while awaiting her decision.

"She hasn't awakened?"

"No, she's exactly the same as she's been since yesterday. We had the broth prepared as you suggested, but she never awakened to take it."

The healer ran her fingers through Tanella's hair, probing the surface of her scalp.

"And she did not strike her head on anything when she collapsed?"

"Not that we've able to find. She was standing near the table, and she did slide to the floor, but I really didn't think there was anything much she could have hit her head on. I was next to her, holding her hand, and I know she didn't hit the table. "

"And there's no bump here to tell us that it was hit, either," the woman muttered, more to herself than to Janna. "Well, 'tis quite a shock she'd had, hearing of the deaths of her father the king, and her father-in-law as well. If she's not roused by this afternoon, send for me again, and we'll do what we can to wake her. She can't go on too long without food, or the babe will suffer for it."

Janna nodded. There was a tap on the door, and Glinndee stepped into the room with a curtsey.

"Beggin' yer pardon, Milady, but there be a courier below, and he says he'll only speak with the princess." Her eyes darted to the still figure on the bed. "What should we be a-telling him?"

"Tell him the princess will be down shortly," the healer instructed the maid. Glinndee withdrew with a curtsy.

"Are you going to wake her now?" Janna asked.

The ancient healer shook her head. "Nay; you must take her place. Yon courier will speak only to a princess, but we must have his news quickly, in order to do her the best good. Change your dress quickly, and go receive him. Wring every drop of information from his lips that you can."

"But,"

"It's for *her* good. And the courier will never know. Heaven knows half the people in this town can't tell when the two of you have switched for the day."

"But how did *you* know?"

The old crone turned and looked at her in surprise. "I'm a healer, child; it's my profession to be more observant than the average yutz. Now, get one of her gowns, and I'll help ye get it laced."

Janna quickly changed into one of Tanella's favorite gowns, and hurried down the stairs to the main hall. One of the footmen moved quickly to a parlor door and opened it for her, announcing her as 'Her Most Royal Highness, the Princess Tanella'.

She tried to still the trembling of her legs, but was unsuccessful in the venture. While it was true that the she and her sisters had often traded places with Tanella for fun, none of them had ever taken Tanella's place when it came time for the performance of her royal duties. She prayed she could carry this off. At least Uncle Jameisaan wouldn't be walloping her afterward for this bit of effrontery, though her father might.

The courier was on his feet as the door opened, and was bent on one knee, in a deep bow, by the time Janna entered the room.

"Your Majesty."

What would Tanella do? Janna's mind wailed in her anxiety, even as she felt her mouth curving in a smile as she approached the man.

"Do please rise, courier Davisson."

The courier rose to his feet, and immediately began digging in his bag.

Janna held her hand out in a gesture that would stay his movements.

"I understand you had trouble with your horse yesterday, and that you bring me grave news?"

"Yes, Majesty."

"Have you eaten yet this day, or have you need of any refreshment?"

"No, Majesty, that is, yes, I've broken my fast this morn, the farmer would not let me leave hungry, and no, I have no need of refreshment. But the news I carry should have come to you yesterday, and for the delay, I apologize."

Janna nodded, and then seated herself in Tanella's favorite chair, gesturing to another chair that sat before the fire.

"Please do be seated, and give me what news you carry."

The courier seated himself, well accustomed with Tanella's ways, and took a deep breath as he faced her. He scrabbled in his pouch again, and withdrew a small scroll, passing it to her.

Janna looked down at the scroll in her hand. It had been hastily tied with a black ribbon, but bore no wax seal.

She opened it and read the hastily scrawled and spidery writing within.

Majesty,

The kings are dead. I have seen their bodies. The battle is won, and the citizens of Jurisse are to return home with all haste.

Tomas

Janna's heart sank. Tomas had written the note. As Fergan's cousin by marriage, he might have been chosen as a temporary leader for the city until Tanella could take over. She turned to the courier.

"Was there nothing else but this scroll? Tell me of the battle. How fares Jurisse, and King Fergan?"

Courier Davisson licked his dry lips.

"I wasn't there, but when I was given the scroll, I was told that the fighting was fierce. The army did take Jurisse, but at a heavy cost. The kings were killed in the battle, and the citizens of Jurisse were needed home as soon as may be, to rebuild before the harvest market. As to His Majesty, I have no knowledge. Is not the scroll from him?"

Janna shook her head. "The scroll is signed by his cousin, Tomas, and as you have seen, it is not sealed by any ring. There is no news of, or from his Majesty, then?"

Davisson stared at the floor for a long moment.

"Majesty, I have told you all I know. I could set out today with a message, but 'twill still take at least ten days to receive a reply from Jurisse."

Janna nodded. "I will have a message for you shortly. Wait here for it. Let the footman know of any needs you have, and they will be met."

She stood, and swept from the room, not pausing to acknowledge the fact that Davisson also stood and bowed to her as she departed.

As soon as the door of the parlor was closed behind her, Janna gave orders to the footman to see to the comfort of the courier, to have writing tools sent to her in the library, and to send for the Lord Mayor at once. It was obvious to her that now the deception had begun, she was going to have to play Tanella's role until the princess, no, the queen, she reminded herself, recovered from her weakness. Decisions needed to be made, and plans carried out immediately. She only hoped she was up to the task.

Chapter Sixty-six

The Homecoming
28th Day of Monleth, 2448

Fergan stood in the open gates of the nearly empty city of Jurisse. Jornn had reported back to him that a train of carriages, wagons, and horses had been seen in the Victory Valley late yesterday evening. His people should be arriving today, and he would be here to greet them.

Sure enough, before the sun had reached its zenith, the first of the evacuees rolled into the city, met by those who had survived the battles. There were tears and smiles; happy reunions all around him, as well as the sadness as those who had lost loved ones were told the sad news.

Families returned to their homes to pick up their lives again as though they had never been shattered by the evil of war. Fergan knew even those families who had not lost members still had lost neighbors and friends. Not a single person in Jurisse would be untouched by this.

The lives interrupted, the livelihoods lost, and the families shattered, Jurisse would never again be the same.

Many, as they arrived over the next few days, brought Fergan tidings of his wonderful wife, who had taken such care of them during their stay in Kwenndara.

They spoke often of the two red-haired ladies, the princess and her lady-in-waiting, who greeted them, settled them, and visited with them during their stay, ensuring they wanted for nothing.

They spoke of how quickly the exodus to come home again had been organized by the princess and the mayor. There were also rumors, whispered here and there. The quiet tidings no one told the young king still came to his ears by other sources. There were many who were willing to speak to Jornn, the innkeeper's son, and as courier, he carried such tidings to his liege.

The story went that the lady-in-waiting had been struck ill, just as they had received the tidings to come home. The Princess had worked with the Mayor to organize them, and to send them home, but she was changed. She was likely stricken with worry over her lady's illness, some said. Others said she was a pale ghost of herself. Many told the tale that she'd forgotten people's names, and things she'd said to them, in the last few days as she worked so hard to see them safely on their way home.

Fergan received these tales, at first with a concern for the welfare of his beloved. The task they had laid on her had been too much for her. Then, as more details, and many similar stories reached his ears, he began to wonder.

He sharply recalled a young woman who had traded places with her maid in order to effect her escape. He wondered whether or not the maid had been forced to fill in for her mistress for some odd reason. Apparently, the changes were noticed immediately after the news of their victory, and her father's death, arrived. Had Tanella suffered some sort of collapse when she received the news? Was Janna now filling in for her?

Fergan shook his head to clear it. There was nothing he could do from here. With his fears for his beloved mounting, Fergan vowed to settle his people as quickly as he could, and to leave for Kwenndara as soon as things here were stable enough for him to depart.

Chapter Sixty-seven

At the Bottom
2nd Day of Aidorth, 2448

Hellenne the Healer stepped through the door softly closing it behind her. Janna stood quickly, her fingers entwined and held chest high, nearly in an attitude of prayer.

"How is she?" she whispered.

Hellenne shook her head, her answer coming in a very soft, low voice. "I'm afraid she's still the same. We've got to find a way to get more food into her, or not only will she lose the babe, but we'll lose her."

"I just don't know how to do that. When I take the nourishing stew into her that you prescribe, I try to talk to her about getting well so the babe will live and be strong. She just turns her head away and cries silently into her pillow. The only thing she'll say is, 'I didn't tell him about the child' and then cries harder. I'm at my wits end."

"I'm about there, myself. Short of resurrecting King Fergan from the dead, is there anyone you know who might possibly be able to reach her?"

Janna stood, biting her bottom lip in thought. "With Shayla at the inn, perhaps Mother and Father could come for a few days. If anyone could help, it may be them. Do you think she'll be angry we sent for them?"

"I don't care if she gets angry or not. Mayhap a little anger could stimulate her more than all the molly coddling we're doing. How many days travel will it be? It's been a dozen days now. I don't know how much longer she can last."

"I know. No matter what has ever happened in our lives, she's always been the one who gave us the courage to go on and face what was in front of us. I've never seen her so low."

"Well, receiving the news of the deaths of her father, father-in-law and husband within the space of thirty seconds, I can certainly see why she's been so afflicted in her mind. Janna, if we don't find something she can hold on to, something to cling to which would give her hope for life and for living, she's going to die. How soon can we get word to your parents to get here?"

"Two days, maybe one and a half on a fast horse, for the messenger to go, and the same for them to be coming back again."

"You write the letter to bring them here in a hurry. I'll go down to the stables and see what's available to us, and who could travel the fastest with the message. I'll be back as soon as I've found a rider. It's about our only chance to save the queen. We'll never be able to gather another army and fight back against the traitorous army in Jurisse if we lose her."

"I'll hurry. Do you think I should tell Mother about the babe? Tanella didn't want anyone to know." Janna bit her lip as she looked for the answer from the healer.

"If you *don't* tell her, she won't realize the full urgency and exactly what's at stake. You tell her everything. I'll accept the wrath of the queen's anger if she lives long enough to bring it upon my head." Hellenne turned and hurried into the hall.

Janna looked once more at the closed doorway into her cousin's bedroom. Pulling herself together, she went in search of parchment and ink. She'd write a letter that would curl Tanella's hair, but would get her parents to come by the quickest route, and in the shortest amount of time. She didn't want to lose her cousin, and not just because she was also her queen.

Chapter Sixty-eight

Together At Last
5th day of Aidorth, 2448

The door opened softly, and Tanella turned her head away from the portal. She didn't want to be badgered about eating again. Food not only didn't sound good, it didn't taste good, either. Who could get excited about eating sawdust? Bleah! She closed her eyes and feigned sleep. That measure had been working very well for several days.

"It won't cadge, my girl. You're not asleep, and it wouldn't matter if you actually were or not, I'd wake you immediately anyway. Sit up."

Tanella turned her head quickly at the sound of her Uncle Fredrick's deep voice. Coming across the room were her aunt and uncle. She didn't know whether to laugh or cry.

Aunt RaeLee sat on the edge of the bed and simply held out her arms, and Tanella fell into them and gave and received a huge hug. She pulled out of it for a second to look at the dear face she knew was like her mother's. One full second later she burst into tears and was gathered back into the soothing embrace.

She felt the pat on the head from her uncle, which only made the tears fall harder. She loved these two people so very much, and hadn't realized how deeply she'd missed them, and their advice, which she knew would be coming as soon as her tears were shed.

She didn't know how long she'd been crying before Uncle Fredrick finally had reached his limit.

"Okay," he said, handing her a soft cloth. "Time to mop up or the bed will be floating out of here, and we'd all look funny bumping along the hall."

The image made her giggle in spite of the tears still flowing down her cheeks. She accepted the cloth, and quipped, "Is that any way to treat your queen?"

"Pish, tosh! When have I ever treated you as royalty? I could spank your sitting spot the very same as I could spank my own daughters' behinds, and if I recall correctly, I actually did on at least one occasion, so don't be pulling your rank on me, my girl!"

"That's right, you did spank all four of us a time or two! Do you realize I could have you put in the stocks for treason now?"

"That's a laugh!" he said. "If you don't behave yourself now, I wouldn't put it past myself to spank the royal behind again, either! Janna tells me you've been acting like a spoiled brat."

"Fredrick! She said no such thing!" Aunt RaeLee said, her voice showing her shock.

"Well, mayhap not in those exact words, but she said as how Tanny just lies here and won't eat. If that isn't the behavior of a spoiled brat, I don't know what is!"

"Well, she's received quite a shock. That would put anyone off their feed, except maybe you!"

"The shock I got when my own Shayla was laying in bed in the arms of a stranger was pretty bad but it didn't put me off my feed, so why should anything put off our most mischievous niece and make her want to stifle the life of her babe what's a-growing inside her by not eating? Doesn't she know that Shayla's own babe won't have anyone to play with or get into the same types of scrapes as the child's ma, her aunts and cousin got into when they were youngsters if her babe doesn't live?"

Tanella's aunt and uncle both stopped speaking and looked at her. Uncle Fredrick had such a look of love on his face that Tanella couldn't take offense at his words. Aunt RaeLee had a tentative but warm look, so full of encouragement, that she felt the first spark of her own spirit stir within her heart.

She gave them back a look that she hoped was full of love, and then the full meaning of what her uncle had just said percolated through her mind, and she squealed. "Shayla's pregnant? That's wonderful! Oh, that's the best news!" and she promptly dissolved into tears once more.

Aunt RaeLee gathered her up, but Tanella pushed her away gently. "I'm all right; I'm just thrilled for them, that's all. I can see I'm going to have to spend at least half of the year at Renthenn so my child," she hiccupped, "will be able to play with cousins. It can be a lonely life in a palace with no one to play with."

She wiped her face once again, and took a deep breath, marred only once by another hiccup. She looked at them through her tears, trying to tell them without words how much their presence meant to her. It didn't work. Uncle Fredrick wasn't having any of it.

"How soon can you be up and around so I can get back to work?" he said in his usual, blunt manner. "With folks coming back from the war and all, my inn's been busier than ever before. Shayla is good, but she still needs a bit of training!"

"Fredrick! I forbid you to bully the girl!" Aunt RaeLee said, holding a hand out to entreat him.

"Bully her? I'm not bullying her. I'm just treating her the way I've always treated her!" The twinkle in his eyes put paid to the gruffness in his voice.

"Bah! Why don't you make yourself useful and go tell the kitchens we'll be staying for the next few days. And don't you dare bully them, I don't want them quitting on Tanella!"

"Talk about bullies!" he said as he turned to leave the room. "*I'm* the one who's being bullied, and I'll be bringing you up something to eat, girl, so get ready for it. If you won't eat it, I'll feed it to you!" As he left, he thumped the door a bit noisily, as if just to let them know he'd gone.

Aunt RaeLee turned to Tanella, her concern filling her face.

"How are you, really, my dear?"

421

"Devastated," Tanella answered bluntly. "I don't know how I'll get on with things. How will I face each day without Fergan? It hurts even to breathe, Aunt RaeLee. I just love him so very much! There's a hole within my heart that has torn me quite asunder, and I don't know how I'll fill it!" She wiped her eyes on the cloth again, and put her head on her drawn up knees.

"When my sister died, Tanella, it felt as though part of me had died, too. We'd been so very close, and had dreamed of such fun things to do with our children. I already had Colette, but we'd planned to have several others as close to each other as possible. Then, when your mother died giving birth to you, I didn't know how I could go on. I really think Colette was my salvation. I had to keep going to care for her.

"I also began to wet nurse you, so that was a 'twin-edged' sword, if you'll forgive the pun. It was a service I could do for my twin, but a dagger because I'd lost her with your birth. Then, a few months later I became pregnant with the twins, and I knew I had to just keep putting one foot in front of the other each and every day.

"It took a bit of time, but eventually with the love of Fredrick, my sense of self, and my sense of humor came back again, and the love of the four of you girls healed my heart wounds. There are times, however, when I still miss her so much it feels like yesterday that she died.

"Although it doesn't feel like it right now, Tanella, you'll be able to do those things you're called upon to do, those things you've been trained to do; to do what is best for the kingdom you rule. You are a strong woman, a strong person, who has always done the right thing when confronted with reality.

"You were willing to give up a marriage of choice so you could combine two kingdoms and rule with a man you'd never laid eyes upon. It's sad you couldn't have had more time together, but this is the way life has turned out.

"Perhaps your babe will be a boy, and you can train him to be the kind of king your father was; full of goodness and love. That's what we have to focus on now; making sure the babe is strong and healthy when it's born. Turn your attention to getting strong, and in pulling the kingdoms together. Eventually, Fredrick says, we'll be able to raise another army and put Liammial on trial for treason and murder, and then you'll be able to rule the kingdom in the way your father and husband would have ruled it had they lived.

"You know I'm speaking the truth, and you know it's because I love you so much that I have the courage to tell you these things. I'll leave you now until dinner is ready, but then I'll be back to help you eat a good meal. You must be strong for you, for your baby, for the kingdom."

She kissed Tanella on the forehead and was nearly to the door when Tanella said, "Thank you, Aunt RaeLee. If Mama were here, she'd have probably said much the same thing. I'll be ready for dinner, I promise." Her cheeks felt stiff but she forced a smile for her aunt.

RaeLee smiled back at her and went out through the door, closing it softly behind her.

Tanella looked at the door for a long moment after her aunt had gone. Finally she looked at her fingers, fiddling with the now-damp cloth. Taking a deep, shuddering breath, she mopped her face once more and realized her aunt was right. She had languished long enough. She doubted very much Fergan would have been very pleased to have her carrying on so.

Although Tanella doubted her heart would ever be whole again, she would get up, she would have this baby and surround it with all the love she could possibly give it, and she would fight Liammial. He was the one responsible for this; for all of it. Her hands balled into fists with her determination. She would do it; all of it! She'd fight for Fergan, for her father, for his father, and most of all for her child. She took in one deep cleansing breath and realized she felt much better than she'd felt since she'd heard the news.

Chapter Sixty-nine

A Thief in the Night
7th Day of Aidorth, 2448

It was only by the light of the moon, shining brightly at just past half, that Fergan could see as he topped the last rise and looked down on the small valley holding the port town of Kwennda-ra. It was very late at night, and the populace had long gone to bed; not a single light showed from any window. The torch-lights that would be alight in the streets of Jurisse were not in evidence. Apparently when Kwenndarans went to bed for the evening, they *all* went to bed.

Fergan noted the path he would need to take to reach the palace, assuming the largest building on the east side of the city was the palace, and nudged his tired horse down the road toward the town.

When things were settled enough that he'd been able to leave Jurisse, he had not waited even for the new day's dawning, but had set out in the late afternoon. This had caused him to end up sleeping not at inns, but wherever he happened to be when darkness was too deep for further travel. He'd carried some travel rations with him, and replenished them at inns along the way, and finally arrived this evening.

The sharp sounds of his horse's hooves echoed off the walls of the silent city, and Fergan reckoned it must be very late indeed. He considered trying to locate an inn, but shook off that thought almost as quickly as it formed. If he was to wake a household, it might as well be the palace, for then he could see his beloved Tanella tonight and be reassured that nothing was wrong with her.

He made his way through the streets to the palace, where the gates were locked up tightly against intrusion of any sort. Fergan rattled the gates and called out, but no one appeared to see to the cause of the noise. Where were the guards that ought to be on duty here?

A feeling of dread filled Fergan's heart. What if the fevers had come and carried everyone off?

Dismounting quickly, Fergan tied his horse to the gate, and set about finding a way inside the stout walls of the fortress. He followed the wall to his right, searching for any way he might gain entry, but the street followed the wall, and there were no smaller gates in evidence.

Nearly a quarter of an hour later, the street ended against the outer wall of the city. Fergan eyed the narrow angle formed where the palace wall and the city wall met. He removed his cloak, and then slipped his boots off, and his hose as well, leaving him clad only in the farmer's tunic he'd been wearing as part of his disguise when he arrived in Jurisse.

Slipping his body as far into the corner as possible, Fergan began to climb, digging his fingers and toes into the small crevasses between the stones and hauling himself upward, inch by painful inch, toward the top of the wall. He gained the top and threw his arm over the crest, only to discover the sharp shards of glass embedded point upward in the mortar cap.

Blood streaming on his left forearm, he carefully avoided the glass with the rest of his body, and soon was on the ground again, inside of the palace's wall. A strip carefully torn from his tunic left the ragged hem falling at mid-thigh, but it served well as a makeshift bandage for his arm, stalling the bleeding.

Fergan set out through the small copse of woods that had been planted in this corner of the palace grounds, and his bare foot almost immediately encountered a nettle of some sort; the stinging sensation on the bottom of his foot was quite painful. Ruefully, he realized he should have thrown his boots over the wall in advance of climbing, but at this moment, he was not about to go back and climb the wall again, twice, in order to retrieve them.

Taking a deep breath, Fergan did his best to ignore the pain, and ran as quickly as possible through the nettle patch and to the edge of the small woods.

With as much stealth as possible, he made his way along the edge of the woods and closer to the rear entrance of the palace. Still seeing no sign of sentries, he made his way along the gravel paths of the formal gardens. The flowers and fragrant herbs were all in shades of gray and silver beneath the moon, and Fergan tried to imagine what they would look like in the full light of day.

He reached the back entrance of the palace without opposition, and all of his senses were on high alert. They were at war, and no one here was apparently interested in protecting his wife or ensuring her safety. The captain of the guards would certainly have an earful from him in the morning.

Fergan cautiously opened the door, and took note he was in the kitchen. Loaves of bread sat on the hearth near the coals, rising for the morning. Three hound dogs slept on the floor near enough the massive fireplace to be warm, and far enough to avoid stray sparks in their fur.

Fergan searched the kitchen for a store of candles. He located a drawer of stubs and chose the longest, a short little candle perhaps four or five inches in length. He held the wick against the coals in the fireplace and blew gently until it caught fire. Looking around the kitchen by the light of his purloined candle, Fergan was pleased with the cleanliness and order he found in the kitchen. He quickly located the main entrance to the room, and moved swiftly in that direction. The draft of his passage caused the thin taper to drip, the hot wax spilling down onto his fingers and wrist. Wincing, he thought this was certainly not turning out to be his night.

Out in the passage, Fergan moved in a direction he hoped would take him to the front of the palace, and the main staircase which would give him access to the chambers of his beloved Tanella.

After several false starts, Fergan managed to find the main entry, and, his short candle stub still dripping on his fingers, started up the stairway. Suddenly there was a shout, and a great weight slammed into his back, throwing him against the stone stairs. His candle dropped from his fingers, and went out. Fergan twisted out from under the body that was atop him, and a short and furious fight erupted with fists flying, clawing fingertips, and the liberal use of elbows, knees, and various other body parts in the dirtiest fighting Fergan had ever experienced in his life.

The shout had apparently raised the alarm, for there were shortly lights and more assailants. One man, wearing a steel glove, smote Fergan on the side of his head, and darkness descended again.

Chapter Seventy

Sweet Reunion
8th Day of Aidorth, 2448

The light of dawn stabbed into Fergan's eyes, producing an instant, burning pain, all along the right side of his head.

He tried to touch his head, to determine whether his skull had been cracked, and discovered his hands were tightly bound behind his back. He could feel the drool leaking out the side of his mouth and tried to swallow, but discovered someone must have hit his throat in the midst of the battle last night, for swallowing caused his dry throat intense pain.

Cautiously, he struggled to a sitting position against the wall, and discovered he was in a stone dungeon, with a small opening high in what was obviously the east wall, and a stout wood door on the opposing side of his small cell. There was no bench, either wood or stone, and not even any rushes upon the floor.

The sound of voices and loud footfalls from somewhere outside the hall prompted Fergan to action. He pushed his shoulders firmly against the wall as he struggled to stand before the guards arrived. Halfway to his feet, a wave of dizziness and nausea swirled over him, and he dropped to his knees, retching.

The guards entered his cell, and a strong hand grabbed the back of his tunic, lifting him to his feet by the scruff of his neck. Three men dragged him into the corridor, where a fourth man waited in silence.

The fourth man, some sort of captain among the guards, judging from the markings on his uniform which differed from the other three, looked Fergan over from head to toe. He snorted his contempt of the prisoner, then turned and silently walked away from them, down the corridor. Two of Fergan's guards slid their arms through the crooks of his elbows, while the third drew a long, wicked-looking knife whose serpentine blade was serrated on one edge and smoothly sharp along the other. He gestured with the knife in the general direction of Fergan's throat.

"No trouble from you today, right?"

Fergan opened his mouth, but no sound came out. The guard laughed. Fergan mutely nodded his cooperation, and the guard resheathed his knife and lead the way as his companions dragged Fergan between them, up the stairs, to wherever they were going to question him.

They took him through the back corridors of the palace and into a well-appointed room with a cheery fire in the grate. The first guard was waiting for them when they arrived. The men on either side of Fergan dropped him on the floor at the feet of their superior. With his hands bound, Fergan fell flat on his face.

One of the men grabbed his arms and pulled them upward, causing Fergan additional pain, then he felt cold steel against his wrists and he held very, very still. His hands were freed, and he slowly, cautiously, raised himself to his feet, rubbing his hands against each other and ignoring the pain of the pins and needles of returning circulation.

The head guard gestured to a chair, and Fergan sat in it, considering the hard and unadorned wood a great improvement over the stone where he had awakened this morn.

In silence, the guard captain poured a glass of water and held it out to Fergan. He eyed it suspiciously, knowing if he was to speak to these men he would need to drink it, but not knowing if they had added any poisons or drugs to the pitcher before he had entered the room.

The guard captain laughed suddenly, and drank from the glass, then handed it to Fergan, who sipped at it. Each swallow of water got easier, and soon he had drained the glass. He held it out, silently asking for more.

The captain of the guards held out a purse.

"Is this yours?"

Fergan recognized the tooling on the covering flap and nodded.

"And the contents are yours?"

"They were when it was on my waist last night."

Fergan's voice was a harsh croak, but at least it was understandable.

The captain laughed again.

"Fair enough." He emptied the purse onto the small table that stood between them.

Several small coins tumbled out, along with his father's signet ring.

"Where did you get this?"

The guard picked up the ring and held it in front of Fergan's face, near enough that there could be no mistake in identifying it.

"From the hand of my father, King Fergasse."

The guard eyed him up and down again.

"You don't look much like a prince to me."

Fergan smiled. "I don't feel much like a prince this morning, either."

"Who, exactly, are you?"

Fergan straightened his shoulders.

"I am Fergan Gamron Lloyd McKaff, King of Kwennjurat. Is her Majesty, Queen Tanella able to come belowstairs? She would be able to identify me, as would her cousin, the Lady Janna."

The guard snorted. "Oh, yes, I'm certain you would want to be conducted into the presence of the ladies. Is yours a mission of assassination, then? Are you one of Liammial's men?

Fergan shook his head.

"How did you come by his Majesty's ring?"

"We were searching the dungeons in Jurisse, and came upon a nearly completely bricked-up cell. My father, King Fergasse, had stretched his hand out through the small opening as he was dying. We identified him by the ring he wore, and found King Jameisaan also in the cell with him. Both had died of lack of food and water. As his heir, I took the signet from his hand, but my fingers are thinner, and I have not had time to have the ring altered to fit me, so I have carried it in my purse."

There was a knock at the door, and one of the guards behind him opened a small window in it, conversing in quietly inaudible tones with whoever was outside.

"And tell me how, exactly, a so-called king comes to be breaking into the palace, disguised as a barefoot peasant."

"I went to Jurisse as part of the army, posing as peasants in order to gain entry to the city. Once the city was re-taken, there was much work to be done to prepare for the citizen's return. I'm sure you can appreciate that the farmer's tunic would wear better for hard work than silk. I heard fragments of news from the people as they returned, which suggested that my sweet wife had fallen ill.

"As soon as I could, I left Jurisse and travelled as fast as possible, to be with her and see to her health. Again, the farmer's tunic was better suited to the travel than more costly garb I had at the palace, so I continued to wear it. My boots and stockings are outside the wall, where the palace wall and the city walls meet, where I climbed over. And I left my horse tied to the front gates.

"None of this would be necessary, had there been guards on the main gates last night."

Fergan added his rebuke in a sterner tone of voice than his explanation had been given in, and was pleased to see the guard color slightly in response.

The door opened, and there was the sound of a rustling of fabric. Fergan did not need to see his lady bride to know who was standing behind him. At the captain's gesture, the two guards closed in and grasped Fergan firmly, pulling him from the chair and turning him around to be seen by the newcomer.

"Fergan!"

Tanella ran forward and flung herself into his arms, pushing the guards aside as though they had never existed. She pulled his head down in a long and tender kiss as he gathered his lovely wife and held her close to him.

"My lady?"

"My lady?"

"Your Majesty!" The captain of the guards was becoming most insistent in his attempts to gain Tanella's attention.

Reluctantly, Fergan broke their kiss, though refusing to relinquish his hold on his wife. He raised his head and stared directly into the eyes of the captain of the guards.

The captain ducked his head, accepting Tanella's identification of the man who was not only his king, but the legal owner of the building in which they stood. He picked the ring up from the table and offered it to Fergan, as he dropped to his knees, silently pleading for forgiveness and mercy.

Fergan reached out and took the ring from his hand.

"Please have food, clothing, and a hot bath delivered to my wife's chambers immediately. And set a guard at that gate, and fetch someone to take care of my horse."

"Yes, Your Majesty."

His arm still around his wife, Fergan turned his complete attention to her, kissing her very thoroughly once more before asking if she would show him the way to their chambers.

Chapter Seventy-one

End of a Journey
10th Day of Pleig, 2449

The coach rumbled to a stop at the front door of Havenhill. Without waiting for their servants, King Fergan opened the door and jumped to the ground, turning back to the door to hold their infant son as Queen Tanella scrambled down from the carriage.

With his son in one arm, and his wife cradled protectively in the other, Fergan walked to the welcoming front door of his home. They had had a busy fall and winter as they settled the running of their kingdom in the wake of the war, and were very grateful to be able to take some quiet time for themselves at Havenhill.

Maggie met the couple in the front hallway, just a step behind Mrs. Palk, and Fergan handed the baby over to her.

"Awww, now ain't he just the perfect little babe? Wot's his name, Milord?"

Smiling broadly, Gamron, Lord of Havenhill, answered.

"His name is Jameisaan Fergasse Crispin McKaff, and you'd best be taking great care of him, for he's the sole heir of Kwennjurat."

Mrs. Palk sniffed.

"Time enough for heir-ing later, Milord, for now, he's jist a wee babe, an 'at's all wot matters. An' fer yerselves, dinner'll be ready soon's ye've washed the dust of the road from yer hides. An' bathwater's bin sent up ta the state rooms alreddy."

With a nod of acknowledgement, Fergan lifted his beautiful Lady from her feet and carried her up the main staircase of his home.

The End

Catching Up with the Story

A large army is poised along the border of Shuell, just south of Jurat. King Fergasse of Jurat and King Jameisaan of Kwenn agree to join their two kingdoms together to defend against the army. As part of the alliance, their children, Prince Fergan of Jurat and Princess Tanella of Kwenn are to be married.

As Tanella embarks on a shopping trip from her home in the Great Krakitts Mountains, she is kidnapped by the army. Posing as her maid, Tanella escapes the cottage where she is being held and begins to make her way home.

Through a stratagem, the kings discover that Fergasse's brother Liammial is involved in the plot to kidnap Tanella. Liammial flees before his brother has a chance to prosecute him.

Tanella stops at an inn to eat, is robbed of her purse and nearly raped, but is rescued by a nobleman, Gamron, Lord of Havenhill. While staying at his estate, they fall in love with each other. She finally is able to leave Havenhill and return home just in time for her wedding to Prince Fergan.

While in Renthenn for the wedding, King Fergasse intercepts a courier from the Black Army to Liammial, and borrows Torresson, one of King Jameisaan's couriers, sending him on an unspecified mission. Lord Gamron is revealed to be Prince Fergan, and he and Tanella are happily wed, joining the two kingdoms, Jurat and Kwenn, into a single kingdom, Kwennjurat. Tanella and Fergan are allowed only one week of honeymoon before their presence is needed in Renthenn to make plans for the troubled times that are coming.

About the Author

A M Jenner lives in Gilbert, Arizona with her family, a car named Babycakes, several quirky computers (one of which has developed a taste for manuscripts), and around 5,000 books. A self-professed hermit with a phobia about having her face in pictures, she loves to interact with her readers online.

Connect with me online

Website: www.am-jenner.com
Blog: amjenner.blogspot.com
Email: anne@am-jenner.com
Facebook: Anne Marie Jenner
Twitter: @AM_Jenner
Google+: A M Jenner

14802739R00244

Made in the USA
Charleston, SC
01 October 2012